Matilde's Empress

"No longer a precocious child but a fiercely resilient, lionhearted, and ruthless leader, Matilde's journey is one that makes the heart howl. Harrowing, breathless, and impossible to part with, *Matilde's Empress* stands as an invigorating testament to fleeting life, everlasting love, and a people's fight to prosper. With a full glossary, maps, and excerpts from historical records, Phillips weaves imagination and research unlike any other. A time-stopping tale that not only seizes but demands something of the reader, Matilde's Empress proves not for the faint of heart; a page-turner that leaves readers repeating 'just one more chapter.'"

Jamie Good, world traveler

Matilde's Empress

Book Three of the Visigoth Saga

Robert S. Phillips

Matilde's Empress

Copyright © 2024 by Robert S. Phillips

ISBN: 979-8-9884074-6-1 (paperback)
ISBN: 979-8-9884074-7-8 (e-book)

Historical Fiction/Antiquity

iv

Dedication

To Frank, Myrtle, Alice, Frances, and Tom.

Growing up, surrounded by love.

Contents

Maps

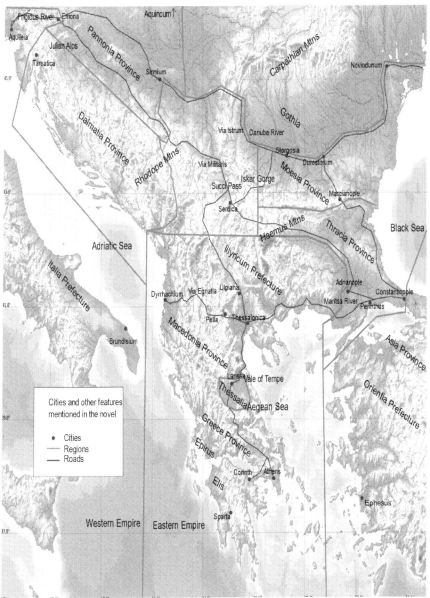

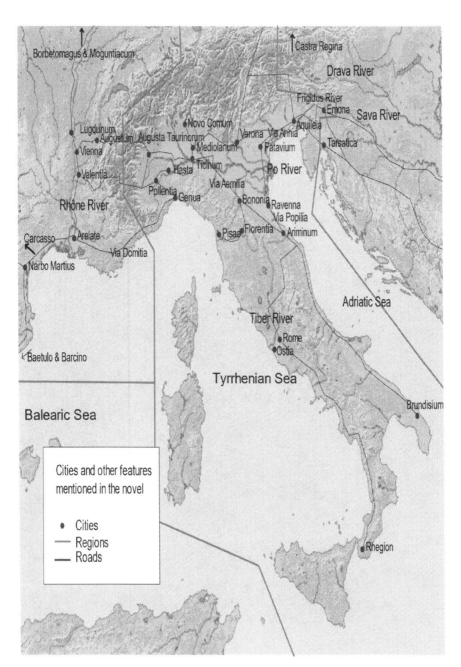

Borbetomagus & Moguntiacum

Castra Regina

Drava River

Frigidus River

Emona

Sava River

Lugdunum

Novo Comum

Augustum   Augusta Taurinorum

Varona   Via Annia

Aquileia

Vienna

Mediolanum

Patavium

Tarsatica

Valentia

Ticinum

Hasta

Po River

Pollentia

Via Aemilia

Genua

Bononia

Rhône River

Ravenna

Via Popilia

Carcasso

Arelate

Pisae

Florentia

Ariminum

Via Domitia

Narbo Martius

Adriatic Sea

Tiber River

Baetulo & Barcino

Rome

Ostia

Tyrrhenian Sea

Balearic Sea

Brundisium

Cities and other features
mentioned in the novel

•   Cities
      Regions
      Roads

Rhegion

A Note to the Reader

Dear Reader,

This work of historical fiction is the sequel to *Elodia's Knife* and *Matilde's General*. It tells the tale of Elodia's daughter, Matilde, starting from her young womanhood at age eighteen. You need not have read *Elodia's Knife* or *Matilde's General*, though I recommend you first read the latter.

Like all good historical fiction, I have woven this story tightly around the historical record. But the historical record of the Roman Empire in late antiquity—360 to 422 CE, years in which barbarian tribes streamed across the Roman frontier and plundered, murdered, and burned their way through Western Europe—is sparse and often inconsistent.

I am sure many of you are familiar with the Rome of Augustus Caesar's time (if you've seen TV series like *Rome* or *I, Claudius*) but are less familiar with the history from Matilde's period until, say, the Renaissance; that is, the historical events around which this story is woven. Because I do not want you to believe this tale is untethered from history, I have included snippets (*in this font*) from professional historians (which I am not) throughout the novel.

These snippets are not essential to the story. Feel free to skip them. Or read them and appreciate how difficult it has been for modern historians to tease out what truly happened "way back when."

Don't forget to consult the glossary for people, places, and other unfamiliar things. Who knew that Mainz, Germany, was once called "Moguntiacum"?

Prologue

Matilde

The days slipped past, and the anguish of my loss slowly faded. Gainas, my life's love, had been killed. Our dream was dead. Our unborn baby had died. Eighteen years of my life—all of my youth—had passed and left me with nothing. Even our hope for a renewed empire had perished. Only the embrace of my family remained to sustain me.

Until now, my life had been a great adventure. As a little girl, everyone considered me bright and pretty (and an irritating know-it-all). I grew up in a village of Visigoths in Moesia, just south of the Danube River, at the edge of civilization. It was a wild place where we children could hunt, fish, and run around like a mob of little savages. My parents, Caius, a retired Roman legionary, and Elodia, a hero of the Visigoths' war with the Romans, fell in love, married, and had me just as the Visigoths and Romans came to an uneasy peace. Earlier, my mother adopted my older stepbrother, Alaric, the son and heir of the Visigoth's king.

But life was not always a fun adventure. I witnessed the horror of a war in which half of my tribe's young men were killed due to Roman indifference, including Gisalric, the love of my eleven-year-old heart. Alaric barely survived. Many of my tribe who avoided the war were slaughtered when the cruel Huns crossed the river and destroyed everything in their path.

Seeing this, Alaric took control of my tribe and, with support from his senior captains, Ataulf and Wallia, led the Visigoths south out of Moesia, looking for a new home, someplace beyond the Huns' reach.

The late Emperor Theodosius had divided the Roman Empire between his young sons, Emperors Arcadius (in the East) and Honorius (in the West). Little love was lost between the Eastern Court in Constantinople and the Western Court in Mediolanum.

Eastern Emperor Arcadius bequeathed us the province of Thessalia. General Stilicho, who effectively controlled the Western empire, opposed this. He marched his army from Italia and confronted our warriors outside of Larissa. To avert war, Alaric traded me for peace, committing me to the care of General Gainas, *my Gainas*. I lived with him and his family in their home in Constantinople. There, I grew into womanhood and, in time, fell in love with him, and he with me.

After I'd been in Constantinople for several years, Alaric found favor with the Eastern Emperor. Arcadius had come to fear General Stilicho more than Alaric, so he appointed my stepbrother *magister militum*, responsible for protecting Illyricum Prefecture. Alaric's Goths provided an armed buffer between the East and West in Illyricum.

At that time, I could have returned to live with my family, but Gainas and I were lovers by then. As Gainas gained power, he and I plotted to seize control of the Eastern Empire. That effort was a disaster. It cost Gainas his life and forced me to flee from Constantinople to Illyricum, where I would be safe with Alaric and my family.

They greeted me with compassion and pity. Only Wallia remained unsympathetic. I overheard him tell Pentadia,

Alaric's wife, "She brought it on herself." Pentadia rose to my defense as usual, but Wallia was not wrong.

In Gainas, I'd had the love of a strong, brave man, and together, we had an opportunity to right the wrongs of this world. Who, given that, would decline the chance?

Chapter 1.   400 CE. The Stranger

Matilde

It was Wallia who first recognized that my troubles were not over. It happened on a day when he was acting as the court magistrate, a duty he performed periodically. He would sit behind a table in the grand reception hall of Thessalonica's palace and deal with petitioners on petty matters of law, dealing justice as he saw fit. Wallia, like the rest of us, was a Goth. We had our own laws and codes of honor and conduct. He would rule based on these, not the Roman laws that pertained before the Emperor gave Alaric control of Illyricum. Wallia was a fair man, though uneducated.

The royal palace in Thessalonica was the jewel of that magnificent city, which itself was the envy of the Eastern Roman Empire. The beauty of the city's gardens, libraries, and monuments, a legacy of Emperor Galerius's rule some ninety years earlier, surpassed anything I had seen in Constantinople.

The reception hall's four walls were constructed with large stones and stood a dozen feet high. These were topped by marble columns separated by brick arches that supported the dome roof. Daylight flooded through the arches into the interior, making the hall as bright as the outdoors. Petitioners crowded the space, seeking a hearing from the day's magistrate.

A few weeks had elapsed since my bodyguard, Brutus, my personal servant, Gaba, and I had escaped from Thracia. Alaric and I assumed that we were beyond the reach of Emperor Arcadius and his vengeful wife, Empress Aelia Eudoxia. They knew my role in Gainas's failed coup. Should they catch me, my head would be on a spike, decorating the walls of Constantinople alongside the rotting head of my late husband. *Oh, Gainas, I ache even thinking of you!*

As Wallia heard petitions and complaints, a man approached with an odd request. "The stranger did not look out of place," Wallia reported. "Perhaps dusty, a little travelworn, and smelling of horse. He waited patiently in line with all the other petitioners. When he finally stood before me, he requested an audience with Lady Matilde. I asked his name and left him while I came into the residence quarter to find you." Alaric used the residence quarter, which comprised one-fourth of the vast palace, to house our family, closest associates, and palace guards.

I said I did not know anyone named Hermengild and asked Brutus to go and study the stranger. He returned quickly. "He has gone," Brutus said.

Wallia blew an alarm trumpet, which startled me. "What? Why?" I called. A half-dozen warriors ran up from throughout the palace.

Wallia described the stranger to them, saying, "He might be an assassin. Search the residence quarter." Brutus strapped on his sword, escorted me to my bedroom, and stood at attention in the door. A minute later, my mother, Elodia, and Alaric's wife, Pentadia, joined me. We sat on my bed, holding hands, waiting nervously.

A half-hour passed before Wallia returned. "No sign of the stranger in the palace. Now we're searching the city, but there's little hope of finding him even if he's here."

Late that afternoon, the family met in the large meeting room where we often relaxed. The room was furnished with couches and opened onto a pleasant courtyard, which featured a small pool with a central fountain and flowering gardens. A gentle breeze wafted from the gardens into our family room.

Alaric joined us. "What was that all about? Not a threat, it seems."

"I'm not so sure," Wallia said. "It was no accident. The man knew Matilde's name and seemed to know she was living here."

"Perhaps he didn't know that," I said. "Maybe that's what he came to find out."

Alaric thought for a minute. "Yes," he said, "It's not as if we announced your arrival. The family and a few servants know you're here, but few other people."

"Well, now the stranger does. And anyone he tells. If the Empress has been looking for me, she knows where to find me."

* * *

After a week without incident, an imperial courier arrived at the reception hall. Intimidating in his official uniform, he pushed through the common people and boomed out, "Clear the way! Clear the way! Dispatch from the *Magister Officiorum* for *Magister Militum* Alaric." His deep voice could easily be heard over the noisy crowd.

Ataulf, who happened to be the day's petition magistrate, was listening to a dispute between two farmers arguing over the sale of a donkey. He had just understood the gist of their argument when the courier thrust a scroll under his nose. Irritated, he glanced at its wax seal and said, "Whose seal is this?"

"From Aurelianus. For Alaric. Are you Alaric?"

Ataulf grunted "No," stood up from his stool, said to the farmers, "Wait here," and walked off, taking the courier into the depths of the palace. The farmers looked at each other and shrugged, wondering if or when he might return.

Ataulf found Alaric in the small, well-lit room he used as an office. His table was covered with papers. He sat half-listening to a clerk rattling off a list of numbers. To his right, sitting on a couch, was Matilde, who seemed to be taking in the figures as he spoke, summing them on her fingers. The clerk stopped when Ataulf and the courier came to the door. "He is Alaric," Ataulf said, pointing. He turned and headed back to the reception hall.

Alaric looked irritably at the courier. "We're busy here. What in Hades do you want?"

The courier handed him the scroll. He, noticing the wax seal, asked whose it was and learned it was Aurelianus's. Matilde noticed Alaric's quizzical look and said, "He must be the new chief minister."

"Never had a message from him before," Alaric said. He cracked the seal and unrolled the scroll over the other papers on his table. Matilde stood by his side, reading.

"Shit," she said.

Alaric, who read slower than her, took a minute longer to say "Shit."

He turned to the courier and asked, "Do you understand this? Tell me the story. The politics."

"I have not seen the message, my lord. I know nothing. I am just a courier, my lord," he said.

"Yes, and I am just a barbarian chieftain who can have you killed before noon. Talk to me!"

"My lord, the court is still reeling from Gainas's failed coup. I believe they continue to look for his wife." The courier glanced furtively at Matilde and back. "Also, since the fall of Gainas, some officials have pushed to remove Goths from every position of authority. Some say they should only be slaves."

"And despite them," Alaric said, "here I am, a Goth and *magister militum*. Emperor Arcadius has always hated Goths. Tell me something new."

"Gainas demanded a seat on the Imperial Council. Now that he's gone, Empress Eudoxia runs the council and has resolved that no general will ever have a seat. She says, 'Lest we end up like the West, where generals govern.'"

"So, General Fravitta is not on the council?"

"No, my lord. He is honored for defeating Gainas and has been appointed this year's consul, but that is all."

"He has become Eudoxia's favorite general?"

"It would seem. They claim his army is now strong enough to prevent another invasion by Stilicho."

"And, perhaps, to crush me? Do they say that, too?"

"I wouldn't know, my lord."

Alaric stared silently at the parchment for a few minutes before asking, "Are you expected to return with a reply?"

"No, my lord."

"Then get out of here!"

As was Alaric's usual practice, he called his family and advisors into the meeting room and read the warrant aloud. "Matilde, Daughter of Caius, and one-time Wife of the Traitor Gainas must Immediately appear before the Imperial Court in Constantinople to answer Charges including Treason, Murder, and Embezzlement, among Others."

Silence ruled for several minutes until Matilde asked, "Must I go?"

"Of course not," Alaric said. "This is rubbish. We will ignore it." In defiance, he burned the parchment.

A laric took the message seriously enough to post an armed squad on the Maritsa River bridge. That bridge marked the border between his territory of Illyricum and the rest of the empire to the east.

A week later, his squad fought a skirmish with a small force of the Emperor's legionaries. They claimed to possess a second warrant authorizing them to travel to Thessalonica and seize Matilde. Alaric's men blocked their crossing, swords were drawn, and one man on each side was killed before the Emperor's men withdrew.

Matilde

Finally, a third message arrived, declaring my stepbrother to be in rebellion. The Emperor suspended all subsidies to the prefecture and appointed General Fravitta to the post of *magister militum per Illyricum*, effectively stripping Alaric of that position.

Alaric called all his advisors together and read the dispatch aloud. Afterward, the room dissolved into a dozen conversations, some quite heated.

"This is Matilde's fault," Wallia declared. "Her rebellion against the Emperor has fouled our relationship with the court and has led to arrest warrants and fighting, and now this."

"Not so," Ataulf said crossly. "I dare say the Empress is displeased that Matilde escaped and that Alaric is harboring her. But to them, she is an irritant, not a threat. Her flight would not justify this action. We must look beyond Matilde to learn why the crown is cutting us off." I quietly thanked Ataulf for his support.

"Is it just to save money?" Alaric asked. That idea set everyone to talking at once again. Finally, when there was a pause, I spoke.

"I believe the answer lies with Fravitta and Stilicho," I said. "No doubt, Aurelianus will be pleased to save the cost of our subsidies. But the Eastern Court now realizes they have a formidable general in Fravitta and a strong army. They do not need our tribe to provide a buffer between East and West. They think Fravitta can stand up to Stilicho. We are not needed."

I looked around to see heads nodding. Even Wallia agreed.

"I judge Matilde to be correct," Alaric said. "But without the subsidies, we are in trouble. We do not raise enough money through taxes and duties to pay for our army. Without pay, our warriors may return to plundering. Or go east and join Fravitta's legions."

"We cannot go back to plundering," Ataulf said. "That would give Fravitta an excuse to attack. If he wins, he will kill or enslave us."

"Perhaps that is what the Roman elite in Constantinople want," Alaric suggested.

"I agree," I added. "I believe the Imperial Council wants us gone. Our whole tribe. I have lived there and listened to their talk. They think we are a tribe of barbarians who refuse to become good Roman citizens and a mob poised to conquer them. Cutting off our money is just the first step. With no money, they expect us to live off the land, to pillage. Now that Fravitta has proved he can conquer barbarians, they will turn him loose on us."

"Then, I must ask," said Wallia, "should we attack Fravitta and the capital now before they get stronger and we weaker?" He answered his own question. "I do not think so. Six years ago, we did not have the strength to conquer the capital. We still don't."

I had a different idea. "Fravitta would not attack us if we were allied with Stilicho. Ever since Emperor Theodorus died, Stilicho has wanted a strong presence here in the East. We could provide that."

The council argued until noon but finally adopted my idea. We would send a delegation to talk to Stilicho. "Who should lead it?" Alaric asked. "It should be someone with a detailed knowledge of the Eastern Court." All eyes turned to me.

With little more discussion, the council agreed that I should lead the delegation, but with Wallia as the nominal head, because the Romans would not accept a delegation led by a mere woman.

Chapter 2. 400 CE. The Marriage

Matilde

When I first arrived at the palace in Thessalonica, Pentadia had a room prepared for me. It looked out on a formal garden, which, as I said to her, reminded me of home. By "home," she understood I meant the home that Gainas and I had shared in Constantinople.

"Your room is right next to Alaric and my bedroom suite," Pentadia said, "and there's a connecting door between them, so we can easily visit each other."

She had an extraordinary sense for knowing when I wished to be left alone and when I was grieving and needed her support. She would open the connecting door after midnight and join me in bed. We often cried together, but in time, we also joked and laughed. Gaba always delivered a large breakfast tray shortly after dawn. Occasionally, Pentadia would come in at dusk. The first time this happened, I said, "You're early."

"Yes, Alaric is using our bed."

I had wondered whether my stepbrother continued to enjoy other women. It was true, explained Pentadia, but she had him most evenings.

"He has another woman tonight?"

"Yes."

I joked, "Your bed is as big as mine. Will it not fit three people?"

Pentadia missed the joke and answered seriously, "Oh, it often does, but he says *this* girl is shy." Pentadia paused for a moment and then smiled. "For the right girl, I think *he* would be shy. Now that would be a sight."

"I find that hard to imagine," I said, giving the idea little thought in that moment.

Some weeks later, Pentadia again joined me in bed shortly after dusk. "Is he bedding another shy woman tonight?" I asked.

"You would know," Pentadia replied cryptically.

"I know this girl?"

"Very well indeed."

When I continued to look dumbfounded, Pentadia said, "I told him that your mourning has lasted long enough. It has been more than six months. I love you, and he loves you, so tonight, you are the shy girl. I think you have gone on long enough, far too long, without a man. We both agree that we want you in our marriage."

Never! Unthinkable!

But then I reconsidered. Growing up, I'd often fantasized about sleeping with Alaric, but I no longer thought of him that way. He was my friend. Yet he held me close when I mourned Gainas. As I still mourned Gainas. I'd received such comfort from the tenderness of being wedged between him and Pentadia with our arms interlocked.

I would never love Alaric as I'd loved Gainas. Not passionately, not romantically. With Gainas, I'd shared enough passion and romance to last a lifetime. Now, I was done with that. Gainas was gone. I expected to be chaste for the rest of my life.

Poets say that love takes many forms. I loved Alaric as a dear companion, someone whose company I might enjoy forever. He was the center of our family, and I wanted to dissolve into it. After carefully weighing the pros and cons, my heart said, *Why not?*

Next, I questioned the specific proposition. "The three of us? Tonight? Here?"

"No. I will sleep in the other room. For tonight, for your first time with Alaric, you need all of him."

Pentadia went to the connecting door, opened it, and whispered, "She says 'yes.'"

Alaric said something I couldn't hear.

Pentadia said, "Oh, Jesus, you're shaking like a leaf! Just go to her. It's not like she's Medusa. You've known her all your life."

Alaric mumbled again.

"No, not like a sister, like a stepsister. And she loves you, too."

And so I entered my second marriage.

At first, Mother was uncomfortable with my relationship with Alaric. "It just doesn't seem proper," she said, though she could never quite put her finger on the impropriety.

"Just because you always treated us as brother and sister didn't make us so," I argued.

"Perhaps that's true," she said. "But it is wrong for a man to have two wives."

"Not under Gothic law," I said. Before my mother could cite Roman law, I added, "Anyway, to the Romans, he calls me his concubine."

Mother soon got used to seeing her daughter and stepson kiss in public. Also, her daughter and her stepdaughter-in-law kissing. If her children were happy, she was happy.

Chapter 3.   400 CE. Delegation to Mediolanum

Matilde

I was so excited! I had never crossed the sea before. (Crossing the Bosporus on a ferry doesn't count.) I drew a map showing our route on horseback using the *Via Egnatia* to cross Illyricum to Dyrrhachium, where we would charter a ship to take us across the Adriatic Sea to Brundisium. From there, we would hire horses and ride up the Italian peninsula to Rome, where I would meet Stilicho. I showed my map to Alaric and described my plan. He hugged me, kissed my forehead, and told me I was "sweet." He could be so condescending!

"First," he said, "we don't know where you'll find Stilicho, but it's unlikely he'll be in Rome. The Emperor stays close to his palace in Mediolanum, where all the court officials reside, so you'll likely find Stilicho there.

"Second, I want you to go on the overland route, north from here, through Ulpiana, and across the Julian Alps to Aquileia."

"Why?" I asked. "Won't that take me down the Frigidus River valley? I never want to go there again. They say the ground is still littered with the bones of the dead. There will be ghosts."

"No, there's another route to Aquileia. I want you to scout it."

"You want me to spy!" I couldn't help but grin.

"Um, I want you to talk to Stilicho and, on your way there, to—um—note the things you see."

"Are you planning to invade Italia?"

"Not unless it's necessary."

Although Wallia was the titular head of our delegation, Alaric made it clear that I was responsible for negotiating with Stilicho. Wallia came along because the Romans would not deign to deal with a woman, though Stilicho might, being half barbarian. Besides, Stilicho knew me.

But facing him would be humiliating. I would have to face his "I told you so" and hear Gainas's flaws again. Yes, he had faults, but I was not the first woman to love a flawed man.

Brutus was coming and, of course, Gaba. And a dozen bodyguards. The preparations were onerous. So many things to bring, including gifts.

The nominal reason for the visit was to present wedding gifts to Emperor Honorius and his bride, Maria, Stilicho's daughter. It comprised a lot of gold rings, jeweled chains, crowns, and other finery, of which I'm sure they already had plenty. Alaric wanted to send a cart so we could carry bulkier presents like bolts of fine cloth, but I argued against it. His *other route* followed a lesser road north of the Frigidus River, which might be difficult for a cart to traverse. So instead, we would bring several pack mules and carry presents that were easily transported.

The journey from Thessalonica to Ulpiana took a week. When we got there, I realized I had missed my bleeding for the second month. There were other symptoms, such as falling asleep in the saddle. I was pregnant with Alaric's child. Brutus asked why I was walking around with a smile glued on my face.

I found it almost impossible to contain my joy, but it was a secret I had to keep until I completed this mission.

A few weeks later, I recognized the town of Emona from my youth. I remembered how our warriors entered, marching proudly with flags fluttering, on our way west to the Frigidus River, that fateful site, and how we returned, far fewer in number, burdened with men in carts, men who would never walk again. To my relief, we took the north road out of town along the Sava River. That narrow road rose high through wild country, carpeted by pine trees pierced by ranks of bald mountains. There were no villages and no farms. At night, we could hear the wolves howl. After two days of trudging up the lonely, overgrown track, we reached the frontier fortress of Ad Pirum. It straddled the pass that separates Italia from Pannonia province, a narrow saddle with steep mountains on each side.

The fortress's wall spanned the entire width of the valley and, being the height of three men, forced all traffic through a single gate.

Ours was not a large party, fewer than thirty horses and a few mules, yet as we approached the gatehouse, we watched the garrison push the gate closed and man the ramparts. Did they think we were barbarian invaders? Perhaps so. Wallia dismounted and approached a small postern door, wide enough for only one person to pass, while everyone else remained two bowshots away. He was carrying a passport we had secured from the governor in Emona. A soldier opened the postern door and accepted the passport. Much to my relief, the garrison pushed the gate open a few minutes later and welcomed us.

Once we passed the gate, we entered a large walled yard containing barracks, stables, and other buildings. On the far side of the yard was another gate. It was the gate by which we would leave the fortress and resume our journey.

I made careful notes about the fortress's structure. Its location was peculiar, being a stronghold that was interior to the empire and not located on a frontier, and designed to prevent an Eastern force from invading Italia. When it was constructed, such a force would presumably be barbarians that had breached the Danube frontier, but now, with ill will between the Western and Eastern Imperial courts, it would block *any* force from the east.

The governor's passport instructed the garrison commander, Proculus Tatianus, to welcome and provide us with all reasonable accommodations, an obligation he seemed happy to fulfill. He was proud of his fort. I requested a tour, which Tatianus granted and conducted himself. By my count, there were about five hundred men in the garrison. I based this estimate on the number of barracks and the size of the eating hall.

The buildings were all stone with steep timber roofs. "We have much snow here, and the roofs must support many feet of it," Tatianus said. "Once snow blocks the pass, I send most of the garrison down to Emona, but I stay here with a skeleton crew. You can see our large storerooms. If the road to Emona is blocked, I can sustain my reduced force for two months."

I asked how many men would that be. He said twenty, a number that I carefully noted.

The commander provided barracks for our men, and I could see that his cooks made a special effort to ensure we were well-fed. As we prepared to leave the next day, I asked if the fortress had ever been assaulted.

"Oh yes," he said. "A half dozen years ago, during the war between Emperor Theodosius and the usurper Eugenius, a cohort of the Emperor tried our strength. Of course, at that time, we were allied with the usurper. The Emperor's men found our walls exceedingly stout, and we turned them back with heavy losses. That is why he chose to bypass us and march down the Frigidus River. Where as you know, he defeated Eugenius. Once we heard of that, we surrendered. Now, we are all loyal subjects of Emperor Honorius." But for this fortress, the bloodbath on the Frigidus River might have been avoided, I thought, and Gisalric might still be alive. Even now, after all these years, my heart still hurt.

Wallia and I thanked him for his hospitality and promised to give a good report to General Stilicho. That report would not mention a portion of the wall that a natural spring was undermining and looked near collapse. My report to Alaric *would* mention that.

It was snowing as we left the pass. Winter was coming. However we returned home, it would not be this way.

Two days later, we descended from the Julian Alps and reached the gates of Aquileia. My father had grown up here, and it was all as he'd described: the great walls, the port, the vast forum. I was enchanted by the nearby flower farms, with so many brilliant colors, where carts of fresh blossoms were harvested and sold in the city market. Every street in the city was lined with pots filled with flowers and shrubs, making the city as green as the surrounding countryside. On our last day in the city, I bought a small perfume bottle from a flower merchant, who said it was produced by pressing blossom oil from unsold florets. It smelled exquisite. I would give it to Mother when I returned.

We quickly crossed the Venetian plain and up the Po River valley, where farm slaves were harvesting the crops. The autumn days were warm and sunny, but the evenings were cold. Our route featured many *mansiones*, which provided adequate shelter, but where we were treated like merchants. Without an official document from Honorius's court, we had to pay full price for food and lodgings. In two weeks, we reached Mediolanum.

A message from the governor of Aquileia had notified Stilicho of our impending arrival, so a cavalry squad met us a few miles outside the city and escorted us in. I was not impressed by the city walls; not that they were insignificant, but they were no more impressive than those of Thessalonica. Where I'd expected to see buildings of marble, most were built from drab red bricks with tile roofs. I saw no color, no flowers, and heard no music. Stilicho later explained, "Emperor Honorius doesn't like music."

The squad captain led us to the palace compound. It was enormous, occupying one-fifth of the space enclosed within the city walls and was, itself, walled. At the palace gate, a sentry found our names on a list and admitted Wallia and me, though Wallia was required to leave his sword. The sentry admitted Gaba once I explained that she was my personal servant. The cavalry squad escorted Brutus and the rest of our party to billets in a nearby military barracks. I was so used to having Brutus watch my back I felt vulnerable, but I did not protest. If the Romans wanted to harm me, having a single bodyguard, even Brutus, would make no difference.

The palace compound contained the imperial residence, home to the Emperor, and the residences of many senior court officials. The buildings varied in size, based (I assumed) on each official's importance, but Stilicho's was the largest, second only to the Emperor's.

Stilicho's wife, Serena, met us at the door of their home. She reminded me of Servilia, Gainas's ex-wife: two hands shorter than me, plain face, slightly crooked teeth, and a quiet voice. Her gown was long and grey, unadorned by any embroidery or embellishments. She wore no jewelry other than a small golden cross on a fine chain around her neck.

"Welcome to my home." Her tone was more formal than friendly. As the adopted daughter of the late Emperor Theodosius and now the mother-in-law of Emperor Honorius, she occupied the highest level of Roman society, higher even than her illustrious husband. To her, I was nothing but the stepsister of a barbarian chieftain. I understood we could never be friends; it was unthinkable. It surprised me that she would greet us in person. Her husband must have insisted I was someone important. If she felt any distaste at entertaining two barbarians, she hid it well.

"These servants will show you to your rooms in the guest wing and will wait on you as you bathe and dress. Then at the dining hour, they will guide you to our *cenatio* where the evening meal will be served. General Stilicho will be home by then." She spoke the Greek of Constantinople, where she'd grown up, and seemed relieved when I thanked her in the same dialect. Wallia tried to express his appreciation but stumbled over words and pronunciation. Serena did not seem to care. I think she realized that I was the more senior emissary despite my sex.

I had not expected Stilicho to accommodate us in his own home. It indicated my delegation's importance, which made me anxious. I was already nervous at the thought of seeing him again and worried that the future of my tribe might lie in my hands.

The servant who showed me to my room was an attractive young woman. The room contained little more than a large bed, almost as large as mine back in Thessalonica. We dropped off my bags, and she led me next door to a bathing room containing a long, deep tub filled with steaming water. The servant was approaching to help me undress when Gaba intervened. "I'll do that," she said, which caused the palace servant to step back out of the way. I sensed a competition, with Gaba trying to demonstrate that she could attend her mistress better than any palace servant. She helped me undress, assisted me as I stepped into the tub, and proceeded to soap and scrub every inch of me. After she rinsed, dried, and oiled me, a palace servant announced that the masseur was at hand. She opened the door to admit a young man, who, with no regard to my modesty, led me to a massage table, where he rubbed and kneaded away all the knots and tension amassed from a month on horseback. I was in heaven.

When he left, my palace servant presented me with a selection of evening garments, all of silk with varieties of silver embroidery and brocade. I tried on several. When I remarked how well they fit, she said, "My master remembered your size." That was quite a feat of memory for anyone, especially for a man and one whose head must be filled with politics and strategy.

I met Wallia as my palace servant led me through the General's vast house to the *cenatio*. I noticed Wallia's servant was an attractive young man. Wallia saw my glance and whispered, "They know my preference." It made me wonder if there was anything Stilicho didn't already know about us.

My servant opened the *cenatio* door and waved us in, saying, "The General should be along shortly."

As she turned to leave, I said, "Make sure Gaba gets something to eat."

"She will eat with us, and we eat very well."

The *cenatio* was a wide hall that connected two wings of Stilicho's home. A long, narrow dining table, with chairs on each side, ran down the hall's center. On either side were windows that looked out onto gardens filled with fountains, trees, and shrubs. On one side was a fountain featuring a marble sculpture of the nymph Daphne being transformed into a laurel tree. From the waist up, she was nude and beautiful, but below, her legs had changed into trunks and roots. In the garden on the other side of the hall was a fountain featuring a statue of Apollo, holding a bow in one hand and reaching out with the other, pointing across the hall toward Daphne.

As we entered the hall from one end, Wallia noticed the statues. "Why is she becoming a tree?"

I was about to respond when Stilicho entered the room from the far end and answered.

"Apollo," he said, pointing at that statue, "wanted her, but she had sworn to remain a virgin. Rather than allow him to rape her, she prayed to her father, the river god, for help. He answered her prayer by turning her into a laurel tree."

"Seems harsh," Wallia said.

"As are the gods," Stilicho said. "Matilde, I am filled with pleasure at seeing you again. I hear that life has not been gentle to you recently. I am sorry."

He looked essentially unchanged from when we met in Corinth, with a few more lines around his eyes and some streaks of gray in his close-cropped hair, but he was still upright and vigorous.

"Thank you, my lord," I said. "Perhaps we can discuss my recent ... adventures later?"

"Certainly. Tonight, we celebrate your safe arrival and my daughter's wedding. I am sorry you missed the occasion, but... But here they come, my darling Serena and my older daughter Maria, the Emperor's consort!"

Entering the room from behind Stilicho were a woman and two girls. The older one, Maria, looked no more than her age of fifteen years. If she had started maturing, I saw no indication.

Stilicho did not mention the other girl, so I asked, "Is this your other daughter, Thermantia?"

"No," the little girl answered for herself. "I am Galla Placidia and I am eight years old and Serena did not want me to meet you but I insisted."

"It is very nice to meet..." I began to say when she continued to talk.

"And Thermantia and Eucharius said they do not like meeting barbarians and my brother Honorius—he's the Emperor—does not like barbarians either, so he is not here, and I have never had dinner with a barbarian before, especially with the Queen of the Goths, so I demanded that I be allowed to come and Honorius is only a half brother because my mother was Galla and his was not."

"They do not hate barbarians," Serena interjected.

"I am happy to meet you, Galla Placidia," I said, holding out my hand for her to shake.

"People just call me Placidia and you have soft hands and are very beautiful, but perhaps not as beautiful as my mother, with whom my father, Theodosius the Great Emperor, fell in love at first sight." Finally, just when it seemed that the little girl had run out of things to say, she added, "No one calls my half-brother Honorius 'Great.'"

Stilicho noticed me craning my neck to see if anyone else would be entering. "If you're looking for the Emperor, my son-in-law prefers to eat in private."

"Oh," I said. "I hope we will have an opportunity to present our wedding gifts to the royal couple."

"I have arranged that for tomorrow. Isn't that right, Maria?"

The girl nodded her head. She had yet to say a word.

"But," continued Stilicho. "My lord has already received many wedding presents and may not be as gracious as you might expect."

"Or hope," Serena muttered, which drew a warning glance from her husband.

"We will keep the presentation as brief as possible. Perhaps lay out the gifts on a table and present them all at once?" Stilicho said. Maria nodded again, approving that approach.

"That would be most acceptable," I said. I didn't care about the gifts or their presentation. They were incidental to my mission. But I thought it interesting that the Emperor's behavior seemed rife with peculiarities and that he had no interest in dining with his bride.

While we'd been talking, servants had emerged with platters of food and filled the long dining table. Stilicho led the way, loading his plate with slices of wild boar, bread, and onions, all slathered with a rich sauce. I noticed he avoided the seafood, the lobster, and raw oysters, which I usually love. He saw me eying them and said, "The seafood is fresh, brought here daily on ice." But, counting the miles on my fingers, I thought it was still a twenty-four-hour ride by galloping horse. "Thank you, but I prefer the pheasant," I said—*rather than day-old seafood.*

As I filled my platter, I glanced at Stilicho occasionally and found he was studying me. He smiled when he saw I'd noticed, and I returned it. He was a handsome man, and I felt comfortable in his presence.

Stilicho had already cleaned his plate by the time everyone was served and seated. Wallia and I sat across from him and Serena.

"As pleased as we are to see you again," he said, "and to receive these wedding presents, I believe there are other aims to your visit, no?" He looked at me and, receiving the briefest nod, said, "Subjects that would be best discussed after eating?"

Placidia approached with a plate ladened with sliced pork and nothing else. "Sir, would you please move over," she said to Wallia, "so I can sit beside the queen?"

Wallia laughed and moved.

"My name is Matilde," I said.

"I see you're not eating the lobster," Placidia said. "I had it once and I vomited."

Stilicho and I exchanged smiles. Such a cute girl. She stopped talking and began wolfing down slabs of pork.

Trying to avoid any controversial topic, I asked, "Are affairs in Africa now all settled?"

"Are you referring to the commotion caused by Gildo?"

"Yes," I said. "We heard a version of the events from the Eastern court's perspective. I would like to hear the story from yours." Stilicho proceeded to tell it.

Gildo had been the *magister militum* of Africa under Emperor Theodosius and was allowed autonomy in ruling the province. After the Emperor's death, Gildo did not report to his successor, Emperor Honorius. Instead, he reported to Stilicho. This was a demotion in Gildo's mind. Feeling vexed, he approached the Eastern court and offered to switch his allegiance to Emperor Arcadius. The prospect of losing control of Africa, particularly the vital grain shipments from Libya to Rome, so frightened the Roman senate that it declared Gildo *hostis publicus*, enemy of the people. Stilicho brought the whole affair to a speedy conclusion by sending a small army to Carthage, led by Gildo's brother, Mascezel. For him, the fight was personal. Earlier, Gildo had tried to assassinate him and his sons. The father survived, but the sons did not. Though Mascezel's force was small, it defeated Gildo's army and quickly killed him.

"Another foolish man dies young," I said.

"Not so young," Stilicho corrected. "Perhaps sixty years of age, but, yes, foolish. Though tell me, Matilde, why you think Gildo was foolish."

After thinking briefly, I said, "Not because he was ambitious. Even a wise man can be ambitious. Not for the killing itself. Sometimes, one's enemies need killing. Though killing his nephews and letting their father escape was foolish."

"I would say unlucky rather than foolish," Stilicho said. "No, he was foolish for threatening Rome's grain supply. Transferring his allegiance from Honorius to Arcadius would have bothered no one—well, *I* would have been bothered!—if he'd promised to maintain the grain shipments. Instead, he threatened to cut them off. That was unneeded and pointless."

"Was Gildo foolish for proposing to change allegiance?"

"Not if East and West were friendly with each other, which they are not, and if they'd both agreed, which they would not."

This answer did not bode well for my commission. If Alaric changed his allegiance to the West, Emperor Honorius might be pleased to take ownership of Illyricum, but the East would oppose it. But would the East go to war over it? Would Illyricum's value to the West make the risk worthwhile? I needed to sit in a room with Stilicho and discuss those questions.

My face showed my worry, and Stilicho noticed. "Not the answers you were looking for?" he asked.

"It is what I expected," I lied, before changing subjects. "Would you be willing to discuss your recruiting along the Rhine?"

"I'd like to. We can compare it with your recruiting experience on the Danube."

The topic was of no interest to Serena or Maria, so they soon left the table, taking Placidia with them. Wallia, pleading exhaustion, returned to his room, escorted by his attractive young manservant. Stilicho could see my weariness, so after a short conversation on recruiting, he said, "Perhaps we should finish this discussion tomorrow. We'll discuss your *real* reason for traveling all this way to see me." He called for my servant to escort me to my room.

Chapter 4.   400 CE. Meeting the Emperor

Matilde

Gaba helped me wash and dress in the morning, and I found my way to the *cenatio*, where Stilicho was already eating. His bowl contained two dozen small fish, which he would put into his mouth whole, pull them out by the head through clenched teeth to scrape off the flesh, then throw away the skeleton. It looked disgusting, so I helped myself to a bowl of oatmeal porridge and prunes.

"Your wife?" I asked.

"Serena attends Mass before eating breakfast."

"And you?"

"I am an Arian, like you. We have a small chapel in the city, which I attend on Sunday and when duty permits."

"If we are still here on Sunday, I will go with you."

"Good. Now let us move to my office. We'll discuss your commission."

I lifted my bowl and drained off the last of the porridge, popped a half-dozen prunes in my mouth, and followed him out of the *cenatio* through a maze of halls, up some stairs, and to a sizeable room with a window that looked north over the city to the mountains beyond.

Stilicho's table, unlike Alaric's, was not covered with papers. He sat behind it in a padded chair while I made myself comfortable on one of the room's two couches.

"From your questions last night about Gildo, I anticipate that your husband—can I call Alaric your husband?" I nodded yes, "wishes to change the alignment of Illyricum from East to West, from Arcadius to Honorius. Is that correct?"

"In essence, yes. Alaric sees adversity closing around us. He owed his appointment as *magister militum* to Eutropius, who is now dead." I wondered if Stilicho would mention that Alaric's appointment was in reaction to Stilicho's invasion. Was he still bitter about his failed expedition? I thought it best to avoid the topic.

"Alaric and my nation have never been viewed with favor by the Eastern court," I said.

"One hundred and fifty years of fighting Goths might account for that," Stilicho said. I chose not to react.

"Following Gainas's failed coup, we are positively despised, even by Empress Eudoxia, who I thought was sympathetic to our plight."

That was my fault, I had to admit. I'd destroyed our relationship by advocating for my foolish husband in the Imperial Council.

I went on. "Fravitta, having destroyed Gainas's army, has proved himself to be a good general."

"He was always a competent general," Stilicho said. "He demonstrated that against Eugenius. Recently, he restored law and order to Anatolia."

"Our worry," I said, "is that Fravitta's next demonstration of competence will be defeating Alaric."

"Really? Based on what evidence?"

"The Eastern court has cut off Alaric's subsidies. The council has signed a *foedus* with Uldin the Hun and plans to take control of the Illyricum arms factories. City administrators who are Goths are being replaced by Romans. These may seem like small things, but we can see where they will lead."

"And where is that?"

"When they have stripped us of every position of power, Fravitta with his Hun *foederates* will occupy Illyricum. He will destroy and enslave us. That has always been the goal of conservative Romans. Men like Synesius."

"That seems unlikely to me, but regardless, what is Alaric's proposition?"

"You should claim Illyricum for Honorius and retain Alaric as its *magister militum*."

"Has he a second idea?"

"You don't like his proposition?"

"If I tried to annex Illyricum, we would have a civil war, East against West. Matilde, I have my hands full with the Franks and Alamanni on the Rhine and the Vandals and Alans on the upper Danube. I haven't got the strength to face Fravitta. If I tried, barbarians would overwhelm my river frontiers. Italia would be endangered. My political enemies would overthrow me."

"But, my lord, if you stood with Alaric, he would stand with you. You say you do not have the strength. With Alaric by your side, you would have more than enough strength. We have thousands of warriors to aid you; young warriors who were born here in the empire. Who were raised among Romans and have been equipped and trained like legionaries. Men who are more Roman than barbarian."

"The Senate would not view them as such. They would still call them Goths. If I tried to fill my legions with Goths, the Senate would not tolerate it. They want a Roman army composed of Romans."

"And yet in the war on Gildo, you did enlist *real* barbarians in your legions, men who have no connection to Rome, no knowledge of its history, tradition, and laws."

Stilicho laughed. "I had little choice. I needed men. I gave the Senate a choice: allow me to conscript farm workers from their great estates or provide me with money to hire barbarian mercenaries. They hated both options, and they hated me for forcing a choice, but ultimately, they provided the money for the mercenaries."

I could not understand how an empire could survive when the rich and powerful cared only for their own interests.

"If you subjugated the East, you could finally fulfill your promise to the late Emperor by providing Emperor Arcadius with the guidance he needs."

"He does not need or want my guidance. He is no longer a little boy, and in Empress Eudoxia he has a competent guide. She would not tolerate my interference."

Stilicho was rejecting Alaric's proposal. I felt sick to my stomach. It wasn't just that my mission was failing; I could now see a future where my family and my tribe would be destroyed. And my baby. We had much to offer to Stilicho, but it wasn't enough.

I had one more idea, a wild idea, but it was worth suggesting.

"You could find us a new homeland. That is why we left Moesia. If we can no longer stay in Illyricum, there must be some other place in this vast empire where a nation of industrious, Christian, loyal subjects could settle. Isn't there? Italia, Africa, Aquitania, Hispania? Somewhere far from the Huns. Somewhere?!"

Stilicho thought for a minute before answering. "The problem is all those places are already occupied. They are settled and prosperous. The rich men who own those lands would oppose any influx of Goths. Those men have great influence with the senate and Emperor. Who, you should know, dislike *barbarians* as much as their counterparts in the East."

"My lord, Alaric would like to be of service to you, but you reject his proposals. Is there no way we can reach some accord?"

"Not that I can see, Matilde. Perhaps if things change. If Arcadius dies ... Who knows?"

"I am afraid, my lord, that Alaric might get desperate."

"Desperate and attack me? Attack the West?"

"I cannot say."

"Be assured, Matilde, that I will defend the West. As much as I would dislike to contend with you, I shall. It would not be personal. My attacks on your people have never been personal. But I have a duty to my Emperor."

"I cannot think of any event worse than Alaric pitting our warriors against your legions."

I was desolate. This entire mission had failed. There would be war. Once again, my husband, my family, and my baby were at risk. I began to cry. I was so ashamed at losing control. Wallia could have negotiated better than an emotional girl.

Stilicho got up from his chair and sat beside me on the couch. He took my hands in his.

"It doesn't have to be a war," he said.

Without thinking about it, I blurted out, "I am expecting a baby. Alaric's baby. I have told no one else. How can I raise a little one if we're at war?"

"These are events that no single man or woman can control. But I promise you, young Matilde, come what may, I will endeavor to ensure no harm comes to you or your baby."

It took some time before I managed to control myself. Stilicho gave me a hand cloth to wipe my eyes. When I recovered, he led me back to my room, where Gaba awaited. She knew I'd been weeping.

In mid-afternoon, after I'd eaten a noon-time meal, bathed, and napped, my palace servant escorted Wallia and me from our rooms into the imperial residence. The reception hall had none of the elegance I expected. I'd pictured a room comparable to the Emperor's reception hall in Constantinople, one with a high ceiling supported by stately marble columns, granite tile floors, and murals showing heroic deeds of Rome's early years. Instead, the servant left us in a gloomy room with bare brick walls and a cobblestone floor. A few narrow windows admitted the only natural light and, apparently, the local birds. Sparrows had built a nest in one window. Someone had placed our gifts haphazardly on two large tables that were poorly lit by torches held in wall sconces.

"Please stay here," the servant said. "The *Augustus* should be here shortly."

There were no chairs. We stood near the door we'd entered by. For a half hour, we waited. Finally, a door at the room's far end opened, and Serena entered, followed by two servants. "He hasn't come, has he," she said, more a statement than a question. When I said no, she turned and left, along with her servants. The door thunked closed. We stood waiting for another twenty minutes when I heard a commotion beyond the door.

"Of course you must. They've come all the way from Illyricum ... no, that's in your brother's empire ... leave the mink stole on, my lord, it covers where you spilled your soup."

Then the door opened, and a small party entered, headed by Serena, who was leading Emperor Honorius by one hand. Her daughter, Maria, was pulling the Emperor's other hand. Wallia and I dropped to our knees.

"You're the barbarians with gifts," Honorius said. He walked to the nearest table and poked at a few of the gold rings.

Maria followed him and lifted a thin gold chain with a ruby pendant. "This is pretty," she said before laying it back down.

They spent no more than two minutes looking at our presents.

"Thank you for coming, and thank you for the fine wedding gifts," she said.

She and Serena looked at Honorius, expecting him to say something, but he was distracted by the sparrows. "My lord," Serena said. "Our guests have honored us with their presence and gifts."

"Yah," he said and then walked out the far door. Maria shrugged and followed him.

Serena said, "I'll escort you back to my home." She did not attempt to explain the Emperor's behavior. I'd heard that he was odd, but he was beyond odd. He was frighteningly strange.

When we arrived back at Serena's home, she instructed Wallia's palace servant about the dinner plans and then led me back to my room, where Gaba and my servant were waiting. They were deep in conversation—I could hear them laughing as we came down the hall—but that stopped when Serena opened the door. She looked at the two of them and said, "Out!" They left.

Serena turned to me and, without any preamble, said, "When do you plan to leave?"

"Our business here is done," I said. "I thought we could leave tomorrow, but would that seem precipitous? You have been most hospitable, and I do not want to offend you."

"Tomorrow would be satisfactory since I suppose it's too late for you to leave today."

I was stunned. Was she pushing us out the door?

"I do not understand. Why the haste? Have we offended you?"

"I object to your presence here."

I stared at her. Perhaps my jaw actually dropped.

"Because you think we are barbarians?"

Ignoring my question, she said, "Do you think me blind? I saw the glances you and my husband exchanged at dinner yesterday. Then, this morning, the two of you snuck off for a private assignation."

"Domina, I swear there is nothing between us. Nothing but goodwill."

"Girl, you do not understand our Emperor or his court. My husband hangs on by a thread. The Emperor has many advisors who hate Stilicho. The Senate is full of men who despise him.

Even the army has jealous men. The only thing keeping him in power is his marriage to me. I am the daughter of the old Emperor and the mother-in-law of this one. The day our enemies believe our marriage is fraying is the day my husband will be deposed. And killed.

"I do not care if he beds girls when he is on campaign. He is a lusty man. But I will not permit it here."

"But," I said, "it is not happening here. Not with me."

"Or," she said, "even its appearance. He was a fool to insist that you stay in our house. Tongues will wag. Are wagging already. You need to go."

I was surprised at how quickly Wallia and Brutus prepared our troop for the trip home. We left Mediolanum the next day. I wanted to see Stilicho again, but his aide said he was unavailable. I explained to Wallia that I did not want to leave, having failed in my mission, and perhaps one more conversation might persuade Stilicho that he should find a post for Alaric and a home for my people.

Although there was no chance to bid Stilicho farewell, he did provide us with a passport that allowed us to stay *gratis* in the better *mansiones*. We quickly traversed the length of Italia, traveling twenty miles each day. It was exhausting. Or *I* found it exhausting, given my condition, but Brutus urged us to keep moving, saying the sea crossing from Brundisium to Dyrrhachium would soon be dangerous or even impossible. The winter storms in the Adriatic could be ferocious.

I marveled at the land we traveled through. It was lush, with fields of corn on the coastal plains and vineyards on every hillside. There were horse farms that could match the best Thracia could offer. I saw pastures white with sheep. Surely, this would be a fine country for my people. The land was not thickly populated. My entire tribe could settle here and no one would notice. Or perhaps they would. The townsfolk gathered at the roadside in every village we passed and stared sullenly at us. They were making it clear that Goths were not welcome. No one threw stones or shouted insults. Any growling stopped when my guards rattled their swords.

At one *mansio*, the innkeeper served us sour wine and rancid pork. Brutus complained while placing his dagger on the man's throat. Fresh food and drink were quickly forthcoming.

And yet the countryside was fruitful and beautiful, which I told Alaric when we finally got home, four months after we'd left.

Alaric was pleased at seeing us safely home, but he could not hide his frustration at our mission's failure.

Chapter 5.   400 CE. Birth of Theodoric

Matilde

Those days of pregnancy were the happiest time of my life. Pentadia greeted my return from Mediolanum with glee, and glee redoubled when she saw I was expecting. Alaric was quick to hug me but slow to notice my condition. Feeling enveloped in his arms brought me a calm I'd sorely missed. When he finally noticed my bulge, he was delighted. He had always proclaimed how he loved babies, to which Mother once remarked, "Which explains why he leaves a trail of them wherever he goes." To his credit, he acknowledged his bastards and supported them and their mothers.

The family debated what we should name him. I wasn't sure the child would be a boy, but Gaba insisted it was true because "you are never sick in the morning." Alaric agreed because he wanted it to be so. Finally, he decided the child would be named "Theodoric."

I saw Gaba shake her head, but as a servant, she could not protest. However, when she and I were alone, she said, "Your husband is saying it wrong. The boy should be named 'Theodor.' 'Gift of God' is 'theo' for God and 'dor' for gift. No 'ric' at the end."

I laughed. "The names sound similar, but Theodoric is Gothic, with 'theodo' meaning people and 'ric' meaning ruler."

Gaba looked skeptical. "Your son will be the ruler of people?"

"That is my hope."

To my surprise, I grew tired of life in the city. One might think that after spending years in Constantinople, I would be used to the noise and bustle, but as Theodoric grew inside me, I longed for peace and solitude. When I told Pentadia this, she confronted Alaric, who took time away from his many tasks to sit down and talk to me. It was a different conversation than I'd ever had with Gainas. Alaric listened carefully. He held my hands as I described my ideal home. A small house, a hut would do, on the edge of a forest with a view overlooking a stream or lake. I wanted to see deer come down to drink. Hear bears breaking through the underbrush and wolves yelping to each other at night.

"You're describing our home in Moesia," he said. "You're homesick."

Then I knew I truly loved this man, my husband, my Alaric. Not with the passion I'd felt for Gainas but with a deep, abiding love. We had shared a house and parents, and though a dozen years of age separated us and we'd interacted only rarely, home meant the same thing to us both. We knew each other in ways that no one else, not even Pentadia, could understand.

He found me a villa in the hills northwest of the ancient Macedonian capital of Pella. It was not as wild as our childhood home south of the Danube, but there were trees and wildlife and, to the south, an excellent view of a vast lake. The smell of pine and fir took me back to my youth. The locals claimed there were bears and wolves, but I saw no sign of them. I spent weeks there, always with Brutus and Gaba and as few other bodyguards as Alaric deemed prudent. Pentadia and Mother came rarely; Pentadia missed the city life, and Elodia's poor health made traveling difficult. Alaric kept me company when his responsibilities allowed. My private time with him was precious. He would help me go down to the lake to fish, a short distance, but one that I found more onerous as the weeks went by. We would sing or play Tabula in the evenings, a board game I learned in Constantinople.

Or gossip. Alaric might ask, "How many lovers have you had?" and I would answer, "No more than a dozen." When I posed the same question, he would fabricate, say, a girl from Ratiaria. His descriptions were always long and detailed. She was always short, petite, and red-headed, which I am not, and "far more beautiful than you." Ratiarian girls, he would say, are coached by their mothers in the art of love, unlike girls from Moesia, and *his* Ratiaria girl had learned her lessons well. I found the only way to halt his babbling was to demonstrate my own knowledge of the art.

One evening, when we finished making love, I asked, "Of all the many women you have bedded, what makes Pentadia different?"

"You are asking why I love your sister-wife," he said. "I love Pentadia because of her joy. Every day, she fills my life with laughter and delight. She accepts me as I am, with all my faults. She doesn't try to change me. She never tries to advise or inform me."

I interrupted. "Has she any advice or information to offer?"

He laughed. "Not that I've ever noticed. But truly, she is never jealous. I love her because she loves everyone and anyone I love. Because she loves you."

"Then why do you love me?"

"I love you because you're Pentadia's friend, even though you have nothing in common as far as I can tell. And despite your endless advice and information. You are my font of wisdom."

"It seems your font is generally dry," I said. He tickled me until I begged for relief.

He replied, "I love you despite your being quite ugly." Then I tickled him.

I prayed to Jesus, to Frigg, even to Eleuthō, who I was quite sure was not a real goddess, that my baby would be born safely and that I would not die. So it happened, though it perhaps also helped that I had the best possible care with Mother, Pentadia, and Gaba at my side. Theodoric was chubby and hungry. My breasts, anticipating this, had grown and swollen to meet his needs.

Chapter 6.   401 CE. Kingship

Matilde

The termination of our subsidies caused endless problems. My husband was not an expert at managing money or doing sums, but even he could see that the funds to retain our warriors were less than we could collect in taxes and duties. We had limited sources of revenue. Illyricum had few cities, factories, or large expanses of farmable land.

Perhaps we could have raised more money from our *fabricati* (arms factories) in Tarsatica and Horreum Margi, but the profits from those operations were relatively small—suspiciously small in my opinion. When Ataulf and Wallia inspected them, the factory owners and overseers impressed them, and they always returned with glowing reports. I noticed they came home with new gem-studded daggers. I suggested to Alaric that we could reduce corruption by installing an inspector in each factory. Alaric adopted the idea, which increased our profits for a while, but they soon fell again. The drop-off coincided with the inspectors acquiring fine estates and beautiful gowns for their wives. When I pointed this out, Wallia accused me of being a nag. Alaric was satisfied because all our warriors had the finest weapons and armor. That was his priority; profits were a distant second. I gave up and devoted my time to playing with Theodoric.

The day soon came when there simply wasn't enough money. Alaric reduced his subsidies to the other clan chieftains and told them to reduce their warriors' pay or let them go. This did not go down well. Especially with Sarus and his clan.

After Alaric was appointed *magister militum per Illyricum*, he allocated Thessalia to Sarus. It was a choice district: fertile and passive. There was no reason for Sarus to maintain a large army, yet he resisted when confronted with the need for belt-tightening. Sarus stood by while his men looted their non-Gothic neighbors, whose numbers still greatly exceeded those of their Gothic overlords. Reports reached Alaric that Thessalia was ripe for a rebellion. In response, he summoned all chieftains to meet in Thessalonica.

Two dozen chieftains arrived at the palace reception hall. They gathered around Alaric, who stood on the table usually used by the petition magistrates so everyone could see him. He held the speaker's rod, an ornate length of brass, which, by custom, one must hold to address an assembly. Hundreds of citizens were present to watch the proceedings, but a line of guards kept them back from the chieftains. It was a dreary rainy day. I suspected half the onlookers were simply there to be out of the weather.

Only clan chieftains were permitted to address the assembly, but I was allowed to watch from the balcony. I had already primed Alaric with my thoughts, and he agreed with my opinion, by and large.

Sarus was too proud to attend; instead, he sent his son Sautus. I had not seen him since he went as a hostage to Mediolanum a half-dozen years earlier. Stilicho released him after Alaric received a military appointment by Emperor Arcadius, and the Goths were no longer considered an imminent threat. Sautus was my age, no longer a boy, but not much of a man: tall, skinny, and almost bald.

Alaric informed Sautus that we—and by "we" he meant all the clans, which he indicated by waving his hand across the assembled leaders—would march on Thessalia and depose Sautus's father if the depredations continued.

Sautus came forward to the magistrate's table, received the speaker's rod from Alaric, and called out in a high, squeaky voice, "It is illegal for a clan chieftain to lead the clans against a fellow clan." Some chieftains laughed at his high voice, but the rest took his comment seriously. The Gothic legal code was unwritten, but Sautus was correct. There was such a law. It was intended to prevent inter-clan warfare, although bride-stealing, cattle thieving, and other similar raids remained common. But those were small-scale, undeclared attacks. What Alaric proposed was illegal. As *magister militum*, his plan would be perfectly acceptable under Roman law, but Alaric was scrupulous about obeying the law, which for him meant Gothic law.

Fortunately, we had considered this objection. Unfortunately, the workaround had its own difficulties. Ataulf took the speaker's rod and turned to address the assembly. "Sautus is correct that a chieftain cannot lead such a war, but it is legal for the *reiks* to make and enforce laws. I propose that we elect Alaric as our *reiks*."

We'd had no *reiks* since Fritigern died. Alaric was just a clan chieftain to our tribesmen, even if the Romans always called him king.

I knew Ataulf's proposal would cause an uproar, and it did. The assembly dissolved into dozens of loud arguments and at least one fistfight. Alaric allowed the commotion to continue for a few minutes, and then he retrieved the speaker's rod and banged it on the table to restore order.

A chieftain named Alfsthan pushed to the front, and Alaric passed him the rod. He did not need to stand on the table to be heard. With a booming voice, he shouted for quiet and said, "We need to stop Sarus and his lawlessness before the Emperor does it for us. If that requires electing Alaric *reiks*, then so be it. We all know that General Fravitta and his legions are sitting across the border in Thracia, just looking for an excuse to come and crush us. Nothing would make the Emperor happier than to see us crushed."

I thought Alfsthan spoke very well. As he should have, given that we had helped him rehearse his speech several times. I'd hoped that would settle the argument, Alaric would call for a vote, and my husband would finally be king. But Sautus had more to say. He received the speaker's rod from Alfsthan, climbed back up on the table, and stood beside Alaric.

"Alaric seems to think that my father has no wish to maintain law and order and that he encourages our young men to prey on their neighbors. That is not the truth. The problem is money. We have no money. Our young men would happily pay for bread and meat if they had money. Is this not a problem that all your men face?" There was a general murmur of agreement from the assembly.

"If you wish to elect Alaric as *reiks*, I cannot stop you, though I must say that my father, Sarus, would be a better choice." This drew a laugh from the chieftains. Sarus had few friends among his peers.

"But the *reiks*, whoever you elect, must address the problem we all face. We Goths are too many for this land. We need a bigger land, a richer land, and one that is further from

Fravitta and our other enemies. I will carry your message to my father that our young men must be constrained, and perhaps he can do it. But only for a time, not forever. If our *reiks* does not provide us with a solution, then, in a year or so, we may see clan fighting clan."

Sautus returned the speaker's rod to Alaric just as Ataulf started a chant, "*Reiks, reiks, reiks.*" Within a few minutes, Alaric ordered a voice vote, and he was unanimously elected *reiks*. I noticed Sautus remained silent.

Pentadia was ecstatic at being a wife of the *reiks*. "I thought it couldn't get better than being the chieftain's wife, but Matilde, can you imagine? Did you ever think it possible? We are wives of the King!"

I could imagine it, thought it possible, and was not overjoyed. As a chieftain, our husband had been in an untenable position. Now, besides the burden of his own clan, he was responsible for the whole tribe. The other chieftains' message had been clear: find us a home, a productive land sufficient for us all and far away from our enemies. They were looking to him for answers he did not have.

"Tell me again about Italia," Alaric would ask, and Wallia and I would answer.

"And the passes through the Julian Alps?" and we would describe the fortifications at Ad Pirum.

We would talk long into the night, discussing why Stilicho refused my proposals and how he might respond to what Alaric called "a little pressure."

As the weeks passed, we received reports of our young warriors—not many, but a few—traveling to Thracia to enlist in Fravitta's legions. "This is what happened to your father,"

Mother said to Alaric. "After Fritigern's victory at Adrianople, he had no money to retain the army, and, bit by bit, it frayed. A young warrior will not pick farming if given a choice between farming and selling his sword. Then, as now, the Romans are always looking to bolster their legions.

"If we end up battling Fravitta, those boys will find themselves fighting their fathers and brothers." It was obvious, but it needed to be said.

"We have to leave," Alaric said. "But where? Ideas? Matilde, you've previously suggested Italia, Africa, Hispania, or Aquitania. What do you think now?"

"Italia would make a wonderful home, but we are not strong enough to take and hold it. It is the home of the Roman people, and they would fight us forever if we tried. Yet, the path to all the other provinces goes through Italia. I recommend quickly crossing Italia into Gaul and *then* deciding where to go next. Perhaps Aquitania or Hispania, or even crossing the narrows into Africa. But we cannot stop in Italia, or Stilicho will crush us."

"When Matilde and I were in Mediolanum, we met the Emperor. Just imagine if we could capture him!" Wallia said excitedly. "If we plan to dash across Italia and climb over the Alps into Gaul, we will travel right by Mediolanum. We could take the city, capture the Emperor, and force him to do whatever we demand!"

Alaric agreed enthusiastically. I did not.

"We cannot *dash* across Italia while stopping to besiege a city. I fear Stilicho will catch us. Our priority must be to move *fast*." But Alaric and the others were enthralled by the idea of capturing the Emperor and dismissed my warning.

Therefore, we planned our migration through Italia. Alaric, Ataulf, and Wallia traveled to every district of Illyricum, consulting with each clan chieftain and telling them to prepare their carts, oxen, and supplies while I stayed home and cared for my little boy.

Chapter 7.   401 CE. Migration

Matilde

In early autumn, Theodoric turned two years old, and we received word from an Aquileian merchant that a large force of barbarians had crossed the Danube from the north into Raetia and Noricum. The merchant claimed the frontier forts at Castra Regina and Lauriacum had been attacked but were not being besieged. It was messengers from those forts who had crossed the Alpine passes to alert Stilicho.

"Barbarians? Which barbarians?" Alaric asked.

"Vandals and Alans," the merchant said.

"What is Stilicho doing?"

"Just before I set sail from Aquileia, Stilicho passed through our city at the head of his legions heading for the passes."

"Which legions?"

"All of them, all the ones in Italia, including the *militiae praesentalis*, the Emperor's own troops."

"What about the garrison of the forts in the Julian Alps?"

"Stilicho deployed them first. I mean, he is not worried about Arcadius invading, is he?"

Alaric dismissed the merchant after rewarding him with forty gold aurei for swiftly bringing the news. Then, my husband called his captains together and passed the information on to them. "The road to Italia is open and unguarded," he said gleefully.

"Ataulf, send out a message to all the clan chieftains. We leave at once. Everyone. We all meet at Sirmium in three weeks."

After he and I were alone again, I said, "The clans in the far south can't reach Sirmium in three weeks. I even doubt if *we* can."

"We don't need everyone. We need enough warriors to seize and hold the passes until the tribe can migrate into Italia. Stilicho will be busy in the north, and by the time he realizes what we're doing, it will be winter, and all the passes will be closed. He won't be able to respond until next spring. Perhaps by then, we'll be in Gaul.

"Perhaps," I said. "But only if we don't stop to capture the Emperor."

"We may have to take that risk. We cannot just sit here. Doing nothing is not working for us."

"I agree with that. We need to move fast and ruthlessly, or we will die," I said. "Fast and ruthless!"

Brutus and I approached the gate of Ad Pirum, mounted but at a slow walk, trying to look insignificant and peaceful. We were neither. Alaric feared putting me in harm's way, but he was also loath to simply assault the fort. Though eight years had passed, the losses and pain from the Frigidus River were still raw. I'd argued that if we wanted to take the fort by ruse, I was the only one who might approach it without alarming the sentries. Though it had been three years since my previous stay, the garrison commander would remember me.

We were high in the Julian Alps; it was very cold, and light snow was falling. In a few weeks snow would fill this corridor. Alaric was threading a tight needle: our tribe needed to traverse this pass *before* the weather blocked our way, but *after* snow had closed the northern Alpine passes to Noricum, thus preventing Stilicho from returning. I dreaded that we might descend from the mountains only to face a Roman legion on the Venetian plains. At the rate the snow was falling, I also feared avalanches might clog the road before our wagon train was through or a slide might thunder down a mountain, sweep our people off the narrow road, and bury them in a grave of snow.

I left little Theodoric with Gaba, sheltered in the warmth and safety of our wagon so Brutus and I could go ahead alone. We reached the gate and casually dismounted. The main gate was closed, but two sentries emerged from the postern door. I did not recognize either of them.

"Who are you?" demanded one. I gave my name and asked to speak with Proculus Tatianus.

"He has been deployed to Noricum. Give me your passport."

Oh, dear Jesus!

I was terrified this would happen. I'd counted on Proculus being present and recognizing me so we could bluff our way into the fort. Instead, we would have to fight, which I dreaded. I began to panic for a moment but then took a deep breath and went ahead with my deception.

"Proculus said that Stilicho might call up the garrison, and so it would appear," I said. "How did you get left behind?"

"Bad luck," he said. "Passport?" he persisted.

"At least the two of you have each other for company," I said with a forced grin while nodding at the other sentry.

"There are more than just the two of us," he said without a hint of humor. He stretched out his hand and waved it impatiently.

I had to assume this man was part of the skeleton garrison, one of twenty, Proculus had said. But that was for the winter garrison. Stilicho needed men up north to repel the barbarians. Would he leave twenty men behind? If there were that many, Brutus and I would soon be dead.

"The passport is in my saddle bag. Can your man hold my horse while I fetch it?"

"I suppose," he said reluctantly.

I moved beside my mount, and as I pretended to fumble with my saddlebags, the other sentry stepped forward and took her reins. I slapped her flank. She stepped forward, butting him with her head and causing him to drop her reins.

He muttered, "Shit," and bent down to retrieve them. While he was distracted, I'd unsheathed my dagger. He stood, arms out, handing the reins to me. He did not see my dagger coming until, I drove it into his chest with all my might, just below his ribs, angling it up into his heart. He collapsed. Meanwhile, Brutus had cut the other sentry's throat. Our whole assault had taken twenty noiseless heartbeats.

We darted through the postern door and lifted the main gate's heavy bar, working together before any other guards appeared. A man emerged from the warm shelter of the gatehouse. He cried out in surprise, and two other men followed. By then, I was slowly, agonizingly slowly, pushing open the massive gate. I heard hoofbeats pounding. Our cavalry was on the way.

Finally, I'd opened the gate enough to squeeze out, but I kept pushing. Brutus had his back to me, protecting me from the three men who, with slashing swords, had formed a semicircle around him. There was no silence now. Steel rang on steel, and the sentries called to each other. I turned and pushed the gate with my shoulder, trying to force it open just a little faster. A glance told me Brutus was holding his own, but for how long?

"Bring your horse," he shouted. That was not part of the plan.

When the gate was open far enough to admit my horse, I slipped out, grabbed her reins, and led her through the gap until we stood just behind Brutus. He was busy stabbing and hacking, whirling and twisting, a blizzard of slashing death.

I nudged him from behind and shouted, "We're here!"

He glanced over his shoulder and saw me standing with my horse partway through the gateway. With one last sword thrust, which his opponent deflected, he turned, tucked an arm around my waist, lifted me off my feet, leaped past my horse, and beyond the gateway. When he released me, I fell, turned, and watched him drive his sword into my poor mount. With a scream, she collapsed, her body filling the gap in the gateway. One of the sentries scrambled over the horse's body to pursue us, but when he saw our cavalry only a hundred yards away, he went back. He and his comrades tried to close the gate, an impossible task with the horse's body in the way. They could not budge the carcass, and, with nowhere to run, they stood shoulder to shoulder in the gateway behind the bulky corpse, swords ready, awaiting their fate.

Wallia was first on the scene with two dozen horsemen. While the dead horse had succeeded in keeping the gate open, it now blocked his access to the Romans.

"Are you safe?" he asked.

"The postern door is open," I pointed.

A dozen warriors entered that way, flanked the sentries, and quickly cut them down. The fortress was ours, and the road to Aquileia lay open.

I walked through the gate and forty paces beyond and vomited in the courtyard. I'd never killed a man at close quarters before. Alaric found me there, retching, and gathered me into his arms.

"You stupid, stupid girl," he said as he hugged me tight. He'd never liked my plan, my ruse, and preferred to demolish the wall where a natural spring was undermining it, leaving it ready to collapse. But, since we both knew that demolishing it would take weeks, time we didn't have before the winter blizzards arrived, he'd reluctantly agreed to my plan and accepted its risks.

Chapter 8. 402 CE. Pollentia

Early Modern Source: Gibbon (1737-1794 CE), English Historian and author of "The History of the Decline and Fall of the Roman Empire," which describes the Battle of Pollentia:

Chapter XXX: Revolt Of The Goths.—Part III "... Stilicho resolved to attack the Christian Goths whilst they were devoutly employed in celebrating the festival of Easter. ... The camp of the Goths, which Alaric had pitched in the neighborhood of Pollentia, was thrown into confusion by the sudden and impetuous charge of the Imperial cavalry; but, in a few moments, the undaunted genius of their leader gave them an order and a field of battle...

"... The defeat of the [Alan] wing of cavalry might have decided the victory of Alaric if Stilicho had not immediately led the Roman and barbarian infantry to the attack. The skill of the general and the bravery of the soldiers surmounted every obstacle. In the evening of the bloody day, the Goths retreated from the field of battle...

"The magnificent spoils of Corinth and Argos enriched the veterans of the West; the captive wife of Alaric ... *was reduced to implore the mercy of the insulting foe..."*

Matilde

It took weeks for our wagon-train to pass through the Julian Alps, and, as I feared, the last dozen wagons were trapped in the snow, and people froze. Alaric created a wagon-fort on the outskirts of Aquileia, where we waited for everyone to rendezvous. Our forces blockaded the city, but with its high stout walls, there was no point in a siege. It was impregnable and could not be starved into submission. The port remained open, and sea trade continued as if we were not there.

By early February, the entire tribe had arrived. We were a formidable force: fifteen thousand warriors and twice that in women and children, twelve hundred oxcarts, and four hundred warhorses.

A delegation came from Mediolanum, where the Emperor resided, seeking our demands. I helped formulate our response, which I wrote out in proper Latin. We were not, I wrote, *not* invading, but migrating. We sought free passage to a new home, a home of the Emperor's choosing, whether that be Gaul, Hispania, or Africa. The choice was his.

I wrote that we had no interest in devastating the countryside through which passed. That is what I wrote while understanding that the Emperor's court might view my assertion skeptically since we had already scraped clean all the land of anything edible or valuable within a day's ride of our wagon-fort.

We received no reply. Our requests were ignored. It was time, Alaric said, to seize Mediolanum and capture the Emperor. Could anyone, he joked, suggest a better bargaining chip? I did not argue. It was an argument I'd repeatedly made and lost before we left Illyricum.

The journey to Mediolanum was slow. It took several weeks, much slower than my previous journey over the same route, because we were burdened by miles of oxcarts this time. Most everyone was on foot, but I, as usual, rode with the scouts. Our march across the Venetian plain and up the Po Valley was surprisingly peaceful. As we approached each town or city, we would stand at the city gates and announce a tariff: so many pounds of flour, of pig, of vegetables, etc. Cities that obliged we left in peace. If a city with stout walls ignored our demands, we just moved on. We had no interest in engaging in a lengthy siege. We sacked and burned any unwalled cities that defied us. They were very few. We maintained our usual vigilance, sending our scouts out to look for any Roman force. But Stilicho had pulled every fighting man north with him, across the Alps, to deal with the barbarians in Raetia and Noricum.

By the middle of February, we were besieging Mediolanum, hoping the Emperor would negotiate a settlement. Our pickets prevented anyone from entering or leaving, which prevented the Emperor from knowing when Stilicho might come to his aid. However, we knew we should expect his army to attack once the Alpine passes were clear in late March. We hoped Honorius would panic and negotiate. Our hope was in vain. In early March, I was awoken by shouting and the clashing of arms. I climbed out of my wagon and found Ataulf striding about, cursing.

"What's happened?" I asked.

"Some Roman horsemen have penetrated our siege lines and entered the city," he said.

"How is that possible? Were our sentries asleep?"

"No, but they were taken by surprise. However, we managed to capture one of the riders. In the morning, we'll see what he has to say."

I dismissed the incident and went back to bed. By morning, Ataulf had interrogated the rider.

As I was feeding Theodoric, Ataulf walked up. "Silco?" my little boy said. It galled me that one of his first words was "Stilicho."

Ataulf patted his head and said, "Good question, lad. Yes, he was leading last night's riders. The rest of his army is only a few days behind. It is even larger than we'd feared. He has bolstered his force with a large number of barbarians. And he has called in support from Britain and Germany."

"What barbarians?"

"The rider reported that Stilicho's army crushed the invading Vandals and Alans. But a large number of those warriors surrendered. He enlisted them as *foederate allies*. These barbarians will do anything for a gold coin."

"Are we any different?" I asked. Before he could answer, I asked, "Are we in trouble?"

"Not if we capture the Emperor. The rider said he left Mediolanum and was fleeing to Gaul. In any case, that's where we're heading. We'll go west, chasing after the Emperor and away from Stilicho's army. Then over the Alps and into the lush fields of Gaul."

I grated my teeth. We would be in Gaul by now if we hadn't stopped to besiege Mediolanum.

"If we cross the Alps, won't we encounter Stilicho's reinforcements coming from Britain and Germany?"

"Alaric has thought of that," said Ataulf. "We'll enter Gaul by some route in the southwest."

As quickly as possible, we got ready to move. We broke off our siege of Mediolanum and marched for a day southwest to the Tanaro River, broad and swift. We marched upstream beside it, confident we were following hard on the Emperor's tail, and laid siege to the small city of Hasta, where the local peasants said the Emperor was taking refuge.

But we were not the only ones capable of a ruse. I later learned that the Emperor was still in Mediolanum. Stilicho had sent one of the Emperor's carriages, surrounded by a large entourage, to Hasta to deceive us, hoping we would besiege that city, a fruitless effort and one that would delay us until his army and reinforcements were at hand. We fell right into Stilicho's trap.

Alaric ordered two assaults on the walls of Hasta, ineffective and costly attacks that took the lives of three dozen young men. After the second, he instructed my scouts, "Tell me the size of Stilicho's force and where they are." I could see he was considering a third assault.

As I prepared to mount up, he approached me. "You don't need to go. Wallia can lead the scouts. Pentadia says she would enjoy your company tonight. As would our boy."

I was sure Pentadia and little Theodoric had said no such thing. I knew there was no point in arguing, so I ignored him. "We'll be back two hours after dawn," I said, leading our small scouting party away from the camp.

My squad returned at dawn, horses blown, and each of us unrecognizable under a crust of dust. I found Alaric sitting with his council by the command wagon, warming their hands by a fire and talking anxiously. Their eyes were asking: fight or flee? Pentadia and our children were sitting beside him. I squatted on his other side and gestured for his flask, which he handed me. I filled my mouth with watered wine, swished it about, gargled, and spat it into the flames. It took another mouthful of wine to moisten my dry throat enough to let me speak.

I talked clearly so the chieftains on the fire's far side could hear. "Stilicho has forty thousand men." I paused to let that sink in. "They are one day's march east of here."

In a conversational tone, Alaric said, "Oh, forty thousand. One day." I marveled at his calm. While others around the fire were cursing and shouting, Alaric spent his time thinking.

"Yes. At least that number," I said.

"We cannot take Hasta in one more day," he said. "We must abandon this siege and flee. We cannot outrun them, burdened as we are with our baggage train."

I could see Alaric was bitterly disappointed at abandoning the siege. His goal had appeared within his grasp. No one doubted that if we'd succeeded in capturing Honorius, our dream of securing a homeland for our nation would be granted. What choice would the weak-minded boy Emperor have? Now, we were running for our lives.

"We can move faster if we abandon our wagons and flee on foot," I said. "Stilicho's army has been marching for a week and must be exhausted. When they find our wagons, they will stop and loot them. That will give us a head start. Perhaps we can outpace them, though it will be difficult with the women and children."

A voice called out from across the campfire. It was Sarus. "Abandon our wagons? Mine contains wealth collected over a decade, everything I have taken since Adrianople. I will die first."

In a quiet voice, I said, "Then you will likely die."

"We will not abandon our wagons," Alaric ordered.

We are doomed.

I had been up all night riding and was weary to the bone, but my horse needed attention. I walked to the horse line and took care of my tired beast. Then, I staggered to the river and dove in, causing a patch of dirt to surface and disappear downstream. I dripped back to the wagon that Pentadia and I shared with our children—Alaric had his own wagon—stripped off my wet garments and climbed under my blankets. I was slightly disturbed when someone hitched the oxen, and we started moving west. Later, somebody, probably Pentadia, put a napping Theodoric next to me. With him by my side, I relaxed and fell back to sleep.

Our people marched long and hard to escape Stilicho's army. On the first day out of Hasta, we traveled over twenty miles southwest beside the Tanaro, finally reaching a village called Pollentia. Behind the village, to the north, stood a great cliff. The paths leading to the clifftop looked highly defensible. I mentioned it to Alaric as a secure site. He and I climbed to the cliff's rim as the others prepared for the night. From there, we could see the camp being organized below, campfires glowing, and tents popping up in the wagon's protective ring. Looking down the river valley, I saw no sign of the pursuing Romans.

Alaric said, "Stilicho is probably spending the night inside Hasta, secure from a sudden attack by us."

I was less sure. Certainly, Stilicho must interpret our withdrawal from Hasta as a retreat. Now, the Romans held the initiative. Wouldn't the Roman general quickly close in for the kill? But the evening's overcast sky suggested otherwise. If the Romans were anywhere near, the clouds would reflect their campfires.

"Besides," continued Alaric, "tomorrow is Easter. Christians honor that day above all other holy days. There will be no fighting."

When it came time to bed down, Pentadia, Gaba, and I, with our two children, slept in the wives' wagon and immediately fell asleep. A short while later, a knock on the wagon wheel woke us up.

"He wants Pentadia," a guard said.

She got up, shook Amalric awake, and the two climbed out of the wagon and went off to Alaric's tent. I fell back to sleep until dawn, then, after kissing the sleeping Theodoric, I climbed down to the ground. We rode east with the rest of the cavalry, trying to locate Stilicho's army. After an hour of riding, having seen no sign of him, we started back to the wagon-fort.

We had not arrived when the Romans attacked. It caught everyone by surprise. Contrary to Alaric's belief, Stilicho had no qualms about desecrating Easter.

His forces struck just as everyone was breaking camp. The wagon-fort was slowly unraveling from the night's defensive circle into the day's line of march. When the Romans struck, the wagon train had already stretched out west for three miles along the riverside road. The remaining wagons were back at the campsite in their overnight positions, waiting their turn to move out.

The Romans and their barbarian Alan allies had quietly snuck along the river's edge, hidden from the road by the riverbank. They swarmed up from the river and attacked our wagon train. When the alarm sounded, the women and children throughout the column abandoned their wagons and ran back to the shelter of the wagon-fort, with our warriors covering their retreat.

Our warriors fought hard to protect their families, most of whom managed to flee to safety. By the time the rest of the cavalry and I returned, the enemy had captured all the wagons strung out along the road and had pushed our forces back into the wagon-fort. Their attack had stalled as the Alan warriors were more eager to plunder our wagons than to press their advantage home.

Wallia, who led our cavalry, called for the attack. Our horsemen, armed with lances, descended on the enemy with a fury. One Roman officer shouted at the Alans to stop looting and resist us. I watched with satisfaction as Brutus, who was riding beside me, drove his lance through the Roman's body. Our surprise appearance provided a short-lived advantage. Soon, another Roman officer restored order among his men, and they began to push us back. I recognized the officer. It was Stilicho himself.

We rode through the gap in the wagon-fort that served as its gate just as men pushed a wagon to fill that hole. The air was full of shouting and weeping, but people moved about purposefully. We had drilled for this eventuality, and people knew their roles.

My mount was lathered and panting, and I was bleeding from a sword slash to my leg. Would I be able to stand? I doubted it. Pentadia ran over to me. "I need a bandage," I shouted. "Fetch me one!"

She had reached my side and shouted in my ear, "Theodoric!"

I understood in an instant. My little boy had been left behind in my wagon, now being swarmed by the enemy. Hopefully Gaba was with him. Without giving it another thought, I kicked my horse and darted through the closing gate and galloped down the line of oxcarts, past surprised groups of Romans and Alans, desperate to save my baby.

The distance to my wagon was not far, and I almost made it before a legionary thrust his sword into my poor beast's leg. She screamed and collapsed. I was able to roll free but could not stand. The pain was unbearable. The legionary raised his sword above his head, readying a killing stroke, when a voice shouted, "Stop!" The pain and loss of blood overcame me and I blacked out.

I woke later as a medicus wrapped a bandage around my leg. He saw my eyes open and said, "It wasn't too deep, though it gushed blood. You will walk again, I think." Then I passed out again.

It was midafternoon when I awoke. A young legionary was squatting beside me, offering me food and drink. I drank—it was watered wine—but said I could not stomach any food. "You must eat before I help you find your boy," he said. "Stilicho's orders."

That motivated me to eat bread soaked in spicy chickpea paste and wine.

"General Stilicho says your name is Matilde, and you are the queen of these Goths."

I nodded my head and asked, "And yours?"

"Constantius. Now, we must hurry to view the prisoners before the slave traders show up. They are like vultures. They can smell a battle and prey on the losers, selling them quickly before the slave market is flooded."

This was not news to me. The slave traders would buy all the prisoners, a windfall for the soldiers. Any not purchased, the old and very young, would be killed. Theodoric was very young.

I could not put any weight on my left leg, but with an arm over Constantius's shoulder, I could hobble down the road, past all our oxcarts, to a rope corral crowded with women, children, and old men. I knew many of them by name and all by sight. One woman, Wallia's sister-in-law, cried out when she saw me. "Oh Gods, Matilde, they got you too!" The crowd was small, no more than two hundred people. Thankfully, most of our people had escaped to the wagon-fort, though that was small comfort for those who'd been captured.

One woman, hearing my name, stood and faced me. It was Gaba and, thank God, she was carrying Theodoric. "Matilde," she called.

"That is my servant," I told Constantius, "and my little boy."

"Release them," he said to a guard, and soon I was holding my baby, and Gaba was draped around my shoulders, weeping. We were all crying except Theodoric, who, laughing and excited at seeing me, kept repeating, "Mama."

"Why did you not grab the baby and run?" I asked her.

"I was too scared," Gaba said. "And then there was Brutus. I am so sorry about Brutus. He fought bravely to save us, but there were too many."

My dedicated bodyguard was dead after years together, never in friendship but always friendly. Servilia had said he would die for me, and he had. I prayed to Jesus that he be given a horse farm in the afterlife, and then I cried and cried.

Chapter 9.   402 CE. Constantius

Matilde

Stilicho kept his promise: Neither I nor my baby had been harmed, not intentionally, though it took months for my leg to heal. Constantius and a small squad of legionaries took the three of us—Gaba, Theodoric, and me—back to Stilicho's home in Mediolanum.

That magnificent city had changed. The Emperor and his court were gone, and with them, the spirit of the city. Honorius had fled to Ravenna, accompanied and protected by an entire cohort of legionaries. It was a seaside city surrounded by swamps and was virtually impregnable. Never again, said the Emperor, would his person be subject to a barbarian threat. The troops that once guarded the palace compound were gone. Anyone could wander through the compound's gates and gaze at the homes of the rich and powerful. Some homes, like Stilicho's, retained a security force, but most were empty, their owners having fled to Ravenna with the imperial family. Stilicho and Serena had also moved to Ravenna, though he kept a home in Rome and retained the one in Mediolanum. Empty homes did not stay empty long. The homeless poor soon squatted in them.

I asked Constantius for news of my friends and family, but he knew no more than I did. "We will talk when I return," he said. "You are safe, under Stilicho's protection, but do not think to escape. That would try his patience, and people who try his patience do not survive."

It wasn't as if I *could* escape, not with a baby, a timid servant, and a crippled leg.

"I have instructed the guards that you are free to move about the house, and when your leg heals, you may go about the city if accompanied by a guard. You may not leave the city."

"What about Gaba?"

"She may go wherever she likes and wherever you wish her to."

"When will you return?"

"I don't know. Whenever Stilicho wishes it," he said.

He was gone from April, when I was first captured, until late summer, by which time Stilicho had pushed my tribe back out of Italia into Pannonia. Every day, I longed for news. Had my family been massacred? Sold into slavery? It was hard to imagine Alaric and Pentadia dead, but my idle mind was more than capable of dreaming horrible thoughts.

There was little for me to do. Almost nothing. Stilicho maintained a few household slaves, a stable of horses, and staff to look after them. It took some begging, but I persuaded the chief groom to let me tend the horses even though the guards would not let me ride. That was a freedom I would request the next time Constantius returned.

Stilicho had an extensive library, which I began to read, systematically working through all his books. I had previously read many of the poets, such as Sappho and Pacuvius, but re-reading them was a great pleasure.

As my little boy grew, I told Theodoric stories about his father and taught him his letters, Gothic, Greek, and Latin. Along with Gaba, we played games, and when a game needed four people, one of the young guards would sit in. His name was Nevitta, and Gaba soon took him as her lover. None of the men interested me, though I had thought Constantius was handsome. I looked forward to seeing him again.

Finally, in early September, he reappeared with a squad of legionaries. They were billeted in a local barracks, but he took a room in Stilicho's house, just down the hall from mine, so we saw a good deal of each other. I peppered him with questions about my family and my tribe. Yes, Alaric, Pentadia, and Amalric were safe. After I was captured, Alaric had defended the hilltop stronghold in Pollentia. There had been bitter fighting and deaths on both sides before he and Stilicho negotiated a settlement. Alaric agreed to return across the Julian Alps to Pannonia.

"What about all the captured families?" I asked.

"Stilicho refused to release them. They were sold into slavery, and the proceeds were awarded as bonuses to the legionaries and the Alan barbarians. The wagons and their treasure were auctioned, and the takings were distributed to the soldiers. Each man's share amounted to two years' pay."

I covered my face in dismay, thinking of Wallia's sister-in-law and her children. One was a newborn. It was worth nothing to the slavers, so they probably killed it. I felt sick.

After I regained my composure, I asked, "Did Alaric go peacefully?"

"Hardly. He promised to retreat past Aquileia and east through the Julian Alps, but when he reached Verona, he led your tribe north, attempting to reach Noricum. But Stilicho was watching. When Alaric made his move, Stilicho pounced. He killed many Goths, and whole clans defected. Sarus and his clan are now Roman allies."

"Sarus is scum," I said bitterly. "Stilicho will regret accepting him as an ally."

"But now, finally, Alaric has gone to Pannonia, and Italia is at peace again," Constantius said as if he were telling the happy ending of a long story.

"What about me?" I asked.

"Stilicho has said nothing about you. He appears to be proud of housing the Queen of the Goths. I think he likes having you nearby and away from Alaric. The general once remarked, 'Alaric is twice as dangerous when Matilde is advising him.'"

I laughed sardonically. "I was the one who advised migrating through Italia. What a disaster that was."

"It was not bad advice. Your suggestion made sense with General Fravitta at your back, no subsidies, and restless clan chieftains. It would have worked if you'd captured Honorius. Too bad you didn't."

"Should you be saying that?"

"Perhaps it is a little treasonous. Keep it as our secret. Anyway, who would you tell?"

I laughed. "Stilicho?" I joked.

Constantius would come periodically, once every two or three months, and then disappear again. On his first visit, he agreed to accompany me riding in the countryside near the city. I was so pleased I kissed his cheek, making him blush. He only stayed for three days, but we rode every day. It was early winter, and even though the countryside was bleak, the air was crisp, clean, and free. I laughed with the joy of being outdoors.

As he was leaving, I begged him to let me continue to ride, but I could see he did not trust me.

"What would keep you from fleeing to Pannonia?"

"My promise?"

"I might accept your promise, but my General would not. Stilicho remembers how you spied back in Thessalia and your ruse at Ad Pirum." I'd foolishly boasted of those deeds, never thinking they might be held against me.

"I would never flee without taking Theodoric," I said. "Would you trust me to return if I left him here with Nevitta?"

With that assurance, Constantius was persuaded.

In time, the guards testified to my good behavior, and Constantius came to trust me. We grew comfortable in each other's company. I felt free to ask him questions: Did he have any news from my family? There seldom was. How did he spend his time away from Mediolanum and me? Was he married?

"I am Stilicho's eyes and ears on the frontier," he said. "And I oversee construction of the new facilities in Ticinum." Ticinum was a city on the River Ticinus, a tributary of the Po, and a half-day's ride south of Mediolanum. Constantius wouldn't talk about the new facilities. "The work is secret," he said, "and you don't need to know."

"Then what, Sir Eyes and Ears, can you talk about? Is anything happening at the frontiers?" I asked.

"Rhine or Danube?" he asked. I knew little about the Rhine frontier, and since my tribe was now living in Pannonia, I asked about the Danube.

"There is a problem with the Huns," he said. Just the name filled me with revulsion. "Their king, Uldin, is on good terms with both Emperors, at least for now. Honorius pays him a subsidy, and I believe Arcadius does too. We have exchanged hostages, including sending them Aetius." That was the first I'd heard of that young man. In a few years, he would feature largely in our lives as the leader who would destroy Hunnish power forever.

"The problem with the Huns," he went on, "is they are cruel masters. All of their subject peoples despise them. I have talked with Godigisel, chieftain of the Asding Vandals, and Goar of the Alans."

"Aren't those the tribes Stilicho defeated last year in Raetia and Noricum?"

"Yes. They came across the Danube to get away from the Huns. In part."

"In part?"

"Yes. They also hoped to settle in the empire just as your tribe did. They watched as Alaric got a position in the military and a subsidy from the Emperor. They want that."

That was a mistake neither Emperor would ever repeat, I thought.

"Have your eyes and ears taken you to Pannonia? Have you talked to Alaric?"

"Yes. Your family misses you and keeps asking when Stilicho will release you."

"What do you say?"

"I tell them I cannot make any promises, but it may happen once Stilicho becomes convinced that Alaric won't invade Italia again."

"We weren't invading. We were migrating."

"Yes, yes," he cut me short and, without answering whether he was married, said, "Let's go for a ride while the weather's good."

"To Ticinum?"

"I cannot take you there. Anyway, it is too far."

But we rode and rode until the weather broke, and we were utterly drenched. The chief groom was amused when we returned with our clothes dripping wet.

Gaba had anticipated my need for a hot bath, so she filled the great tub with searing hot water. As I settled in for a long soak, Constantius poked his head in the door.

"Oh." He seemed momentarily confused. "Gaba, come tell me when the tub is free." He stood there waiting, hair still dripping, naked except for a small towel wrapped around his waist. Broad shoulders, well-muscled chest, rippled stomach, legs of steel.

Gaba said, "Yes, Dominus, of course. But there is room in the tub for two!"

Constantius made a choking sound, retreated into the hallway, and slammed the door.

Gaba and I laughed until we ached.

Constantius visited regularly, sometimes more than once per month. Each time he came, he brought Theodoric a toy. It might be something simple like a carved horse painted brilliant red or a wooden chariot with wheels that actually turned. He would sit on the ground with my son, marching miniature soldiers around garden fortifications and bathing mud-covered unicorns in puddle-sized lakes. The garden had a sundial that stood waist high, high enough that Theodoric had to stretch to perch his wooden animals on its edge. The height of hilarity was when Constantius flew a stuffed doll named Apollo around and around the sundial until it landed, knocking off all the wooden animals. As they fell, Theodoric would voice their cries of "Aaaaa!" And then, "Again, Contans, again!" I dearly loved my son, but Constantius's pleasure and patience with him—feelings I could never match—left me wondering whether I was a good mother.

While Constantius was away, I had time to think about our failed migration, which the Romans insisted on calling an "invasion." Why, I wondered, didn't Stilicho simply destroy us the way the Romans eradicated the Carthaginians? He'd had the opportunity. Two opportunities: once at Pollentia, when I was captured, and then again in Verona, which I only knew about through Constantius's description. After Stilicho captured me, he had Alaric pinned in a hilltop redoubt near Pollentia. Why did Stilicho negotiate rather than fight? And likewise in Verona. Why?

When Constantius was home, I asked him those questions one morning at breakfast. He said he had his own opinions but would not divulge them before swearing me to secrecy. That was curious since he claimed he didn't trust me, but I readily agreed. Who would I betray him to, even if I wanted to (which I didn't)?

"It's all politics," Constantius said. "Stilicho versus Roman senators. They belittle his victories and throw our ancient triumphs against the Carthaginians in his face. Back then, we lost army after army—fifty thousand dead at Cannae alone—and then, we raised another army every time. Our armies comprised strong farmer citizens. We did not fight with German mercenaries. When we finally won, we made mountains of our enemy's bodies. To Stilicho's adversaries, that is what a proper victory should look like, not some negotiated settlement where the enemy lives to fight another day.

"But today, Stilicho has only one field army of citizen soldiers. He cannot risk losing it because he can't raise another. The rich Senators have blocked conscription since it would strip them of their plantation workers. They would rather pay a fine than lose a farm hand. Which is why Stilicho is cautious with his army. Rome would have been left defenseless if he'd fought Alaric at Pollentia and lost."

"Do you think he might have lost?"

"It is possible. Your people spent years in Illyricum, with all its arms factories. They have fine swords and armor, every bit as good as Stilicho's, and they are trained in Roman tactics. Your Goths are good soldiers. Stilicho would rather hire than fight them. But then Stilicho hits another problem. The Senate hates it when he hires mercenaries. They pay him money rather than allow him to draft Romans, but when he uses that money to pay for barbarian troops, they hate him for *that*. They want citizen armies, not mercenary armies. Stilicho cannot win. So he avoids battles."

"But he fought at Pollentia," I pointed out.

"Yes, he did, and he lost many good men—Roman citizens—at Pollentia. It was a pyrrhic victory. But a good victory because it encouraged many Goths to change sides. He recruited those barbarians to fill the gaps left by his casualties."

I nodded. "That explains why he negotiated at Verona rather than crushing Alaric," I said. "Stilicho could not risk pitting his new Gothic recruits against their friends and cousins in Alaric's battle line."

"Yes. The Senate is correct in one regard: our legions *should* be filled with Roman citizens, not barbarian mercenaries. But to do that, Stilicho ought to force the Senate to legalize conscription and raise taxes to pay for it."

"Won't they resist?"

"Undoubtedly. When they do, he should crush them. Kill a few dozen senators, and the rest will fall into line."

"Surely Honorius will oppose that?"

"If he does, then Stilicho should kill him, too. He's useless anyway."

"It's hard to believe Stilicho would kill the Emperor."

"True, unfortunately. Stilicho is loyal to a fault. He is a much better servant than Honorius deserves."

"Would *you* do it?" I asked.

He just smiled at me, a smile I took to mean "yes."

"All this talk borders on treason," I remarked.

"Which is why I swore you to secrecy."

Over the subsequent years, Theodoric grew, and Constantius returned more often. Their play evolved from ball games to mock stick fights and then wooden swords. My host found a gentle pony, and the three of us (with a few bodyguards) would ride through the countryside. On cool evenings, we would sit on a couch before a merry fire, Theodoric between us, and talk. My boy would fall asleep, leaning against Constantius, and when I couldn't keep my eyes open, he would carry my son to my room and put us to bed.

One evening, Constantius bade me goodnight and kissed me. I lifted my head to return it, but he had gone to my sleeping son to kiss him, too.

I lay awake, looking at the ceiling, wondering what this meant and what I felt for Constantius. Did he love me? He never said so. Did I love him? I didn't know whether it was love, but I realized something had changed. Every time he drew near, every time our hands touched, my heart raced, and my breath shortened. I knew these feelings; I'd had them with Gainas. When he died, I thought my ability to feel such things had died with him. I'd been wrong, as Constantius was now proving.

I'd done nothing wrong—yet—so why did I feel guilty? Gainas was long gone; I owed his memory no loyalty. This passion, these feelings, were nothing I'd ever felt for Alaric. It was always a calm love with him, two souls that fit together like a hand in a soft leather glove.

But I was getting ahead of myself. Constantius had kissed me, nothing more. He had not wrapped his arms around me, pulled me to the floor, and smothered me with caresses and kisses. And then I had not returned his passion, stroke for stroke, and—

I put those thoughts away. Did I want another affair, an emotional storm like I'd had with Gainas? That had ended so tragically and, in truth, was ending even before he died. He was not the man I wanted and imagined him to be.

Constantius was different. Here was a man who knew what the empire needed and how to get it. Unlike Gainas, Constantius was a native Roman, a Catholic Christian from a good family. The aristocracy would accept him as Emperor, and he would make a good one. That got me thinking...

One morning, I said, "You've never told me whether you are married."

"I was, but she died along with our baby. That was a year before I met you." I saw his eyes turn red, but no tears fell. I took his hand, gently pressed it to my cheek, and kissed it.

"I am so sorry."

He shrugged. "The day is young. Are you ready for a long ride? We could get to Ticinum and back today."

"Is that allowed now?"

"If I say so, then it is so," he replied. We rode south, leaving Theodoric in Gaba's care.

By the time we got to Ticinum, it was midafternoon. Constantius largely ignored me as he set about inspecting his *project*. His project was transforming this small Italian city into a massive army depot. A palisade, which surrounded the town at some distance from its walls, enclosed a port along the Ticinus River, barracks for a dozen legions, warehouses for arms and armor, granaries, forges, and other workshops, kitchens, pastures for livestock, and fields for military drill.

His tour, with me trailing behind, felt endless. He seemed to spot every flaw, whether from a leaking armory roof to rat droppings in a granary. When a blacksmith complained of the charcoal's poor quality, Constantius instructed an aide to "fix it and fix it quickly." We finished our tour at one of the kitchens, where the staff fed us a passably good meal of pork pie.

When we finally had time to ourselves, I asked, "What is it all for? Is Rome in some war that I haven't heard about?"

"Not yet, but soon. There is great barbarian unrest along the Rhine frontier and the upper Danube. Whenever they come—probably the Vandals and Alans—and wherever they appear, we need to have our supplies here, in the foothills of the Alps, so we can quickly respond. There won't be time to bring wheat from Africa or shields from Tarsatica. Stilicho and I were of like minds when he ordered me to create this depot. Our only regret is we don't have enough men to fill the barracks you saw today. The Senate won't permit more recruiting. I expect they will change their minds when they see Siling Vandals torching their villas."

"When I was with Gainas, Eutropius allowed him to recruit both native Romans and barbarians," I said. "I even went with him on one trip to Aquincum, where he recruited Goths from across the Danube."

"Were those the men of Chieftain Radagaisus?"

"Yes. Gainas recruited perhaps seventy-five warriors on that trip."

"Do I understand that you have met Radagaisus?"

"Yes. I can't say I liked him. I thought better of his son Guitabert and became good friends with Guitabert's wife, Ralamunda."

"Hmm," said Constantius. I could see him tucking away that information for future use.

By the time we finished eating, it was too late to ride home, but Constantius said there was a *mansio* nearby, within the palisade. "I had it built as part of the depot."

His men rode to one of the barracks while he and I entered his new *mansio*. The innkeeper welcomed us—he said he'd known we were coming—and told us our room, the finest room in the building, was ready for us. "*Our* room?" I asked Constantius, "*One* room?"

"Do you mind?" he said.

"It contains a tub, already filled with hot water. The attendants and masseurs are standing by," the innkeeper offered.

I laughed and said, "No, I don't mind." I'd toyed with several plans to coax Constantius into my bed, but as his project demonstrated, *he* was the master planner.

Chapter 10. 406 CE. Radagaisus

Ancient Source: Zosimus (fl. 490s–510s), a Greek historian and author of "Historia Nova," which describes how Stilicho defeated Radagaisus:

[5.26.3] While Alaric waited for his commands, Rhodogaisus [Radagaisus], having collected four hundred thousand of the Celts and the German tribes that dwell beyond the Danube and the Rhine, made the preparations for passing over into Italy.

[5.26.4] This intelligence, when first communicated, occasioned a general consternation. While the several towns sunk into despondency, and even Rome itself was filled with apprehension of its danger, Stilicho took with him all the forces that were stationed at Ticinum in Liguria, which amounted to about thirty cohorts and all the auxiliaries that he could procure from the Alani and Huns, and without waiting for the approach of the enemy, crossed the Danube with all his forces.

[5.26.5] Thus attacking the barbarians before they were aware, he completely destroyed their whole forces, none of them escaping, except a few, which he added to the Roman auxiliaries; Stilicho, as may be supposed, was highly elated by this victory and led back his army, receiving garlands from the people of every place, for having in so unusual a manner delivered Italy

from the dangers which she so much dreaded and expected.

Matilde

Constantius returned often over the next several months. He claimed the work in Ticinum kept him busy, but I believe our new relationship drew him back. On each occasion, he continued to bring a toy for Theodoric. A recent favorite was a leather ball stuffed with wool. The four of us, for Theodoric insisted that Gaba join, played a game where we would kick the ball around a field, trying to elude the other players.

One evening, when Gaba and I were alone, she knelt at my feet and clutched my knees. "I have something to say. Something to ask."

Then she hemmed and hawed until I said, "Well? Well, what is it?"

"I am expecting a baby. Nevitta and I are expecting a baby."

She always wore a loose-fitting tunic, so if she had a bulge, I never noticed it. "That is wonderful! When is it due?"

"Um, thank you. In five months. Nevitta wants to marry me before then."

"I approve. Does he need Constantius's approval? I'll talk to him."

"Thank you, but there's a problem."

It was late, and I was tired, so it took me time to realize her problem: citizens could not marry slaves. I gently pressed her cheeks between my hands and kissed her forehead. "Of course, you shall be freed. Immediately." She hugged me and cried and laughed.

I fulfilled the promise I'd made when we escaped from Constantinople, that I would purchase her freedom from Gainas whenever he returned, now a meaningless promise. Constantius drafted the necessary legal documents, and I stood with Gaba as she and Nevitta married. She continued to assist me, but now as Theodoric's auntie and not as a servant.

Constantius brought me the latest news. After a fine meal on a stormy evening in early winter, he reported that Augusta Eudoxia had put General Fravitta to death. Her official reason was treason: Fravitta had accused John, one of Arcadius's advisors, of exacerbating the tension between the brother Emperors. But Constantius said that was just an excuse. The actual reason lay in a secret. Eudoxia had given birth to Theodosius II, the heir to the throne, a few years earlier. Members of the court were surprised because it was widely accepted that Arcadius (like his brother Honorius) was impotent. So who was the father? General Fravitta learned the answer from the household slaves: Eudoxia and John were lovers. Fravitta was doomed once he revealed to Eudoxia that he knew her secret.

As if in divine punishment, Eudoxia herself died in childbirth. I cannot say I was sorry. I still blamed her for the death of Gainas.

Saving the best news for last, Constantius informed me that Honorius had appointed Alaric as *dux Pannonia Secunda*, military leader of lower Pannonia.

"What does this mean?" I was breathless with excitement.

"It means he is responsible for securing that portion of the Danube frontier and preventing any barbarians from crossing.

He will receive a subsidy from the Emperor, and his warriors are now Roman allies, *foederate allies*."

Constantius was grinning at me. He knew what I was actually asking.

"No, you ass, what does this mean for *me*! Can I finally go home to my family?"

"Technically, you're still a prisoner, but I am empowered to release you whenever you want."

I sat silently, mulling the implications. Constantius watched without speaking for a while before asking, "Don't you want to go back?"

"Yes, of course ..."

"But?"

"I love Alaric. Not with the same passion that I loved Gainas. And now there's you."

"You know we cannot marry," he said. "Asking Alaric to divorce you would risk making an enemy of him. Again. Rome cannot risk that."

"I don't want to anger Alaric. But I don't want to lose you."

"That is a dilemma. You need to decide."

He'd never said he loved me or expressed any such sentiment. Would he marry me if I weren't married? Not wanting to hear the answer, I didn't ask.

"I will go back to Alaric," I said.

He embraced me, kissed my forehead, and said, "That is the right choice. I will be gone for a week, but I'll provide a squad to accompany you home when I return. You should be home before New Year's."

Instead, Constantius was back in two days. "I've come to take you to Ticinum. Things have changed. Your friend Radagaisus has invaded Italia with his whole nation. My scouts estimate he has twenty thousand warriors, so perhaps forty thousand people altogether. They swarm like locusts over the land."

"Aren't I safe here?"

"The garrison of Mediolanum is weak. You and your son will be safer in Ticinum."

"What about my journey to my family, to Pannonia?"

"Out of the question. Too dangerous. Hurry, we don't know precisely where the invaders are, but I have had reports that they have overrun many towns in Venetia and along the Po River."

Constantius arranged for a small carriage to carry Theodoric, Gaba, and her children while Constantius and I rode along on horseback.

"Did Alaric try to stop them?" I asked.

"Whether by luck or intelligence, Radagaisus bypassed Alaric's province to the west," Constantius said. "They traveled south over the Alps on the military road, the *Via Claudia Augusta*. Our first reports came from Verona, which they were besieging. I have sent scouts there for more information, but they have not returned. I fear they are dead."

Constantius installed me in the same *mansio* where we first made love. Stilicho soon arrived from Ravenna. The depot was a hive of activity, with couriers heading to Gaul to summon all the Rhine frontier troops. He even called in his Alan and Hun allies.

"Why bring in the Huns?" I asked.

"They volunteered. Uldin claims Radagaisus's tribe are his slaves, and he wants them punished." That matched what Radagaisus told me years ago in Aquincum.

Squads of what Constantius called "recruiters" were sweeping the countryside looking for young men who could be "volunteered" into service. Soon, I watched as battalions of these men, supervised by regular legionaries, came marching into the depot.

"They march well," I said to Constantius.

"That is all they do well. It will take months to turn them into soldiers, months we don't have." Constantius's depot was the right place for the effort. After only a dozen days, I saw the recruits, equipped with armor, shields, and weapons, running for miles, then halting and conducting sword drills. The depot kitchens provided good food, and the barracks provided sound rest. A few tried to run away but found the depot's palisade challenging to climb. When a small group of recruits cut a hole through the palisade, a cavalry squad soon caught up with them. They were dragged by their heels back to the depot, tied to stakes, and publicly lashed to death. There were no more breakouts.

In the spring, Stilicho set about using the vast army he'd amassed. He received reports from the mayors of Florentia that Radagaisus was besieging their city. "We will move fast," Stilicho said, "and surround the barbarians before they know we're coming."

And we did. In only three days, our army raced down the *Via Aemilia*, crossed the Apennine mountains, and came up behind Radagaisus's forces, catching them unawares. (I say "we" because Stilicho insisted I come along, though I had no idea how I might be helpful.) The fighting was ferocious. Radagaisus had brought his Goths all this way to escape from his overlord, Uldin the Hun. When the Goths found they were facing Huns, they fought with superhuman zeal, but Stilicho's army was massive. It forced Radagaisus back into the hills northeast of Florentia, where they quickly established good defensive positions.

There followed a three-day standoff, which left the defenders near starvation. Radagaisus refused to negotiate with Stilicho, saying he didn't trust any ally of the Huns. That is when Stilicho called on me early one morning.

"You know this man, Radagaisus?" he asked. I explained my earlier encounter with him.

"Then he may trust you. You will approach him under a flag of truce and offer him terms of surrender." An order, not a request.

The mountain on which the barbarians sheltered rose a thousand feet above the plains below, a hillside of rocks and forests. I scrambled up the hillside carrying a white cloth on a stick, stumbling many times, scraping my hands and knees, but always keeping the flag aloft. I cried out, "Friend. Don't Shoot!" in Gothic and sometimes Greek because Stilicho had said that not all the barbarians were Goths.

"Stop, stay where you are," came a voice. "Who are you, and what do you want?"

"I am Matilde, wife of Alaric and a prisoner of the Romans. Stilicho has sent me to offer terms."

I remained stationary for many minutes until a man climbed down to me. It was Guitabert, Radagaisus's youngest son. He led me up to the mountaintop, where Radagaisus and his captains had gathered around a campfire.

"It *is* you," Radagaisus said. "I wondered what happened to you after we met in Aquincum. You were Gainas's hostage, yes? What did he do with you? He must have released you; otherwise, the Constantinople mob would have killed you along with all the other Goths."

"It was a near thing. I barely escaped," I said before giving him a brief recap of my story, and he shook his head in wonder. "So you've gone from being a hostage in the East to a prisoner in the West. You are unlucky, indeed.

"Now, tell me the terms Stilicho proposes."

"Stilicho says," I began but then coughed. My throat was parched. Guitabert brought me a cup of water. I sipped deeply and went on. "He offers the same terms he gave to the Vandals and Alans when he bested them in Raetia and Noricum a few years ago. Stout warriors who disarm, submit to Roman discipline and swear allegiance to the Emperor will be taken into the ranks of the Roman army. Stilicho will settle their families in Italia."

"What of those who refuse?"

"Stilicho did not discuss their fate," I said.

"We can imagine their fate. Did he mention my fate or the fate of my captains?"

"No."

"Ralamunda, take this girl aside while we talk."

From the far side of the firepit came a person I knew well. Ralamunda's figure had thickened in the years since we last met, evidence of bearing babies to Guitabert, and her face had lost some of its youthful vitality. This migration had taken a toll on her, but she remained gorgeous.

We talked for an hour, mostly about our children. She'd borne three. The oldest, a boy as she'd hoped, was the one she'd been carrying when we first met; the second had died after only a few months, and the youngest came tottering towards us as we spoke, her hand clutched by her older brother's. Both children promised to grow into their mother's beauty.

"Will they enslave us?" Ralamunda asked. She assumed her father-in-law would surrender. Indeed, what choice did he have? They were starving.

"Stilicho says no. He says he will settle the warriors' families here in Italia."

"But as free people or slaves?"

It was a good question. Stilicho had not specified. "If the Romans enslave the families, the husbands would not make good warriors," I said.

She seemed somewhat relieved.

Finally, Guitabert came to escort us back to the firepit. "We will surrender," Radagaisus said. "At noon tomorrow, we will descend into the valley, drop our weapons, and throw ourselves on the Romans' mercy."

That's a rare thing.

When I told Stilicho, he just nodded at me. There was no "thank you."

At dawn the following day, an alarm went up. One of the squads tasked with encircling the barbarian's hilltop had captured three of the enemy. Their captors brought them, hands tied, to the great tent where Stilicho, Constantius, his other officers, and I were eating.

"Do you know any of these men?" Stilicho asked me.

Before I could answer, the oldest prisoner said, "Matilde knows me. I am Radagaisus, and these are my sons." I had seen the other two men standing by the firepit yesterday but had not been introduced to them. They were Guitabert's older brothers.

"You promised to surrender," Stilicho said. "Now, instead, you try to escape."

"We did not trust your promise of mercy," Radagaisus responded.

"Is there any reason I should not execute you here and now?"

"We did not come here as your enemies," Radagaisus said. "We came to find a new home, a place to raise our children in peace, away from the perfidious Huns."

"Why did you think we would welcome you?"

"We knew you Romans always need good soldiers. We provided Gainas with many fine warriors. The girl, Matilde, can verify this. But now Gainas is gone."

"You say you did not come as our enemies, but you have sown destruction wherever you went."

"We came in winter, and our people were hungry. We just took what we needed."

Even I knew that to be a lie.

"Have you any last words?" Stilicho asked.

"We will not beg for our lives," Radagaisus answered.

"Take them away and kill them."

With the surrender of the barbarians, Stilicho had no more tasks for me but resisted allowing me to return to Mediolanum or to my family in Pannonia. "For your own safety," he said, and he had a point. The barbarians who had surrendered at Florentia were only one-third of Radagaisus's people. His horde had split into three groups to make provisioning easier, and no one was sure where the other two groups were. I stood and watched as the Romans processed the thousands of barbarians descending from the hilltop.

Stilicho's officers had staked a large pasture, dividing it into three fields. As the barbarians emerged from the woods, legionaries disarmed them, taking care to search for knives and daggers. Then, they were herded into the first field, the largest. From there, each family was brought forward for inspection. If the inspecting officer judged the husband to be a stout warrior, he and his family were pushed into the second field. But if he was absent—perhaps the victim of recent fighting—or infirm in any way, the family was pushed into the third field. Legionaries gathered those people into groups of one hundred and marched them off at spearpoint to the slave market in Florentia.

The warriors in the second field had a few minutes to say farewell to their wives and children before they were gathered into groups of fifty. When a group was formed, a squad of legionaries would escort it to a town—its new home— somewhere in Italia. I watched as the group containing Ralamunda and her children headed to Patavium. That walk would take a week, which would be hard on the little children, but better than walking the length of Italia. We'd traveled that length six years earlier when my delegation rode through dozens of Italian towns. I remembered the chilly receptions we received. Radagaisus's people would not be warmly welcomed in their new country.

Chapter 11. 406 CE. Seize Illyricum?

Ancient Source: Zosimus, which describes how Stilicho and Alaric planned to seize Illyricum from the Eastern Empire:

[5.26.2] Stilicho, perceiving that the ministers of Arcadius were averse to him, intended, by means of the assistance of Alaric, to add to the empire of Honorius all the Illyrian provinces. Having formed a compact with Alaric to this purpose, he expected shortly to put his design in execution.

Matilde

After Radagaisus's defeat, Constantius escorted me back to Ticinum and installed me in Stilicho's new home, which my lover had designed and built. It was every bit as spacious as the home in Mediolanum but far more utilitarian. It lacked an atrium and garden, but there were meeting rooms and many bedrooms. Constantius procured a room for us and a second room for Gaba and her family. Stilicho's room had a tiled tub, which we could use when he was away. He traveled often abroad to Ravenna, waiting on the Emperor, and Rome, dealing with the Senate. We never saw Serena. Stilicho's wife moved between Ravenna and Rome and avoided what she disparagingly called "the military camp."

Constantius was also frequently absent. He commanded a cohort tasked with combing the Piedmont region, looking for more of Radagaisus's people. The victory at Fiesole had captured most of the warriors, but it was only one of the three groups. One group had disappeared, probably fleeing West over the mountains into Gaul, and the third group was scattered around the countryside. Constantius's troop was rounding these up, sometimes peacefully, with deadly force otherwise. The strong warriors were recruited. Everyone else was sold to the slavers.

By the end of the year, as chilly weather crept in, Stilicho and Constantius were back in Ticinum, and the three of us sat comfortably around a table, drinking. When Constantius designed Stilicho's house, he included hypocausts, which ran hot air channels under the floors. It was a luxury I could get used to.

"The time has come," Stilicho announced, "to take Illyricum." He looked at Constantius, who wore a sour face.

"You speak as if you have already decided this." Constantius spoke skeptically.

"I am leaning in that direction, but I would like your opinions."

"Mine too?" I asked.

"Yes. You are smart for a woman." After I helped negotiate Radagaisus's surrender, Stilicho began treating me with more respect. For a woman.

"You've failed to take Illyricum twice before," Constantius said bluntly. "Why would this attempt succeed?"

"I believe I can take the prefecture without a fight. This time, I will have overwhelming strength. I will include the twelve thousand barbarians recruited from Radagaisus's army, and I hope and expect to get Alaric's support. Especially once the Emperor appoints him *magister militum per Illyricum*."

"Which you can persuade Honorius to do?"

"Yes. I will explain the benefits to him."

"In very small words," I whispered. Both men laughed but did not contradict me.

"Won't the East resist?" I asked.

"They've lacked a competent general since Augusta Eudoxia executed Fravitta, and their administration has been in disorder since she died. Now is a good time for us to act."

"Even so, I believe they would put up a fight," I said.

"I will make them a deal. Emperor Theodosius charged me with managing the entire empire, East and West. They know this. I will promise to abandon my claim on managing the East if Constantinople returns Illyricum to me."

"What do you mean *returns*?" I asked.

"It may seem like ancient history, but the West controlled the Prefecture of Illyricum until Emperor Gratian elevated Theodosius—Honorius's father—to be Emperor of the East and *loaned* him the prefecture. The two Emperors agreed that the East could better control the mountain passes from Illyricum to the West."

"Which the East has shown it cannot do," I said. Arcadius had failed to stop both Alaric and Radagaisus from invading Italia.

"The East cannot even keep peace in Thracia," Constantius added. "How many times have the Huns crossed the Danube and devastated crops and towns, going all the way to the gates of Constantinople?"

"So," said Stilicho, "this is my proposition. I offer to take Illyricum off their hands while promising not to interfere with Eastern politics anymore."

"An offer made persuasive," I said, "by having twenty or thirty thousand soldiers at your back."

"Fine," Constantius said, "Then please explain why you want Illyricum."

"Money and men," Stilicho said. "I'm already paying a subsidy to Alaric in Pannonia. Having him control the entire prefecture won't cost that much more, and I'll have the prefecture's tax revenue to help. Then there are the men. I need a place where I can recruit Roman citizens."

"Yes," I said, "Gainas had the same concern. That's why we recruited from Pannonia."

"He recruited *in* Pannonia," Constantius corrected, "but *from* across the river. Gainas hired Ostrogoths, Eastern Goths, Radagaisus's men."

"Well, *some* were from within the empire," I replied defensively.

Ignoring me, Constantius said, "It's important that we recruit citizens, not barbarians."

"That would make the Senate happy," Stilicho said. "They pine for the days when the army comprised citizen farmers, even as they ignore that all the citizen farmers work on their estates and aren't permitted to join the legions."

"The Senate also longs for a time when a victory meant slaughtering all the enemy, not recruiting them as we do now," Constantius said.

"I see a problem," I said. They waited for me to continue. "As I walk around Ticinum, attending the market, for example, I hear the men talk, the regular Roman soldiers, and they are unhappy. They don't like all the foreign recruits. They say the barbarians take Roman jobs and Roman women, and they have too much influence."

"Jobs? I would hire Romans if I could and if the Senate would let me," Stilicho said.

"Yet your bodyguards are all Huns," I said. Stilicho knew I hated Huns, so this was a weak argument.

"I completely trust my bodyguards. As for the rest, foreign recruits are not permitted to marry Roman women. I don't care if the legionaries are unhappy about my barbarian warriors so long as they obey my orders."

Stilicho was turning red with anger. There was no point in arguing.

"I have written orders—a proposal, really—for Alaric, which you, Matilde, will deliver to your stepbrother in Pannonia. It includes a commission for him, making him *magister militum per Illyricum,* and a plan to move his forces down the Adriatic coast to Epirus. I will meet him there, with the Western army, in the spring after the storm season. I expect he will agree to my proposal, but whether he will or won't, you must return with his answer."

"You trust me to return? Am I not your prisoner?" I asked.

"In principle, yes. But, to be honest, I trust Constantius to come back, and I trust you to stay with him." It was a fair assessment of my motivation. As much as I yearned to see my family, I did not want to leave Constantius.

"Then, Constantius is coming with me?"

"Constantius will lead a cavalry squad to escort you."

Did this truly mean that my captivity was ending? The next answer would tell all.

"May I take Theodoric with me?"

"Your boy? Of course. My trust means I will not keep your boy as a hostage. You should leave as soon as I have the Emperor's approval."

I had dreamed of this day for so long that I had trouble maintaining my composure.

Constantius, Theodoric, and I rode swiftly to Sirmium, the capital of Pannonia Inferior. As we approached Alaric's palace, I was surprised that the building was hung with black drapes. I asked a sentry on the street for the reason. He responded only, "It's the fever, Domina."

I entered the building with the other two trailing behind and made my way to the residential wing. It was eerily quiet. There were no guards or servants. We were walking down one corridor when we encountered Alaric coming the other way. He looked terrible. His hair was gray, his skin looked sickly, and he was gaunt.

"Matilde," he said, "Oh, my dearest, you've come too late."

"Too late for what?" I asked.

Without answering, he led us to a living room and sat us on a couch. He shivered, even though a crackling fire was keeping the room warm.

"What is it, Alaric? What is happening?"

"They are dead," he said. "The fever took them just three days ago. It almost took me."

"Them?"

"Mother, Pentadia, Amalric. In good health one day and gone two days later."

I could not believe it. I dissolved in sorrow. For five years, I'd been parted from my family, and now, when I could finally see them again, I'd missed them by less than a week. I do not remember the rest of that day. Someone found me a room and put me to bed. I woke several times in the night, hoping the nightmare I'd arrived in was unreal. I lay awake until the exhaustion from my journey pulled me back to sleep.

When morning finally arrived, a servant helped me dress and took me to the living room where Alaric, Constantius, and Theodoric were talking. "I'll bring you food," she said and disappeared before I could stop her. I knew I would never eat again. But when she returned with a tray of breads, fruits, and cheeses, I nibbled at a few figs.

I listened as Alaric talked to his son—our son. He told Theodoric of Elodia, her life and heroism, and her firm mothering of himself and me. Of how she killed Commander of the Guards Barzimeres with her lance at the Battle of Dibaltum. Theodoric knew all these tales, though he could not remember his grandmother. I'd recounted them over and over when he was little.

Finally, Alaric asked, "Do you remember Pentadia? Or Amalric?" Theodoric did and told his father what he remembered about my sister-wife and his half-brother. He'd been only two years old when we'd been captured, so he soon ran out of remembrances. Alaric picked up the threads and talked about Pentadia, how he'd had the pick of all the girls and had chosen the most beautiful one of all. He tried to tell how she had been clever and kind and... But his voice broke, and he could speak no more.

We sat quietly until Alaric could compose himself. Finally, he spoke. "Young Theodoric, you are now my heir. Amalric is gone. Pentadia is gone, and it is unlikely that I will marry again and father another boy."

"You are still married to my mother," my son said. "She is old, but not so old that she couldn't give you another child."

Alaric laughed like Theodoric had made the funniest joke in the world. "Oh, the wisdom of youth," he chuckled. "Your mother and I love each other, but that time has passed. It ended when you were born. If she is to bear another baby, it will be with Constantius, not me."

I was amazed. Constantius and I had said and done nothing to reveal our relationship, and I never credited Alaric with the ability to notice such things. He saw my astonishment and said, "Oh, I have my sources, but even without them, the way you look at him tells me everything."

"You aren't angry?" I asked.

"I became your lover because Pentadia wished it. She is gone. You've been gone for five years. I would not expect you to suspend your life for so long. You are no Penelope."

I was about to reply, "And you are no Odysseus," when I realized he really was. They had both been on a journey to find their home.

Later, when Alaric and I were alone, we talked about Theodoric and our future.

"Our son needs to stay here and live with me," he said.

Internally, I howled, *No!* but as I reflected on it, I could see he was correct. With Alaric, Theodoric could grow up to be the son of a king and his possible successor. I could offer him no such future.

"If I give you my son—our son—would you give me something?" I asked.

"Name it," Alaric said.

"A divorce."

He agreed. "Yes, your future is with Constantius, not here."

I devoted the rest of my time in Sirmium to Theodoric. We explored the city. I showed him the place where Caius's axle broke, and I finally caught up with my parents' medical wagon. He quizzed me on what life would be like living with his father. He asked when he would see Constantius or me next and if we would get married. I had far fewer answers than he had questions. Rather than being afraid of these changes, he was excited.

Meanwhile, Constantius and Alaric discussed Stilicho's plan to seize Illyricum. Their discussions were hurried because we needed to return to Italia before winter closed the mountain passes. By the end of our visit, Alaric looked much better. Perhaps it was the prospect of another military operation, one that would return control of Illyricum to him, or maybe the joy of having his son restored. Of course, I was sad to leave my son, but to my surprise, Constantius felt crushed. Though he did not weep openly, he clung to Theodoric and repeated, "Do not forget me, my son." Indeed, he seemed to love my son as if he were his own.

Chapter 12.   407-408 CE. Messages from Gaul

Matilde

Constantius and I, feeling pleased, returned to Ticinum toward the end of the year, just as the winter snows arrived in force. In my hand was a document, signed by Alaric, committing him to Stilicho's plan. He would move his army of Goths down the Adriatic coast to Epirus as soon as conditions permitted. Stilicho had assumed Alaric would agree and was already preparing for the invasion of Illyricum.

We arrived at the house in Ticinum, hoping to enjoy a relaxing and lusty evening together, when a message from Stilicho called him to a meeting in Ravenna. There, the General assigned Constantius responsibility for organizing the troops that would cross the sea from Ravenna to Dyrrhachium. I hoped to go along to see my son and Alaric again.

Just as Stilicho had employed Constantius to organize the supply depot in Ticinum, now Stilicho depended on my lover to gather all the supplies our army would need in Illyricum. The General did not want a repetition of his earlier invasion, where the troops in Corinth ran out of food and began plundering the countryside.

It was a week before Constantius returned home. He was exhausted. We bathed together in Stilicho's great tile tub and retired to our bed, where he immediately fell asleep. But in the morning, he woke refreshed and eager to address that earlier neglect.

We enjoyed breakfast in bed and discussed our mission to Pannonia.

"So you feel it was a success?" he asked. "You don't seem happy about it. It's your son, yes?"

"Yes. I will miss him. I *do* miss him. But I have you, and now, with the rest of my family dead, his father has no one else. Alaric needs him. And Theodoric needs to live with his father so he will grow up to be a strong and proud Goth. Not the son of a general's mistress."

"Is that what you are? Just a general's mistress?" Constantius teased.

"It is enough. I'm happy being with you."

"Would general's wife be better?"

I sat silently for a long time. "Are you asking?"

"Yes. You have a fine son, and he suggested that you might have more."

"While saying I am old! Twenty-five is *not* old!"

"If this morning's activity becomes our morning habit—and that would be most pleasant—we will soon test whether you are too old."

"And?"

"I miss Theodoric, too. I would like to have a son, and not with a general's mistress, but with a general's wife."

I said yes. I'd come to love Constantius, watching him play with my son. If one only watched him as a legionary officer, all orders, discipline, and, when necessary, ruthlessness, one would miss half the man. He was not effusive. He never said he loved me, but his actions spoke louder than his words, or lack of them. If the gods should bless me with another child, I could not imagine a better father.

He was due back in Ravenna the next day, but he postponed it for our marriage. It was a small affair, attended by only a few of his officers and their wives. Stilicho did not attend, for which I was happy. It was a joyous occasion, and he was such a dour, humorless man. Anicius, one of Constantius's officers and the chief of his bodyguards, located a Catholic priest to officiate at the ceremony. The priest protested at the rush, saying marriages must be proclaimed at least a week in advance. Anicius brought the priest before Constantius, who did not want to hear of any delay. My lover pulled out his dagger, balanced a gold aureus on the flat of its sharp steel tip, and pressed it against the priest's chest. The cleric stepped back from the weapon, took the coin, and agreed that "exceptions were permitted."

After the wedding, everyone gathered at Stilicho's house and drank a toast to the married couple. Gaba served an apple cake. Then Constantius kissed me, mounted his horse, and rode back to Ravenna.

Three weeks later, he returned.

"What have you been doing for the last few weeks while I was gone? I see no sign that you've taken up weaving." I elbowed him playfully. He knew I had no patience, skill, or interest in the creative arts.

"I read from Stilicho's library, I practiced sword and archery drill, then I grew bored, then I read some more."

"Since you're good with numbers, I have some work you could do," he said.

From that description, it sounded like scribe's work. Boring. "I want you to determine the amount of wheat in my Ravenna granaries. I suspect pilfering."

In anticipation of Stilicho's Illyricum venture, Constantius had been buying quantities of grain to feed the troops once the operation was underway. He stored the grain in four great concrete cylindrical silos close to Ravenna's port. Constantius gave me manifests that named each of the ships that had delivered grain and their owners, the amount of grain purchased, and the silo where it had been stored.

"To measure how much each silo contains, there is a series of horizontal lines drawn on its interior. The first line marks where the silo contains ten *amphora quadrantal*, and the next line higher indicates twenty *amphora quadrantal*, and so on.

"Two weeks ago, I had an inspector check each silo. Each is five *amphora quadrantal* lower than the manifest amount. The port master claimed it was normal for the grain to settle. I don't believe it. I think someone is stealing my grain. Can you find out what's happening?"

Not boring at all. After weeks stuck here, anything would be an improvement. I kissed him enthusiastically and said, "I would," *kiss, kiss*, "love to!"

The next day, I was riding to Ravenna. Three legionaries accompanied me because Constantius insisted I needed an adequate bodyguard. We made good time on the *Via Aemilia*, the ancient road from Placentia to Ariminum, arriving in two days. The next morning, I was up early and told the port master I wished to inspect the silos. He objected until I presented him with Constantius's authorization warrant.

A tile roof covered each of the silos. Over the objections of the port master and Anicius, my chief bodyguard, I scaled a forty-foot wooden ladder to the roof, opened a hatch, and descended an interior ladder until I reached the grain. I'd carefully affixed an oil lamp to my hat, which provided just enough light to see the measurement lines. When I'd repeated this for each of the silos, I took my measurements, manifests, and abacus and found a seat outside a local bakery, where, after buying a loaf of fresh bread, I sat eating and calculating.

I didn't have enough information, so I spent the next week riding up and down the coast to all the neighboring towns, buying bread from every bakery I could find. Finally, I had my suspect. Each of the four silos was shy by about five *amphora quadrantal*, as Constantius had said, but the fourth silo had only half as much wheat as the other three. If compaction were the problem, the fourth silo's loss would be much less, perhaps only three *amphora quadrantal*. The port master was lying. He would tell the truth when Constantius had him tortured, if that became necessary.

The men listed as shipowners in the manifest were local grain merchants. I interviewed each man in turn. Actually, I had Anicius ask the questions. His voice was deep and authoritative—he scared even me—and he would have been a match for Brutus physically. When he asked, the merchants cheerfully acknowledged that they were agents for a shipowner named Neoterius. My suspicions grew when the port master claimed he knew no such man. Neoterius lived in a fine urban home in Ariminum, a city just south of Ravenna. We rode quickly to Ariminum and were dismounting at Neoterius's house when an exhausted-looking man ran up behind us. I had him arrested after I recognized him as one of the port master's slaves. He had run all the way from Ravenna, and his body was dripping with sweat. Anicius saw him carrying a small scroll, which he seized and handed to me.

"That's private," the slave said. "It's for Neoterius."

"Good," I said. "That was my hope."

The slave dared to touch me, trying to retrieve the message, but Anicius smacked him to the ground. I broke the seal and read, "CAVEQUAERENTEMMULIEREM," which, though the writing was smeared and barely legible, I interpreted as "Beware questioning woman." It was the most decisive proof yet of collusion between the port master and Neoterius.

Anicius hammered on Neoterius's door. When the porter opened it, my bodyguards pushed through and found the shipowner sitting at a long wooden table, eating his midday meal. He jumped up, angrily protesting against this home invasion, and called my bodyguards "meat makers" and "water snakes." I stopped Anicius just as he was about to overturn the dining table. "Let the man finish his meal," I said. "He might not get another." Neoterius sat down but did not resume eating, his appetite lost.

Leaving Anicius to guard Neoterius, the other bodyguards walked through the city, arrested all the local bakers from whom I'd purchased bread, and herded them into Neoterius's house. I asked each in turn, "Who do you buy your wheat from, and how much do you pay?" Their costs were very similar and much less than bakers paid in other cities. All had purchased their grain from Neoterius. Finally, I accused him of theft.

"You conspired," I said, "with the Ravenna port master to short your delivery by twenty *amphora quadrantal*. The two of you hoped to mask the theft by spreading the shortage over all the silos. You profited by selling the stolen grain at bargain prices to local bakers. Do you deny it?"

Of course, Neoterius denied it and offered to assert his honesty under the most profound oaths.

"Why deny it?" I said. "The port master has confessed. One of you must hang, but if he was the instigator, it should be him. Perhaps you could escape with some lesser penalty." I was lying but for his own good, I hoped he would confess and save himself the agony of torture. He confessed.

The port master was more obstinate. It took hours of torture to break him. His claim was that neither Neoterius nor he was the instigator. Their patron, a senator in Rome, devised the entire scheme and reaped most of the profits. All probably true.

I knew enough of Roman society and politics to realize that pursuing a senator was hopeless and dangerous. I turned the two men over to the local mayors to be tried, declared the mission a complete success, and returned to Ticinum. The two men were tried, but the Roman senator must have bribed the jury because, as I later learned, both were acquitted.

Still, my mission had not been pointless. Stilicho now had proof of the senator's fraud. When the senator realized it, he became one of Stilicho's steadfast supporters.

Ancient Source: Zosimus, in which Stilicho learns that barbarians crossed the Rhine into Gaul on New Year's Eve 406 CE:

[6.3.1] … The Vandals, uniting with the Alans and the Suebi, crossed [the Rhine River].

Matilde

I returned to Ticinum expecting Constantius's thanks, but his appreciation was muted. "Good work," he said, "but it doesn't matter now."

"No?"

"The whole Illyricum operation is canceled, or at least postponed, until the crisis in Gaul is settled."

"Crisis? What crisis?"

Constantius explained that thousands of barbarians— Vandals, Sueves, and Alans—had crossed the lower Rhine into Gaul on New Year's Eve and blown through the Roman frontier defenses.

"They knew we'd withdrawn most of our *limitanei*, our border legions, to fight Radagaisus. Reports are coming that the enemy has attacked and sacked Moguntiacum, Borbetomagus, and maybe other cities."

"What is Stilicho doing?"

"To start with, as you now know, he has canceled the entire Illyricum project. He has ordered all the troops intended for that operation to come here. I am working to ensure we have barracks and supplies for them."

"Is Alaric coming too?" I asked hopefully.

I knew he'd been waiting in Epirus for the operation to start.

"No, he has been ordered to move his army back north to Noricum to secure the frontier there and in Pannonia. The *limitanei* who *were* in Pannonia have been dispatched to garrison our cities in Gaul and will bolster our Frankish allies battling the intruders." Constantius noticed a perplexed look on my face.

"Weren't the Pannonian *limitanei* just *foederate allies*, the Vandals that Stilicho hired a few years ago? They are also barbarians. How loyal might they be?" I asked.

"Yes, I know what you're thinking, and I posed that same question to Stilicho: how effective will those soldiers be in subduing their tribal cousins?"

"What did Stilicho say?"

"He said *his* Pannonian Vandals are from a different clan, so they should be trustworthy."

As it turned out, they were *not* effective. The cities of Gaul, fearing a ruse, refused to open their gates and admit the new garrison troops. The Pannonian Vandals soon ran out of supplies, began to plunder the countryside, and ended up joining the invading Vandals.

Ancient Source: Zosimus, in which a usurper named Constantine arises in Britain:

[6.2.1] The troops in Britain revolted … delivering the empire to Constantine. He, having entrusted to Justinian and Nebiogast the command of the Celtic legions, crossed over from Britain….

To make matters worse, a Roman general in Britain named Constantine declared himself Emperor. He gathered all the Roman troops on the island, crossed the English Channel, and began to subdue the invading barbarians. With his help, the Franks defeated a swarm of marauding Saxons and drove the other barbarians back toward the Rhine. The Franks, who had received no effective support from Stilicho, quickly changed their allegiance from Honorius to Constantine.

I threw up my hands. "So now Stilicho is dealing with invading barbarians *and* a usurper. What is his plan?"

"Until our troops have gathered here, there's little he can do. In the meantime, he has instructed Chariobaudes, our top general in Gaul, to crush the usurper. Defeating him is the top priority."

I could do little to help Constantius, so I tried to stay out of his way. I occupied myself by re-reading many of the books in Stilicho's library. Sadly, none of the other officers in Ticinum owned any books. Sword and archery drills filled the rest of my time. My husband provided an instructor to help with the latter. "Your stance is poor," the master archer said. "Your grip is too tight, and your left eye is ruining your aim." My aim improved markedly when I corrected those faults and learned to shoot with my left eye closed.

My swordsmanship likewise improved once Constantius provided me with a sword master. I would be the first to admit I was not proficient with the weapon, but with practice, I became competent.

Growing up in a warrior culture, I'd always kept a *gladius* sword under my bed (except when I was a prisoner). It was smaller than the *spatha*, which most warriors wielded, but I lacked the strength to handle the heavier weapon.

"Just how long do you think a duel lasts?" my sword master asked. I had no idea. "When faced with an opponent, the fight will last for three, maybe four blows. Because your arms are weak, he will knock the sword out of your hand on the first strike and then kill you. Whoever taught you all that fancy footwork has never been in a battle. Fighting is not dancing. To be a better sword fighter, you need to be stronger."

He gave me a set of exercises to strengthen my arms, like hanging from an overhead bar and pulling myself up until my chin cleared it. It was very difficult—impossible—to start with, but it got a little better every week. Whenever Constantius was home, we would arm-wrestle. That activity frequently left us lying on the floor and practicing other, more relaxing exercises.

After one such bout left us lying in bed, Constantius asked, "Why do you work so hard at the warrior's art?"

"I haven't really thought about it. I enjoy it, and it keeps me busy."

"Do you imagine being a warrior like your mother?"

"Elodia would never call herself a warrior, but she rode in a Gothic warband and needed the skills of a warrior."

"Do you picture yourself riding with me when I go off to war? Which will happen soon. The preparations here in Ticinum are almost complete."

"I do not want to be left behind when you go," I said.

"I understand, but I will not need another warrior. A woman warrior would not be welcome in a Roman legion."

I'd thought and worried about this. "What about a woman medicus? My mother was a good medicus, and I learned many of those skills while caring for our wounded after the Battle of Frigidus River."

Constantius admitted that I would make a good healer. He arranged for me to work daily with a legionary medicus to learn the Roman ways.

The news from abroad just got worse. A trader from Hispania reported that the provincial governors had gone over to the usurper. The barbarian attacks on Gaulish cities had stopped, which we initially thought was good news until we learned that the usurper had recruited the invading barbarians. Rather than fight them, he enlisted them. I was not surprised. It was a common tactic and one that Stilicho had used when dealing with Radagaisus's men. It turned enemies into allies. It saved the lives of his Roman troops and bolstered his forces with proven fighters who did not need to be trained or equipped.

Chapter 13. 408 CE. Siege of Valentia

Ancient Source: Zosimus, in which Stilicho dispatches a force under Sarus to suppress the usurper Constantine:

[6.2.3] At the same time Stilicho sent Sarus at the head of an army against Constantine. Having encountered with the division commanded by Justinian, he slew that general with the greater part of his soldiers. Having acquired great spoils, he advanced to besiege Valentia, where he understood that Constantine had placed himself, it being a strong city, well fortified and a secure residence.

Matilde

By early in the year, we'd learned that the Pannonian Vandals and the legions in Gaul had gone over to the usurper and that he was marching south from Bononia. Where would he stop?

The Senate in Rome was terrified the usurper would cross the Alps and invade Italia. They blamed Stilicho for the failure of his *limitanei* to stop the invaders and for the damage inflicted by the barbarians on their Gallic estates. He tried to explain that the Rhine *limitanei* had been redeployed into Italia to defeat Radagaisus and that his defeat was a credit to Rome's glory and to him personally. The Senate's armchair generals brushed aside his reasons. They dismissed his victory because he had failed to enslave or slaughter all the vanquished. Instead, he had hired the defeated warriors and planned to use them in an unauthorized plan—now aborted—to seize all Illyricum. Why, they asked, hadn't he sent the *limitanei* back to their outposts on the Rhine? Why hadn't he foreseen the barbarian invasion? Why? Why? Why?... The senators considered every setback to be another of Stilicho's personal failures. Financial problems compounded the military problems: with the usurper controlling Gaul, Hispania, and Britain, tax revenue from those provinces had ceased.

In April, Stilicho planned an attack. I showered Constantius with questions about the operation. "Have you met this usurper, General Constantine?"

"Yes, about ten years ago. Stilicho sent me to Britain during the Pictish War. I watched as Constantine crushed that rebellion."

"It bothers me that he has almost the same name as you."

"I suppose his father, like mine, hoped his son would become a powerful leader like the original Constantine. It seems like this man plans to do just that." The original Constantine had gone from being a general in Britain to Emperor of the whole empire.

"And have you such an aspiration?" I asked with a smile.

"Hush," Constantius hissed. "If the house slaves hear such a joke, it could mean my death!"

"Sorry." I kissed his ear. "I will joke more quietly. What else do you know about this Constantine re-born?"

"He had two sons when I met him. I don't remember their original names, but he renamed them Constans and Julian after those two Emperors. I suppose he hopes they'll grow up to be great rulers.

"He has two faithful followers named Justinianus and Nebiogastes. They were his tribunes during the Pictish war, but our spies now say that he has named them *magistri militum*. I thought highly of Nebiogastes. Justinianus was lazy and unimaginative. The spies have named some other lesser officers, like Gerontius and Edobichus. I have never met them. I assume they are legionaries who followed him from Britain."

"Tell me about our force," I asked. "Who is going to lead the attack?"

"Sarus."

"Sarus? That slimy turncoat? Why him?"

"I do not know," said Constantius. "Perhaps it's a test of his loyalty. Will he abandon Stilicho as readily as he abandoned Alaric? Anyway, Stilicho is not giving him a large force. That suggests he doesn't fully trust him. He'll take his own Gothic followers and a small number of Roman soldiers, perhaps two thousand men altogether. I will watch him to see what kind of a leader he is."

"*You?!* You're going? With that criminal?"

"Yes, those are my orders. It will be a lightning attack, all cavalry. We hope to take Constantine by surprise, kill him, and end this rebellion quickly. In just a few weeks."

"If you're going by cavalry, you won't take a medicus wagon." I could not hide my disappointment. I'd hoped to go into battle by Constantius's side. That now seemed unlikely.

"We will take two mules ladened with medical supplies: bandages, splints, and the like. Someone needs to lead them." His look made it obvious who "someone" might be. I smiled.

"Won't Sarus object?"

"He is the overall commander, but I command the Roman contingent. If I say you are coming, then you can come. But perhaps you should emphasize that Alaric divorced you. Try to put as much distance between your stepbrother and yourself as possible."

It turned out that Sarus did not recognize me, but his son did, though that worked in my favor. Sautus played up my divorce from Alaric with taunts such as, "She's so ugly even Alaric had to ditch her."

Our journey took us west through Augusta Taurinorum and over the Cottian Alps on the Mont Cenis pass. Two days after leaving the Po River valley, the road grew steep, and the mountains grew tall. "How can they be so high?" I asked Constantius. "Why don't they fall under their own weight?"

"Some do," he answered. "As we climb, you will see great rock slides. I just pray that none will strike us or block our road."

We had to dismount and lead our animals. Though it was spring, portions of the way were still snow-covered and icy where creeks crossed. One of Sarus's captains insisted on riding his mount. He boasted of its strength and endurance, claiming it was "more sure-footed than your mules," shortly before his horse lost its footing on an icy patch and tumbled over a three-hundred-foot precipice, taking him with it.

That night at the campfire, Constantius tried to reassure the party. He knew the route and claimed, "It's an easy journey. Be happy we're not climbing Hannibal's Pass." Then, he entertained everyone with the old fable of how a Carthaginian named Hannibal launched an attack on Rome by crossing the Alps with a herd of elephants. The story got a good laugh.

Everyone knew there were no elephants in Europe outside of Rome's Colosseum. Sarus made an uncharacteristic joke, for he was known to have no sense of humor. He claimed his giant, black wolfhound, Caracalla, which had a very long snout, was descended from one of Hannibal's elephants. From then on, everyone called the dog Hannibal, which irritated Sarus, who continued to call him Caracalla.

Constantius's story helped reassure Sarus's Goths that the Romans frequently traveled this route. The Goths had traversed the Julian Alps, but the Cottian Alps were bleak and twice as high. The high pass offered no trees, animals, or people, just rocks and snow, and snowmelt had transformed every brook into a roaring torrent. After spending two weeks fighting the elements, we emerged into the valley of the Rhône River, where spring had arrived. The fields were green with new growth, and buds decorated the trees, promising leaves in the next few weeks. Constantius privately expressed his relief that our passage had been so smooth. Other than losing one obstinate horseman and a few frostbitten toes, our force was intact.

Our attack depended on catching Constantine unawares. We'd left Ticinum and crossed the Alps so early in the spring we assumed no word of our approach could precede us. We were wrong. It was never clear how the usurper knew of our approach, but as we approached the town of Augustum, our scouts captured several enemy legionaries. They were brought into camp, bound and blindfolded. It took only the threat of torture for them to talk. They revealed that one of the usurper's *magistri militum*, Justinianus, had staged an army of three thousand men just west of Augustum. "He expects you to arrive in a week or two," one of the prisoners said, "and rest in Augustum for a few days while you recover from the mountain crossing. That's what most travelers do. That's when he would invade the town while you are asleep and slaughter you."

When we were alone, Constantius asked me, "What do you think?" In private, he always welcomed my opinion. As a Roman officer, he was reluctant to be seen taking a woman's advice. We agreed it was a stupid norm, but his personal opinion was unlikely to change a custom as old as Rome itself.

"I think Justinianus is afraid we will outnumber him," I said. "He imagines Stilicho will send perhaps ten thousand men. Rather than risking defeat in open battle, he will attack at night and catch us off guard."

"Yes, those are my thoughts, too."

Constantius consulted with Sarus, and they agreed to use Justinianus's tactic against him. Constantius led our little army on a midnight ride to within five miles of the enemy's position, dismounted, silently surrounded their camp, and attacked just before dawn. A few boys and I were left in the rear to hold the horses. Constantius quashed my dream of riding into battle with him. "Somebody needs to guard the horses," he said, "and we need to keep you safe to care for our wounded." Of course, he was patronizing me. I found it irritating.

We had a few wounded and even fewer dead. We obliterated the enemy force and killed Justinianus himself. Constantius's Roman soldiers took several prisoners, but Sarus's warriors took none. He justified this, saying, "This is a lightning strike force. How am I supposed to manage prisoners?" He *did* have a point.

Constantius's prisoners were a mix of legionaries, who had come from Britain with the usurper, and barbarian warriors, who had joined opportunistically, hoping, as allies of the

Romans, to get regular pay, food, and arms. Constantius allowed the captured legionaries to swear allegiance to Emperor Honorius. Only a few refused. He had them executed, along with all the barbarian prisoners. I thought that brutal, but, indeed, how *were* we to manage prisoners?

The turncoat prisoners, having watched the others die, were eager to prove their value by providing information. They told us everything they knew, whether helpful or not. One exclaimed, "You're heading for Lugdunum? Constantine has moved south from there. He's heading for Arelate." Arelate was the seat of government for the prefecture of Gaul and the obvious destination for someone who planned to rule this part of the empire.

Constantius and Sarus agreed that, with some luck, we might overtake the usurper on the road, exposed and vulnerable. We set off immediately, trotting through the night, our way lit by the full moon. We reached Vienna at noon, where we learned the usurper had passed through three days earlier. After giving our horses six hours to rest and feed, we headed south along the Rhône River.

The road was smooth and flat, which allowed me to fall asleep in the saddle. When I awoke, we were passing through a gardener's paradise. The country on either side was newly tilled with young stalks of grain already six inches high. Rows of elm trees decorated with the light green leaves of spring separated the fields. To the east were verdant hills covered with vineyards. I could see rocky foothills to the west, hinting at the high mesa beyond.

At dusk, we were well south of Vienna. Our scouts encountered a picket, a force of six Vandal barbarians left behind by the usurper. They had been tasked with alerting their commander if anyone should appear on the road. They might have done so if they hadn't been drunk. As we surrounded them, a local farmer appeared. "Your men broke into my barn and stole several *amphorae* of my best wine," he complained.

I saw that the usurper's men had taken three of the large ceramic jars. One was already empty, and until they noticed us, they'd been drinking their way through the second. The farmer said, "I humbly request compensation, your lordship." The farmer mistook us as members of the usurper's party. To him, all barbarians must look the same.

Sarus, in his Gothic-accented Latin, replied, "Your compensation is that I shall let you live. Return to your hovel." When the farmer saw Sarus draw his sword, he turned and ran.

"Where is Justinianus?" slurred the least drunk of the sentries.

"Still in Augustum, as far as I know," Constantius answered. I smiled at my husband's macabre joke. It was unlikely that the *magister*'s corpse had moved far from where it fell. "I am Gerontius," Constantius lied.

"Oh, good. Constantine was not expecting you for another week. But I understood you would be leading a much larger party."

That was worrisome. Would our two thousand men face twice or thrice our number in a week? "Yes, they will arrive in a week or so," Constantius said. "The last I heard, King Godigisel is still collecting his force." I had forgotten who he was.

"That cannot be," the sentry said. "The Franks killed Godigisel last year." This news had not yet reached Italia. The sentry suddenly looked much less drunk, and his posture suggested Godigisel's death was old news and should be known to everyone. I could imagine the sentry asking himself, "Who are these men who have not heard of the King's death?"

The sentry asked, "Perhaps you mean his son, Guteric?"

I sensed a trap. Was the sentry baiting us with a different, perhaps fictitious, name?

Constantius did not take the bait. "No, the lad's name is Gunderic, and he is too young to lead." When the sentry relaxed, I did, too.

"Indeed. Gunderic is a fine young man and will be a good leader in a few years. No, it is your British legionary, Edobichus, who will soon come with the rest of our force. Maybe ten thousand men, I have been told."

Constantius paused for a hundred heartbeats, staring at the sentry. Then he turned to Sarus. "I think we've learned all we can here." Sarus waved his hand, and his men slew the drunk sentries. They did it coolly, professionally, and quickly. Only their spokesman realized what was happening, but neither he nor the others were sober enough to flee.

We continued riding south at a walking pace. "Please remind me what we learned," Sarus said to Constantius.

"We learned that Counts Edobichus and Gerontius will arrive from the north within a week, leading a force vastly superior to ours. We learned that the usurper is just a few miles south of us and likely already camped for the night, which is why he placed the picket here," Constantius said.

"Then we should move on immediately and catch Constantine in his camp, just as we did with Justinianus," Sarus said.

"May I make another suggestion?" Constantius asked. "We have ridden hard for two long days. Our men are exhausted. So are our horses, and a few have broken down. If we rest overnight, we will be in much better shape to attack tomorrow. Time is short, it is true, but we *do* have a week. We can afford to spend one day preparing for battle."

"And yet, as tired as we are, we all want to quickly finish this campaign. Successfully," Sarus said.

"How far are we from Valentia," I asked quietly.

"What does it matter, woman?" Sarus hissed.

"We are four hours away from Valentia," Constantius said. His calm voice soothed the sting of Sarus's tone. "Tell me your thoughts, Matilde."

"We are tired," I said, "and tired men make mistakes. If we surprise and kill the usurper, then well and good, but if something goes awry, the usurper will flee to Valentia. He will shut the gates and wait patiently for Gerontius's men to appear."

"We will not make mistakes," Sarus said. "My decision is final. We will rest here for a half hour and then attack."

It turned out as I'd feared. A barking dog alerted the usurper's forces before we could ring his camp. A small rearguard blocked our advance while Constantine and most of his men fought south to Valentia. Its gate remained open until his people were inside, then slammed closed in our faces. His rearguard fought bravely and was slain to the last man, but that was small consolation for failing to capture the man who now styled himself Emperor.

And so, our siege of Valentia began. We had enough men to surround the place but not enough to seal it. We caught several men trying to slip through our lines with messages for Gerontius, begging him to hurry to the rescue. I assume other messengers managed to evade capture. Constantine never tried a sortie, though that might have succeeded, given how few we were.

Ancient Source: Zosimus, in which Sarus treacherously slays General Nebiogast during peace negotiations:

[6.2.4] Nebiogast, the surviving commander, having made overtures of peace to Sarus, was received by him as a friend. But Sarus, although he had both given and received an oath to the contrary, immediately put him to death without regard to what he had sworn.

One evening, a solitary man carrying a white flag approached our line. He did not resist when a guard captured him and escorted him into the tent where Sarus, Sautus, Constantius, and I were having a simple meal. Constantius recognized him immediately.

"Nebiogastes! How good to see you!" Constantius said. The other man laughed, saying the pleasure was his, while they shook hands, just like old friends. Sarus did not look amused.

"What business can a *magister militum* of the mighty *Emperor Constantine* have with us?" Sarus asked sarcastically.

"Ah, you must be Sarus, the man who would be king of the Goths if only heaven did not favor Alaric," Nebiogastes said. Sarus sputtered in anger. "I come with a proposal, one that will bring peace and may save your lives."

"We would appreciate staying alive. Speak on," said Constantius.

"We know how many warriors you have—we can count— and it's not many. Within a few days, a great number of our men will arrive. *Comes* Edobichus and Gerontius have suppressed the barbarians who crossed the Rhine and have recruited many of them into our ranks. Now that the north is at peace, those forces are coming south. They should be here within a week. In addition, *Magister Militum* Justinianus will soon arrive with his three thousand soldiers. By telling you this, I am giving you a chance to withdraw to Italia before you are overwhelmed and killed."

"Justinianus and all his men lie dead on a field outside of Augustum," Sarus boasted.

"That seems unlikely," Nebiogastes sniffed. "Regardless, if you want to stay alive, I advise you to head for Italia immediately. When you go, you can take a message to Stilicho and the dolt Emperor that he serves." I noticed that nobody bristled at Nebiogastes's insult. Honorius *was* a dolt, and everyone knew it.

Nebiogastes continued, "Emperor Constantine has no interest in dethroning Honorius. He is satisfied with his current possessions: Gaul, Britain, and Hispania. Honorius has all but abandoned Britain, and his neglect of northern Gaul is evident for all to see."

"How has Honorius shown disinterest in Britain?" Constantius asked.

"We went almost two years without being paid. Why do you think the British legions rebelled?"

Constantius had no answer except, "The war against Radagaisus was costly. It also forced Stilicho to strip all the troops from the Rhine River outposts."

"Leaving northern Gaul prey to the barbarians," Nebiogastes said. "Whom Emperor Constantine has subdued."

"Stilicho would have dealt with them this summer if there were no usurper to deal with," Sarus said testily.

"A year late. It wasn't just the Vandals and Alans. Stilicho turned the security of the northern frontier over to the Franks. While they are good allies, they are also unpaid and neglected, which is why they've welcomed Emperor Constantine. They are barbarians. Roman settlers do not want to live in a land controlled by barbarians! They are abandoning their farms and moving away from the frontier to where it is safer."

I could see tempers were getting hot, so I decided to intervene. *"Magister Militum* Nebiogastes, what is your proposal?" I asked, using his assumed rank out of politeness. "That Honorius acknowledge Constantius as a fellow Emperor and cede him half of the empire?"

"Yes, indeed. I urge you to return to Italia and present this proposal to Stilicho and Honorius. While they are considering that offer, I can assure you that Emperor Constantine will not invade Italia. However, he will not be so generous if matters come to battles and bloodshed. I recommend you leave now so you can return to Italia safely. Do not wait until Justinianus's army catches you."

"If you hope to avoid battles and bloodshed, you have come too late," Sarus said.

"How so?" Nebiogastes asked.

"I already told you. We met Justinianus at Augustum. We fought. We killed him and all his men."

"If that is true, then I *have* come too late," Nebiogastes said. "Please convey my message to your Emperor."

Sarus curled his lip. "We certainly shall," he said sarcastically. "My son will escort you back through our siege lines."

Sautus waved Nebiogastes ahead as they pushed open the tent flap and left.

"Well?" asked Constantius.

"Nothing changes," said Sarus. "You could see he was lying when he claimed that a flood of men will soon arrive. We will besiege Valentia until everyone starves or until the citizens rise up and toss the usurper out the gate."

"You don't believe Edobichus and Gerontius are leading thousands of men here?"

"No. It is a lie to scare us, to make us lift the siege."

I felt compelled to speak. "Nebiogastes's story is the same as the drunk sentry's: that Edobichus will soon arrive with an army, and we will be outnumbered by three to one. Yes, I believe Nebiogastes's story, and I am scared."

"You are scared because you are a woman," Sarus said. "That is the nature of women."

I was trying to articulate a response—that any sane person, given the evidence, would believe Nebiogastes—when Sautus reentered the tent.

"It is done," he said proudly.

"What is done?" Constantius asked.

"I killed Nebiogastes. When we got to the siege line, I ordered a sentry to hold him while I ran him through. Tomorrow, when the usurper looks from the town walls, he will see the head of his *magister militum* mounted on a pole."

I was outraged. "He came under a flag of truce!"

"You were always a naïve girl," Sautus said. "No wonder your husband dumped you."

Nothing more of value could be accomplished that evening.

Chapter 14.   408 CE. The *Bacaudae*

Ancient Source: Zosimus, in which Sarus abandons the siege of Valentia:

> *[6.2.5] Constantine then conferred the command, vacant by the death of Justinian and Nebiogast, on Edobinch, a Frank by extraction but a native of Britain, and on Gerontius, a Briton. Sarus, being in dread of the courage and the military experience of these two, raised the siege of Valentia after he had continued in it seven days.*

Matilde

Constantius posted a picket a few miles north of Valentia, just as the usurper did. Unlike the usurper's, our sentries were not provided with wine but with swift horses.

Six days later, they galloped into camp and reported that a large body of infantry was approaching and would arrive before nightfall. Because Constantius believed Nebiogastes's information, our legionaries had prepared to evacuate, and within a half-hour, we moved out. Sarus had stubbornly refused to credit it, and his Goths' departure was chaotic. His men had collected wagons of loot from Justinianus's camp. In their panic to leave Valentia, they abandoned all the bulky items: looted tents, warm clothes, and extra weapons.

Constantius and I had plotted a route back to Italia. Our Roman troops could not return the way we came because that would involve marching back north to Vienna straight into the oncoming enemy. Instead, we picked a more southern path over the Argentarius Pass.

"Have you gone that way before?" I asked.

"Once, when I was eighteen. It was a well-maintained road, and though the locals were wary of strangers, they would not be unfriendly if the strangers had gold. At the foot of the pass, there is a village with a *mansio*. The villagers expected us to stay in the *mansio* and purchase other items like food," Constantius said.

"And if one chose to stay in one's tent and eat one's own food?"

"We thought it wiser not to find out."

"Argentarius means silversmith. Why is it called the Silversmith Pass?" I asked.

"Because the men there harvest silver."

"Harvest? Do you mean they mine silver?"

"They did when I was last there, but things may have changed. Now, I fear they harvest any silver that travelers carry."

"They are robbers?"

"They would call themselves toll collectors."

Once we left the valley of the Rhône river, the road grew rough and hilly. It was not a well-maintained Roman road like the one over the Mont Cenis pass.

As we forded a frigid mountain creek, I asked Constantius, "Was the road this bad before?"

"It is much worse now. Back then, there was a bridge here. All that remains are its abutments." Two great rock foundations faced each other across the water. These once supported the bridge deck and raised it high above the current.

"Why doesn't the governor fix it?"

"Who knows? Corruption? He might prefer to pocket the repair funds than fix a road he never travels."

Day after day, we followed the road as it rose uphill and down. Once, when we spent an entire day climbing a steep slope and descending the other side, I said, "Surely that was the Silversmith Pass, wasn't it?"

Constantius laughed. "You will know when we are approaching the pass because snow crowns all the nearby mountains."

Just when I thought the road could not get worse, it became too steep to ride. We walked, leading our horses. "Why is there so much 'up'?" I asked, and the legionaries laughed.

Although Sarus and his Goths had abandoned much loot when they left Valentia, they were still pulling two carts laden with gold and silver, which made traveling through the Alps difficult. When we reached Silversmith Pass, Sarus's warriors were several days behind us.

A barrier blocked the road at the foot of the pass: a long log stretched across the road. It was mounted on a pivot so it could be turned out of the way. Behind it stood a tall man dressed in a sheepskin coat, woolen hat, and stout leather boots. Constantius, leading our party, dismounted and gestured for me to do likewise. As we approached the man, Constantius called out, "Hail, village headman!"

"Hail, Constantius!"

"You know me?"

"Of course. You came this way a dozen years ago and enjoyed our hospitality. As I recall, you bought a few of our silver bangles and gave some to my niece, who you also enjoyed."

"I am astonished you remember me!"

"We get few enough powerful Romans. It befits us to remember them."

"I remember your hospitality fondly. And your niece. Did she have my child?"

"Alas, no. To bear the child of a great patrician would have brought much prestige. No, she married a mineworker, a good man but no aristocrat.

"I am Dumnorix. You are welcome, but things have changed since you were last here. We are now obliged to collect a toll to help keep the road open. Two of my men are counting your party and assessing your goods. From that, I will determine a fair and reasonable toll."

I looked around and saw that archers had suddenly appeared down the length of our column from behind every roadside boulder. They stood quietly at attention, displaying their bows prominently, but I saw no arrows nocked and drawn. Two men climbed down to the road and walked past all our men. I saw our legionaries loosen the swords in their scabbards, but no one made any threatening moves. They all looked to Constantius for direction.

Several minutes passed while we waited for the two assessors. Dumnorix had been looking at me curiously, perhaps wondering why a woman would accompany a Roman war party. "This is your woman?" he asked Constantius.

"Yes, this is my wife, Matilde, daughter of Caius and stepsister of Alaric, King of the Goths."

I could see that Dumnorix was impressed by my family connection. "How many children have you given Constantius?" he asked.

"None so far," I said.

"Then it is good that you travel with him. You cannot make children when apart."

The two assessors approached Dumnorix and whispered in his ear.

"My men tell me that the toll for you, your horses, and your goods must be ten pounds of gold."

Constantius looked at me. "Is this a good and fair price?" Dumnorix would expect us to haggle over the price, and Constantius was delegating the job to me. He counted on my skill with numbers. If we foolishly paid ten pounds of gold or an amount close to that, the humiliation would be mine, not his.

The discussion went back and forth, with me pointing out that we had no goods—we were a party of warriors, not merchants—and our saddlebags contained food, clothing, and weapons. I had several legionaries open their bags to prove it. I also asked several of our men to demonstrate the quality of their weapons, a not-very-subtle warning that if our negotiation failed, the mountain people would suffer. Dumnorix argued that maintaining the road was very expensive, a curious claim since we had seen no sign of maintenance. As we came close to an agreement, Dumnorix sweetened his proposition, saying the toll would include a night's lodging in the village *mansio* plus a sumptuous feast.

We settled on four pounds of gold plus my two mules with their panniers of medical equipment. Since we were not likely to fight the usurper, the bandages and medicines were of more value to these remote mountain people than to us. Once we paid the toll, two village men pulled the barrier out of the way, and one guided us to the *mansio,* which had adequate room for all our beasts. It was, perhaps, the most decrepit *mansio* I'd ever stayed in. The outer wall had crumbled in several places, the main gate had fallen from its hinges and could not be closed, and sunlight shone through the dilapidated roof thatching. But, significantly, the courtyard was flat. Finding a flat spot to erect a tent in these mountains was difficult.

At dusk, a parade of local men entered the *mansio*, set up a grill, and began to cook two newly slaughtered sheep. Others brought *amphorae* filled with local beer. A handsome young woman arrived with a fruit pie on a metal dish. She said it was a special treat for the Roman commander. The pie had a typical flour crust, but its filling was novel. She explained she had filled it with a celery-like vegetable with a red stalk and large leaves. The stalk was stewed and mixed with honey. It was tart and sour but also sweet. I thought it was superb, but Constantius quietly confessed he did not like it, though he ate it out of politeness.

I did not like his familiarity with the woman and her with him. I was jealous. But nothing came of their flirting. I guessed she was Dumnorix's niece even before Constantius confirmed it.

Dumnorix sat with us while we ate. Constantius asked, "Who is your lord? Who collects your taxes?"

"No lord, no taxes," Dumnorix said. "We are free people."

"You are *bacaudae*," Constantius asserted.

"That is what Romans call marauding bands of peasants who loot and pillage. We don't do that."

"What happened to your lord? To the owner of your silver mine?"

"Well, I can tell you if you don't mind a sad story."

Constantius and I urged him to continue.

"Many years ago, when you came this way, numerous travelers passed through our town. They stayed in this *mansio*, purchased supplies from us, and bought the beautiful jewelry that our silversmiths produced. Then there was the year of the floods. We had so much rain and snow, perhaps enough for one hundred years. Many of our people died when hillsides slid down on their homes and covered the road. As you have noticed, the rivers flooded and washed away the bridges." Yes, we said, we had certainly noticed.

"We petitioned the governor for relief, money to feed ourselves, and men to clear the roads and rebuild the bridges. He did not respond, though we have been told the Emperor did allot money. We think the governor took the money and put it in his money chest.

"The only outsiders who came were soldiers hired by our lord, the mine owner. They took the silver ingots we produced and demanded more. They guarded the mine entrance, refusing to let our miners out each day until they'd produced a certain amount of ore. When the soldiers were hungry, they entered our homes and took our food. If they felt lusty, they took our girls for their pleasure." Dumnorix stopped to drink from his pail of beer.

"So," Constantius said, "you rose up and killed the outsiders."

"Yes. The mine owner tried twice more to retake our village in the next few years. He sent men who we filled with arrows. In these last ten years, he has left us alone. We train our men in archery and sword skills. Sometimes, I wish the mine owner would send more men because they were a convenient way of acquiring swords and armor."

I laughed.

"We no longer look to the governor, Emperor, or anyone else for support. We quarry our mine, sell our silver, and collect tolls from travelers."

"Some day," Constantius said, "perhaps in a year or maybe twenty, a great general will come through your pass. He will clear the roads, rebuild the bridges, and refuse to pay your tolls."

"That will be a shame," Dumnorix said. "We are happier now than when the road was in good repair. We don't want more travelers, and the tolls from just one troop like yours will sustain us for a year."

"Then this will be a bountiful year," Constantius said, "because another troop, allies of ours but much bigger, is hard on our heels."

With that, we retired to our sleep rolls. The day had been exhausting, and with the prospect of crossing the pass tomorrow, we needed our sleep.

Before we tackled the pass the next day, I asked Constantius if we should remain here until Sarus appears. He said no.

"I will not wait for Sarus," Constantius said. "We dealt well with these *bacaudae*, but he will not. They demanded money, which we paid, and now they will let us go unmolested. That is how these *bacaudae* do business."

"You don't trust Sarus to do the same?"

"He has much more gold and silver and will be loath to lose it. If he resists and fights, the *bacaudae* will fight back, and they are more than capable of fighting. This is their country, so there will be a few dead *bacaudae* and many dead Goths. I want to be far away when that happens."

Ancient Source: Zosimus, in which Sarus loses his loot:

[6.2.6] The officers of Constantine attacked [Sarus] so briskly that he had much difficulty to escape with life and was under the necessity of giving up all his spoils to the Bacaudae, a tribe of freebooters, to allow him to pass into Italy.

Once Sarus had passed through the Alps, his force could move more swiftly, having left their wagons with the *bacaudae*. The toll rate leaped when Dumnorix's assessors uncovered Sarus's two wagons full of gold and silver. The haggling between Dumnorix and Sarus was long, intense, and angry and only concluded when one of Sarus's young warriors grew impatient and unsheathed his sword. Dumnorix's archers promptly slew him. The two leaders calmed their men and decided to compromise rather than battle. Dumnorix had demanded a toll consisting of the two treasure wagons with all their gold and silver, but he settled for only nine pieces out of each ten. The remaining treasure was small enough not to require a wagon.

We learned this when an angry Sarus caught up with us. He and a few followers had raced ahead of the rest of his men and had ridden hard to overtake us. He accused us of leaving him behind. My husband responded calmly.

"No," he said, "we did not ride ahead. You were slow, burdened as you were with those wagons. You could have kept up if your men hadn't been greedy."

It did not improve Sarus's humor to learn of our cordial relationship with Dumnorix, our comfortable stay in his *mansio*, and the feast his village provided. Sarus had not been offered those amenities.

After Sarus offered Constantius a few more curses, he and his followers rode ahead. He was hurrying to ensure *he* could be the first to report on the expedition. Sarus cast the operation as a great success by emphasizing the death of the usurper's generals, Nebiogastes and Justinianus, and the destruction of the latter's force. He did not dwell on the fact that the operation had failed in its prime objective: capturing or killing the usurper. Several senators noted this and laid the blame at Stilicho's feet.

Constantius and I settled into a house of our own in Ticinum. He was busy with the troops returning from Ravenna, men who'd been slated for the invasion of Illyricum but who now needed housing, food, and other provisions. I returned to improving my archery skills. I'd also purchased a set of plain but well-balanced knives and was working with one of Constantius's *centurions*, an expert knife-thrower. "Lady," he said, "you will never stand against a seasoned warrior with a sword. You have not got the strength. But you won't have to if you can bury a knife in his throat before he closes with you." He was lecturing me on the hazards of close combat when the news came that Maria, the Emperor's wife, was dead.

I'd known she was sick, but I did not expect her to die. Of course, people, even healthy people, die all the time. When Constantius and I were dining that evening, I offered a theory. "Did she die with a baby in her?"

Constantius laughed bitterly. "As far as I know, she died a virgin. Honorius has never shown any interest in women. Or men or children, for that matter."

"Surely he could feign an interest in his wife long enough to father an heir, shouldn't he?"

"The Emperor's only concern is to be safe. And to be left alone. He is a coward. He was motivated to flee when he thought Alaric might capture him in Mediolanum. Since then, he has done little beyond what Stilicho and Serena tell him."

I looked around, hoping no servants were listening to Constantius's treasonous comments.

"But wouldn't Maria want an heir?"

"Of course. In any other marriage, the wife would take a lover and claim the resulting child was her husband's, but Honorius is not stupid. He would disavow the child and probably kill his wife."

"Perhaps that's what happened," I suggested.

"I doubt it. Honorius himself could not kill a chicken, and if he ordered her killed, the whole palace would know."

Ancient Source: Zosimus, in which Serena presses Emperor Honorius into marrying her daughter Thermantia soon after the death of Maria:

[5.28.1] … the Emperor Honorius, who had long before lost his wife Maria, desired to marry her sister Thermantia. But Stilicho appeared not to approve of the match, although it was promoted by Serena….

[5.28.3] … Maria died a virgin, and Serena, who, as may readily be supposed, was desirous to become the grandmother of a young Emperor or empress, through fear of her influence being diminished, used all her endeavors to marry her other daughter to Honorius.

Matilde

Only two weeks later, Honorius married Thermantia, Stilicho's younger daughter. He was twenty-four, and she was twenty-two. The ceremony occurred in the Ravenna palace, and Stilicho ordered Constantius to attend and witness the event. I was not invited. Serena always behaved coldly toward me, as if I might steal Stilicho from her. Why would I want Stilicho when I had Constantius?

"I don't understand," I said when Constantius returned home. "Stilicho has already sacrificed one daughter to the imperial dolt. Does he think Honorius will find Thermantia more attractive? That Thermantia might produce a son and heir when her older sister failed?"

"No. I think Stilicho opposed the marriage. He is still grieving for Maria. It was his wife who was the matchmaker. Serena is the only one who can force Honorius to do anything, and her interest is in remaining the Emperor's mother-in-law."

"Because it gives her power and prestige?"

"Yes."

"Is there any chance that Thermantia might seduce her husband?"

"None whatsoever. However, Galla Placidia might."

"What?!" Placidia was Honorius's half-sister, only sixteen years old at the time. It was well-known that she disliked her half-brother, and really, who could blame her? But incestuous feelings?

Constantius laughed at my reaction. "Not that she ever would. He disgusts her, and after this wedding, perhaps she hates him. When Thermantia sat next to him during the wedding feast, he told her to move over to make room for Placidia. When she sat beside him—quite reluctantly, I must say—I could see his hands moving under the table. I could not tell what he was touching, but by the disgusted look on her face..."

"That is horrible!" I said.

"He is horrible," Constantius agreed.

"Isn't she engaged?"

"Yes. She is betrothed to Eucharius." Eucharius was Stilicho's nineteen-year-old son. "They've been engaged since they were children. I don't suppose Serena is rushing to have them married now that she has reconnected her family with the throne."

"I would if I were Serena," I said.

"Why?"

"Because if the dolt should die or be killed, that would leave Placidia as the late Emperor Theodosius's last surviving child. Her husband would be a strong contender for the throne."

"That would be a two-edged sword," Constantius said.

"How so?"

"On one side, it would help secure Stilicho's position. Opposition to his authority is increasing, and he needs all the support he can get. Matilde, there are times when I fear for his life."

I'd seen the same threats. Many Senators hated him, and he had surrounded himself with a bodyguard, all Huns. Constantius and I had argued about the danger posed by that heinous race. He thought that, as individuals, they were trustworthy. I was sure they were not. Regardless, I sympathized with the good Italian legionaries who resented their exclusion from Stilicho's inner circle and the benefits and privileges afforded those barbarians.

"What is the sword's other edge?" I asked.

"The dolt values his life above anything else. Having Eucharius poised to become Emperor would provide an incentive for someone to kill him. He might see Eucharius as a threat."

I had to agree. Eucharius would be a better Emperor than Honorius. Anyone would. I'd only met Eucharius a few times, but he was amiable, educated, and strong. A devout Christian like his mother, Serena.

"Matilde, have you received any messages from your stepbrother?"

"No. Why?"

"There are rumors in Ravenna that Alaric is planning to invade Italia again."

"Why would people think that?" I asked.

"I have ordered him to move his army north from Epirus, back to Noricum, but not to Italia. Perhaps people misinterpret that."

Ancient Source: Zosimus, describing Alaric's response to Stilicho's command:

[5.29] In obedience to Stilicho's order, Alaric marshaled his Visigothic army to assist in taking Illyricum for the Western Empire. However, after canceling that operation, Alaric requested reimbursement for his expenses. The Roman Senate vehemently resented paying this.

Matilde

Stilicho had ordered Alaric to take his forces from Noricum to Epirus as part of the plan to wrestle Illyricum away from Constantinople. Alaric obeyed those orders, paying his men out of his own treasury. Then, Stilicho canceled the plan when he heard of the barbarian invasion across the Rhine and usurper Constantine's crossing from Britain into Gaul. By the *magister militum*'s order, Alaric moved his army back to Noricum and then asked for four thousand pounds of gold to pay his costs.

He was not threatening to invade, at least not openly, but he *was* seeking his due. Constantius thought it only fair, as did Stilicho, who traveled to Rome to argue on Alaric's behalf in the Senate. Even that sluggard Honorius went to Rome and spoke in favor of my stepbrother. I asked Constantius if I could go, but he said it would be unwise. Women were not allowed on the Senate floor, and Gothic women doubly so. My presence would only antagonize those rich old men.

The senate paid, most begrudgingly, especially the senators from Gaul and Hispania, whose estate revenue was now going into the usurper's pocket. Alaric did *not* invade.

Chapter 15. 408 CE. Genocide

Ancient Source: Zosimus, in which the Western court learns that Emperor Arcadius is dead, and Stilicho and the Emperor argue over who should travel to Constantinople to manage the affairs of his young successor, Theodosius II:

[5.31.1] Before this juncture a report had been circulated at Rome that the Emperor Arcadius was dead….

[5.31.3] … Stilicho was desirous of proceeding to the east to undertake the management of the affairs of Theodosius, the son of Arcadius, who was very young and in want of a guardian. Honorius himself was also inclined to undertake the same journey, with a design to secure the dominions of that Emperor.

Matilde

Constantius and I were out hunting when word came that Emperor Arcadius was dead, leaving the Eastern throne to his seven-year-old son Theodosius, Second of that name. Arcadius was only thirty-one years of age. I do not know what he died of, but he died even earlier than his father, Theodosius, who died at age forty-eight. It gave me hope that Honorius might die younger still. I did not like Arcadius or Honorius and had wished them both ill.

Constantius left me in Ticinum and immediately rode to Ravenna to meet with Stilicho and the Emperor. A formal delegation needed to travel to Constantinople, one that would convey the great pomp and majesty of Honorius's court. Organizing it was a significant undertaking requiring a master of planning like Constantius. He didn't know whether Stilicho or the Emperor would lead the delegation, but either way, he was confident he would go and promised that if he went, I could go too. I felt the opportunity to see Constantinople again was the best thing about Arcadius's death.

My husband returned a week later with disappointing news. He told me the details over dinner.

"I witnessed," he told me, "a most astonishing argument between Honorius and Stilicho. At issue was which of the two would lead the delegation. It was surprising because Honorius stood up to Stilicho. Actually defied him! His arguments were foolish, but he made them stubbornly."

"Surely they agreed that *somebody* had to go," I said.

"Yes, and they both agreed the visit should demonstrate the empire's unity and bury any past East-West enmity. But then Honorius claimed if there'd been any animosity, it was Stilicho's fault. He cited Stilicho's past campaigns in Illyricum and the one just planned and canceled. At one point, Stilicho got quite angry—angry at his Emperor!—but I was able to restore civility. Honorius thanked me for interceding. Prior to that, I don't know if he'd ever even noticed me!

"Both were concerned that competent and honest ministers should be appointed to act in the young Emperor's name, men who would see to his welfare. However, Honorius claimed that as the senior Emperor and the boy's uncle, he had the authority and skill to make such appointments."

"Has Honorius ever shown any such skill? Or skill of any kind?" I asked.

He held off answering while a servant served us lamb in gravy. We were careful about our conversation when slaves were nearby.

Constantius shook his head and continued his account.

"Though it tried Stilicho's patience, he explained why *he* (not the Emperor) should lead the delegation. He emphasized the danger such an arduous journey would pose, knowing any suggestion of danger would frighten the Emperor. He also reminded Honorius that, as Emperor, he was the head of the army, and with him present, the usurper wouldn't dare to invade Italia."

"Is that true?"

"Constantine will invade whenever he thinks he might win. But the army does indeed idolize the Emperor."

"They don't know him," I interjected.

Constantius shrugged and went on. "If he went abroad, the troops might think he was abandoning them. Then, they would go over to the usurper. True or not, Honorius believes it."

"Did Stilicho point out the cost of sending an imperial delegation to the East?"

"He didn't, but there was no need. Stilicho had already convinced Honorius that to keep his throne, he had to remain here. Anyway, he doesn't understand money. He thinks we have a bottomless treasure chest. The loss of tax revenue from Britain, Gaul, and Hispania means nothing to him.

"He also doesn't understand manpower. Stilicho is trying to gather as many troops as possible here so we can launch an attack on the usurper this summer. An imperial procession would draw away at least a dozen legions," Constantius said.

"How many legions would a Stilicho-led process require?" I asked.

"Perhaps four."

"And who will lead this attack on Constantine? Not you, I hope. Of course, you would make a fine general, but I'm counting on going to the East with you."

He stopped chewing, swallowed, and gave me a sad smile.

"I have to tell you this. I'm not going to the East. Neither will I be part of the great attack. Apparently, Honorius likes me and wants me by his side this summer."

Constantius saw the disappointment on my face before I could wipe it off.

"I'm sorry to disappoint you," he said. "So, to answer your question, no, I won't be leading the attack. Vincentius will lead the attack against the usurper." I didn't know him.

"And I have some news that will truly surprise you."

"Which is?"

"Alaric will go as Vincentius's second in command! Stilicho will appoint him *magister militum per Gallias*."

Now *that* was exciting. Finally, after all these years, my stepbrother would have an opportunity to prove himself a valuable member of the Roman military. Ever since his invasion of Italia, back when I was captured, he'd been cooperative and trustworthy. He was obedient to Stilicho's orders. He deployed his forces to Epirus, as ordered, and when the Illyricum campaign was canceled, he moved them back north. Although he and Stilicho had been on opposing sides more than once, it wasn't personal. Their history went back to the Battle of Frigidus River. Of all the generals engaged in that conflict, only those two were still alive.

"Oh, how wonderful for Alaric!" I was about to say more when the servant entered with our next and final course, a sweet pie. She dished each of us a bowlful, and I dug in.

Constantius looked skeptically at the pinkish pudding. "It's that dreadful Gaulish stuff, isn't it?!"

"Yes, it is. When we got home from Gaul, I asked around. Poor people here eat it all the time. It's called *rhabarbarum*, and the *medicus* says it is good for you."

Constantius took one spoonful, grimaced, and pushed it away. "Too sour."

I laughed and signaled to the servant who brought Constantius a dessert he loved: cherry pie. He dug into that with pleasure.

"Will Alaric and his warriors be here soon?" I asked.

"In several weeks."

When Alaric and his army joined the force already assembled in Ticinum, he and I could eat, hunt, and sing together. Then, they would all set off to crush the usurper.

"Will the women and children come too?"

"I believe so. I think your whole nation will come because after the usurper is put down, Stilicho will give them land in Gaul or Hispania."

That idea stirred up doubts and bad memories. The idea of having Alaric lead a Roman army began to seem unwise.

"Constantius, my love, is this a good idea? To bring all these Goths here only a few short years after Radagaisus pillaged the north? To put all these legionaries under Alaric's command? In general, you Romans fear and hate barbarians, especially Goths. What if the Romans rise against them? I remember when that happened in Constantinople. I lost many friends when the mob killed anyone who spoke with my accent. I lost my Gainas." My voice cracked, and I bit my lip to keep from sobbing.

We sat quietly until I could regain my self-control. Then Constantius said, "I have wondered that myself, but I've always had confidence that Stilicho could control the army, that it would obey him because the Emperor backs him. But the argument between those two has me worried. I've never seen Honorius dispute with him before. Suddenly, the Emperor has a backbone, and I'm afraid I know why."

"And that is?"

"There's a court official named Olympius. He's the *magister scrinii*, master of the imperial secretaries, a position Stilicho appointed him to. He was there during the great argument. Although he said nothing, whenever the Emperor contradicted Stilicho or made a reasonable argument, he would glance at Olympius, who would return a slight nod. It was like Olympius had coached the Emperor on how to stand up to Stilicho. I came away thinking that Olympius is trying to undermine him."

On that uncomfortable note, we finished dinner and walked through the town to where Constantius was having additional barracks constructed to house all the incoming troops.

Ancient Source: Zosimus, in which Olympius instigates a mutiny by the legions in Ticinum (Pavia), killing many of Stilicho's officers:

[5.32.1] Olympius ... an officer of rank in the court-guards, concealed ... the most atrocious designs in his heart. Being accustomed ... to converse frequently with the Emperor, he used many bitter expressions against Stilicho and stated that [Stilicho] was desirous to proceed into the east, from no other motive than to acquire an opportunity of removing the young Theodosius and of placing the empire in the hands of his own son, Eucherius.

Matilde

I had changed into my riding clothes and had just reached the stables when Constantius ran up behind me. He was gulping great gasps of air and could hardly speak. "Is your horse saddled?"

"No, I just got here," I said.

"Saddle her. Do it quickly. We go immediately."

"Why? What's happening?" He didn't answer but brushed by me, heading for his own roan's stall.

"I'll tell you when we're on the road," he called over his shoulder. "But hurry!"

Two minutes later, we were trotting east on the *Via Aemilia*. "Keep a steady pace," Constantius said, "Don't gallop. Don't talk to anyone or stop. Just keep going."

We were ten miles from Ticinum when we came to a tavern. "I think we can stop here, at least long enough to rest our mounts and get a drink," he said.

We sat outside at a table sipping our wine when I finally asked, "What was that all about? What's happening?"

"Mutiny," Constantius said, taking a great quaff of his drink. "That bastard Olympius has roused the army. The troops heading for Gaul were mustered for the Emperor's review. *Magister equitum* Victorianus was speaking, then there was a commotion, and a soldier strode forward, sword in hand, and ran him through. The troops broke ranks, and a hundred or so legionaries—I recognized them as Olympius's chosen men— surrounded the Emperor and all the reviewing officers and began slaughtering them."

I felt sick to my stomach. I'd seen it all before, the day Brutus slaughtered Rufinus. Was this the way the Romans always solved disputes?

"Did they kill Stilicho?"

"No. He is at the camp outside Bononia."

"How did you escape?"

"I'd been accompanying the Emperor—that seems to be my role, now—and, a few moments before the commotion started, he turned to me and said, 'I have no honorarium for Victorianus. Do you have a purse? Give me your purse.'"

"Your purse?" I asked.

"I'd taken to carrying around a leather purse containing a dozen gold aurei. The Emperor would call for a coin or two to reward anyone when it struck his fancy. But I'd left the purse in the pocket of my heavy cloak back in his carriage, which was parked on that low hill overlooking the parade ground. I ran up there and was a hundred paces away when I heard an uproar. I turned and witnessed the killings, just as I said. The men— Olympius's men—were killing anyone appointed by Stilicho. I saw Olympius pointing them out. He didn't see me up on the hill or they would have killed me, too."

We finished our wine and kept riding east. We did not stop until we got to Stilicho's encampment outside Bononia a full day later. That encampment had almost six thousand tents, surrounded by a protective berm and a wooden palisade with watchtowers, just as one would see in a temporary camp on the frontier. The whole camp was hazy with the smoke from hundreds of campfires and the smell of meat cooking for breakfast.

Constantius knew the way to Stilicho's tent and every other tent because he'd been responsible for constructing the camp. After the twelve thousand survivors of Radagaisus's force were sworn in as *foederate allies*, they needed shelter, which Constantius had provided.

We were not the only ones to escape the massacre. Men straggled in over the day. Not officers—they'd all been killed—but rank and file *centurions* and *optiones*, men loyal to Stilicho.

Within a day, his supporters had gathered, including leaders of the *foederate allies* like Guitabert. While we waited for news, Constantius and I slept in a spare tent. The next morning, we arose, donned our clothes—the same clothes we'd just ridden one hundred miles in—and made our way to Stilicho's tent. A slave served us bowls of salty porridge, and we ate greedily while waiting for everyone to gather.

Ancient Source: Zosimus, in which Stilicho decides how to respond to the mutiny:

[5.33.1] When intelligence of this reached Stilicho, who was then at Bononia, he was extremely disturbed by it. Summoning, therefore, all the commanders of his confederate barbarians who were with

him, he proposed a consultation relative to what measures it would be most prudent to adopt.

Matilde

Stilicho stood on a wooden box from which he could oversee the small crowd. With no introductory remarks, he said, "I learned before dawn today that Emperor Honorius is alive. Olympius," this name was accompanied by hisses and boos, "stopped his mutineers before they could kill the Emperor. Now, the question for me is: What next? I have an opinion, but I can see that Constantius wishes to speak."

"Thank you, my lord," my husband said. "I was there when the mutiny started. I watched as Olympius's criminals slaughtered Victorianus, Limenius, Chariobaudes, and a dozen other fine, loyal men. My lord, there can be only one response. We take all the soldiers here, including Guitabert's many *foederate allies*, march to Ticinum and crush this rebellion, leaf, stalk, and root."

"So advises General Constantius," Stilicho said. A few other men stood and offered their advice, but it was all variations of Constantius's with, perhaps, more specific punishments that should await Olympius.

Finally, Stilicho spoke again. "Thank you for your advice. It is precisely what I'd expected to hear. It is the course of action I spent the entire night pondering. Last night, I thought everything hinged on whether the Emperor was alive or dead. If he were dead, I would lead you in eradicating the mutineers, just as Constantius suggests. But if Honorius were alive, then only the ringleaders would be arrested.

"I do not want a battle. We cannot afford one. Those men in Ticinum are good soldiers, though badly misled, and the Emperor needs them to eliminate the usurper.

"Now that we know the Emperor is alive, I have changed my mind. I cannot lead a force to arrest the ringleaders. That would surely lead to a battle. Perhaps someone else can lead such a force. For my part, I must obey my Emperor's orders. His last order was to travel to Ravenna and prepare for the trip to Constantinople. That is what I shall do. That is my duty."

From all over the gathered crowd came cries of "No! No!"

Constantius stood and, with arms outstretched, said, "My lord, your plan is suicidal! If Olympius controls the army, he will send men to kill you! We support you. We have enough men. Lead us against him."

"Constantius, if the Emperor still supports me, then I will be in no danger. If he does not, then I am doomed. In either case, I will go to Ravenna tomorrow. You and my other followers are free to go wherever you like and do whatever you think best."

With that, Stilicho turned and entered his tent. Constantius and I returned through the maze of tents to ours. In the morning, Stilicho was gone, heading for Ravenna. We and his other loyal followers gathered at the center of the encampment to discuss our plans. Guitabert and the other *foederates* captains joined us. The talk seemed to go round and round until Constantius stood on a box, the same box Stilicho had used, and called for quiet.

"We know that Emperor Honorius is alive and that the troops in Ticinum are loyal to him. But we do not know who the chief magistrate is. Is it still Stilicho? Has Honorius entrusted that post to Olympius? Or to some other? For my part, to avoid being indicted as a rebel, I shall step aside until this question is answered. I leave this morning for Patavium, and I invite any of you who feel likewise to join me."

Before noon, Constantius and I headed north accompanied by a train of thousands of men, mostly Guitabert's *foederate allies* plus the many men who felt a personal loyalty to Constantius. We were not surprised when Patavium's city gates were closed to us. The captain of the guard called to us from atop the southern gate to explain. "With the utmost deference and apologies, General Constantius, we have received a message from *Magister* Stilicho explaining that barbarians are on the move and all cities should protect themselves. Our gates shall remain closed until he or the Emperor directs us."

Constantius did not argue; there was no point. Instead, he directed his men to create an encampment outside the city walls where we could live until the power struggle ended.

Ancient Source: Zosimus, in which Stilicho is murdered:

[5.34.2] … Olympius, who was now become master of the Emperor's inclination, sent the imperial mandate to the soldiers at Ravenna, ordering them immediately to apprehend Stilicho and to detain him in prison without fetters.

[5.34.5] Thus, while Eucherius, his son, fled towards Rome, Stilicho was led to execution. The barbarians who attended him, with his servants and other friends and relations, of whom there was a vast number, preparing and resolving to rescue him from the stroke,

Stilicho deterred them from the attempt by all imaginable
menaces and calmly submitted his neck to the sword. He
was the most moderate and just of all the men who
possessed great authority in his time.

Matilde

At dusk, a messenger arrived with the news we expected but feared. Stilicho had been executed in Ravenna. He'd taken sanctuary in the city cathedral, but when a squad of killers, led by a certain Herclianus, arrived with a letter from the Emperor promising Stilicho his life, he left the sanctuary. Thereupon, Herclianus flourished a second letter, one that bore the characteristic language of Olympius but was signed by Honorius, ordering his execution. Always a servant of duty, Stilicho obeyed his Emperor's command and submitted to the sword without resisting.

Constantius wept. I did not. Stilicho was a good man, but like Gainas, he demonstrated that even a good man can be a fool.

Ancient Source: Zosimus, in which the Roman civilians
massacre all the Goths in their midst, and Stilicho's men
join Alaric:

[5.35.3] … The Emperor Honorius commanded his
wife, Thermantia, to be taken from the imperial throne
and to be restored to her mother, who, notwithstanding
was without suspicion. He likewise ordered Eucherius, the
son of Stilicho, to be searched for and put to death.

[5.35.5] … The soldiers who were in the city, on hearing of the death of Stilicho, fell upon all the women and children in the city who belonged to the [Goths]. Having, as by a preconcerted signal, destroyed every individual of them, they plundered them of all they possessed.

Matilde

Constantius posted guards on all the roads leading into Patavium. His men diverted all produce and other foodstuffs into our camp after paying fair prices. We intercepted all messengers for the city officials, which is how we learned about the hateful edict of November 22. This order, sent to every city throughout Italia, asserted that Stilicho had encouraged the *foederate allies* to conquer the country. It claimed these barbarians meant to kill or enslave all Roman citizens, and it provided a list of Stilicho's allies who should be arrested and tried. The order bore all the hallmarks of Olympius's writing style and reflected Honorius's delusional fears. He had always hated my people and was seizing this opportunity to eradicate us.

Constantius did not pass this message into the city. Instead, he demanded that the city's mayors release all the Gothic families living there. They agreed—why shouldn't they?—and soon Ralamunda, her two children, and dozens of other barbarian wives and families were pushed out a postern door. The relief and joy on Guitabert's face was reflected on his wife's.

Within a day, refugees began to trickle into our camp— women and children from Hatria, Mons Silicis, and even

Vicentia—all traumatized, all telling the same story. The edict had heightened the hatred and fear Romans already felt for the Goths. Soon, they were falling on their foreign neighbors with knives and cudgels, killing the aged, the babies, and everyone in between. The trickle soon became a flood when all *foederate allies* abandoned their posts and converged on Patavium.

Rather than face the regular Roman army, now under Olympius's control, Constantius led the throng north toward Noricum, where we could seek protection from Alaric. Our people marched along the *Via Annia*, which ran through Venetia along the northern shores of the Adriatic Sea. We filled the road from side to side, and as far as I could see, our column stretched back toward Patavium. Some people, fearing to be overtaken by Olympius's troops, ran ahead, but most stayed near Guitabert's *foederate allies*.

We were on the road for no more than a half day when we encountered Alaric's scouts, and by the end of the day, Constantius's and Alaric's forces were united. Alaric's army had come to participate in the great attack on the usurper. Instead, they were saving Radagaisus's Goths from being massacred. It was the largest army I had ever seen, perhaps forty thousand people. Anger and joy filled me. Anger that the Romans in every small town in Italia could hate all our innocent women and children and massacre them as casually as one might slaughter a sheep. Joy, when I saw that we now, with all our numbers, could force the Emperor to meet our demands, which had been unchanged since we left Moesia. We only sought a province where we could live by our laws and safely raise our children.

When, in that vast crowd, I finally located Alaric and Theodoric, I was overjoyed. It had been almost two years.

Chapter 16.   408 CE. Matilde and Honorius

Ancient Source: Zosimus, in which Honorius refuses to negotiate with Alaric:

> *[5.36.1] But Alaric ... still preferred peace, being still mindful of the league into which he had entered with Stilicho. He, therefore, sent ambassadors with a desire to procure a peace, even if he acquired for it but a small sum of money. ... A peace being made on those terms, he would lead his army out of Noricum into Pannonia.*

> *[5.36.2] When Alaric demanded peace on those conditions, the Emperor refused to grant it.*

Matilde

Once the forces led by Alaric and Constantius joined, we camped for the night and arranged for the captains to meet at dawn the next day. Our throng spread out beside the road with people having tents erecting them, those with wagons sleeping under them, and the rest trying to make themselves comfortable sleeping out under the stars. Fortunately, it did not rain. I remarked to Constantius that many among us possessed nothing, so we would soon be plundering every nearby farm and settlement for the necessities of life. If those Romans didn't hate us before, they soon would.

The following day, the captains planned our next step. Of course, Alaric and Constantius were present, but the group also included Ataulf, Wallia, Guitabert, and myself. I participated as an equal, with no one mentioning my sex. Alaric started the discussion with a proposal.

"We need to send an emissary to the Emperor, someone who can convince him that we are not his enemies but loyal subjects. We are only here to protect members of our tribe from the merciless attacks by foolish, ignorant Romans."

"He will not believe that," Constantius said, "when he sees you at the head of thousands of men. How can he view you as anything but a threat?"

"But he knows Stilicho ordered me to come." Alaric sounded exasperated. "I have Stilicho's written orders summoning me and my men. We were supposed to cross the Alps and lead the assault on the usurper."

"Stilicho is dead," I said, "and Honorius has a short memory. What he now sees is a tribe of barbarians at his doorstep set on destroying him."

"We—our emissary—must convince him otherwise. If he agrees to help me, I will return to Pannonia tomorrow," Alaric said.

"What help do you need?"

"Money, to pay my men, no more than one thousand pounds of gold, and food. Surely, he will provide food; otherwise, my people will be forced to plunder everywhere we go."

"He might see these are reasonable requests," Constantius said. "But who should deliver them? I cannot go. So long as Olympius has the Emperor's ear, I would be considered a public enemy. Olympius would have me arrested the moment I step inside the city walls."

The captains agreed that Honorius would not welcome Alaric, "that barbarian king." One by one, all the heads turned toward me. As a Goth, I was representative of the mob facing Honorius; as Constantius's wife, Honorius knew me; and as a woman, I was not a threat.

I agreed to go. Constantius asked that I avoid mentioning him lest Honorius think him a confederate of Alaric and a traitor. My husband emphasized that he was no traitor but Honorius's most loyal subject.

"Honorius does not deserve such a worthy subject," I snapped. "The empire would be well-served if Jupiter were to fling a thunderbolt at the Emperor."

"That is quite enough, wife," Constantius insisted. I was angry, but I bit my tongue.

Our army, led by Alaric, marched down the *Via Popilia* to the outskirts of Ravenna, where the Emperor had taken refuge. I entered the city, accompanied only by Anicius and two other bodyguards. The only road into the city was bracketed by salt-water marshes on either side. Walls and gates fortified the way. Any invader would have to overcome barrier after barrier before reaching the city. At the first gate, we were stopped and kept waiting for most of a day until a courier could reach the city and return with the necessary passports. A dozen soldiers accompanied the courier. These men provided a close escort and never left our side until we reached the palace, where only I was admitted. The soldiers told my bodyguards to remain out of doors.

It was late afternoon when Olympius met me in the palace's reception hall, a large, dark room with few windows and lit mainly by torches. It was a plain room that pre-dated the transfer of the royal court from Mediolanum to Ravenna. It had no tapestries, mosaics, or any other art and smelled vaguely of mold. This was not surprising since Ravenna was a city built in a swamp. Olympius was seated in an ornate throne-like chair halfway down the room's length.

"Lady Matilde, I do hope you and your husband are in good health," he said. His unctuous voice felt greasy to my ear. The long black hair from the back of his head was swept forward, ineffectively covering the bald spot, which the torches highlighted.

"I could never have imagined being honored with your company at this troubled time."

I explained my mission in simple language, omitting the ornate phrases that usually decorated speech at court. I finished with, "And so, I humbly petition for an audience with our lord, Augustus Honorius."

"My dear," Olympius said in a condescending tone, "anything you might wish to say to the Emperor, you can say to me."

"That may be," I said, "but my commission directs me to speak directly with the Emperor."

"I am afraid that is impossible. His lordship..."

Olympius was interrupted by the crack of a door being flung open at the back of the reception hall. Out stepped two *protectores,* followed immediately by Honorius. Two more *protectores* came immediately after. "I will speak with the Lady Matilde," he said.

I was astonished by both the man and his speech. He spoke with precision and authority, unlike the mealy-mouthed youth I'd last seen following his marriage to Maria. His posture was upright, he spoke clearly, and he stood up for himself, which he'd never done before.

Later, when I tried to understand this change, I reasoned that Stilicho's murder had transformed him. Once free from that man's domination, he'd resolved to never be dominated again. One thing hadn't changed; he was still a coward. I stood before him, an unarmed woman, but his four *protectores* stood in a line between us. Did he think I would leap forward and bite him?

"Why are you here?" he demanded.

I explained I'd come representing Alaric, who had come to Italia as ordered and wanted nothing more than to return to Pannonia since the campaign against the usurper was postponed. However, he needed food for his men and money to pay them for their time away from home.

"How many men?" Honorius demanded.

"He came from Pannonia with six thousand."

"You lie," Olympius spat. "My sources say he has twenty thousand."

"With respect, your sources are wrong," I said. "Alaric now has forty thousand people. They include the six thousand he brought from Pannonia, plus the warriors who fought under Radagaisus. They joined with Alaric to protect their wives and children, who you"—I rudely pointed a finger at Olympius—"have targeted for death. And thousands of runaway slaves have swollen Alaric's ranks. Would it not be best, my lord, to meet Alaric's requests—a small sum of money and food—and have this whole throng leave Italia in peace and go back to Pannonia?"

"You talk," Honorius said, "as if I were powerless. I am not. My legions are strong, even without your traitorous *foederates*, and I have a new ally in the West.

"Lady Matilde, are you familiar with the story of Spartacus?" he asked. I was, but he did not wait for me to respond. "The legions of Rome crushed that rebellion. The slaves who died in battle were the lucky ones. The rest—six thousand of them—were crucified and lined the *Via Appia* from Rome to Capua. I believe I can decorate the road from here to Crotona," a town at Italia's southern tip, "with Alaric's twenty or forty or however many thousand." The Emperor wore a snide smile as he made this threat. I sincerely wanted to slap his face, so it was good that four *protectores* separated us.

"Perhaps, my lord, with God's help, you could. But are you not afraid of the usurper? While you are engaged with my stepbrother, won't he cross the Alps and attack you?"

"The man you call 'the usurper,' I call Constantine, Third of that name. I have acknowledged him as a fellow augustus. Emperor Constantine and I are now allies. With northern Italia secure, I shall concentrate on crushing Alaric, not negotiating with him. He shall get no food or gold from me. You may go and tell him so."

I turned to leave when Olympius said, "Yes, you may return to your brother or husband or whatever man or men you are currently sleeping with and tell them of our decision. Guards, show her out!"

It was clear that Honorius would never negotiate with Alaric until forced. One of the *protectores* took me roughly by my upper arm and led me out the door. As we passed Olympius, he grinned widely at me, revealing two missing teeth on his upper jaw and a black and dead tooth on the lower.

Chapter 17.   408-409 CE. Blockade of Ostia

Ancient Source: Zosimus, in which Alaric starves Rome:

> *[5.39.1] … Alaric blocked up the gates all round and, having possessed himself of the river Tiber, prevented the arrival of necessaries from the port to the city. …*

> *[5.39.2] But none coming to their assistance … and all their provisions being consumed, the famine, as might be expected, was succeeded by a pestilence, and all places were filled with dead bodies.*

Matilde

The captains were angry and frustrated by Honorius's refusal to bargain.

When I relayed Olympius's final remarks, Constantius went beyond angry. "Truly? Olympius said, 'Whatever man, or men'?" Though my husband and I fought occasionally, he was protective of me.

But Alaric just laughed. "Did he really say 'and tell them of *our* decision'? '*Our* decision'? Honorius won't forget that. Perhaps the old Honorius might, but this new man, the one who knows how to stand erect, will punish Olympius someday."

The question facing the captains was this: how can Honorius be forced to bargain? Everyone agreed that Ravenna was impregnable. Attacking it would simply squander time and men. Ataulf suggested sacking Rome, but that city was well fortified. It had withstood attacks for eight hundred years since barbarian Gauls sacked it.

"Why not starve the city into submission," I suggested. "Honorius would not stand by while one million Romans starve."

"Besiege Rome?" Constantius asked.

"That wouldn't be necessary. All we need is control the harbor at Ostia."

"Oh, clever girl," Constantius said. "All of Rome's grain arrives there."

"And its olive oil, salt, and wine," I added. "The city will starve over the winter or until Honorius is willing to bargain."

With a settled strategy, Alaric led us south to Rome. Most people found nightly shelter in tents or wagons, but Constantius and I were welcomed into *mansiones* along the way. The innkeepers enjoyed the protection that a Roman general could provide. Alaric and the rest of his entourage were satisfied with camp life. They'd had decades of practice.

We put our strategy into motion, locking down the warehouses, mounting armed guards, and intercepting all arriving ships. As the winter progressed, the common people suffered, and those who could afford to leave did so. We did not prevent it. This was not a siege, and we wanted word to get out, especially to Ravenna, of the local pain.

In December, we learned that the Romans were organizing a local militia, many hundreds strong, hoping it could break our hold on the storehouses. Alaric doubled the guard, and when the militia appeared, our warriors cut them to pieces. Only the gods know why these untrained city boys thought they could stand against men who had practiced the art of war from childhood.

I entered the city twice, guarded by Anicius and several other legionaries, men whom Constantius trusted. It was not safe to be a Goth in Rome, not when Alaric was starving the population, so I dressed carefully as a Roman matron, and when forced to speak, I pretended to have a stutter, anything to avoid revealing myself as a Goth. At one time, the city had thirty thousand Goths, but when mobs began murdering them earlier in the year, they left the city to join Alaric. Now, as part of Alaric's forces, they resided in tents just outside the city walls. Ironically, they were within a mile of their original homes, places they could no longer go without risking life and limb.

My purpose for entering Rome was to visit Serena and Placidia. They had moved into the Suburra—probably the city's most disreputable neighborhood—after Stilicho's murder and were trying to stay out of public view. My first visit caused a commotion, with dozens of little children gathering around me and begging me for something to eat. Anicius tried to shoo them away, but with no more luck than one has keeping flies off a sweet melon. They would not believe that we had no food.

Serena and Placidia lived in a tiny, squalid apartment on the fourth floor of a crumbling tenement. They had no slaves, so Placidia had to walk down to the ground floor twice daily to refill their jug—they only had one—from the public fountain. Both women had to avail themselves of the public latrines just a few yards from the fountain. For food, they were eking out a desperate existence using the small cache of coins left over from their days of prosperity. They looked thin but otherwise healthy, though neither was in good spirits. Serena was still in deep grief over the loss of Stilicho. Placidia was bored and scared. "The people here curse the Emperor. I honestly believe they would kill me if they knew I was his half-sister." She was young and attractive and had expected her life to be filled with hunting, dancing, and flirting with young men.

"Why don't you leave?" I asked. "Constantius would welcome you to our encampment."

"We are guarded all the time. You won't have noticed it, but men in the neighborhood are paid to ensure we do not stray. Every week, they collect a few *siliquae*, money they would forfeit if we escaped. It's not much money, but it keeps their families fed."

I gave them the few coins I was carrying before I left. Serena said, "Next time you come, bring a few small coins, a handful of *nummi* for the hungry children." I promised I would.

Ancient Source: Zosimus, in which the Roman Senate, believing Serena might betray the city to Alaric, has her executed:

> *[5.38.1] When Alaric was near Rome, besieging its inhabitants, the Senate suspected Serena of bringing the barbarians against their city. The whole Senate, therefore ... thought it proper that she should suffer death for being the cause of the present calamity.*

Matilde

I returned the next week to find Placidia living alone. "Where is Serena?" I asked.

"Dead." Placidia's voice cracked, and she wept as she explained. A dozen men had come to the door bearing a death warrant from the Senate. "They said to me, 'Serena, you are charged with treason and have been found guilty of encouraging this attack on Rome by Alaric, King of the Goths.'" She had to pause to control her jagged breath. "And then, without thinking, I pointed at Serena, who was sitting in the corner on that cot, and said, 'I am not Serena; she is.' When my stepmother confirmed it, the men strangled her to death right before my eyes. They did not give her time to say a prayer or bid me farewell. Nothing. Then they dragged her body away. I am," here she halted again, "haunted by the sound of her head banging on the steps as they all descended. Haunted by my role in her death. It was my fault. They would have taken me if I had kept quiet, which would have been so much better."

There was little we could do to help. I offered to smuggle Placidia out, but again she declined. I did leave her with one hundred *nummi* for the neighborhood children. Perhaps she would be a little safer if the children loved her.

By New Year's, senators were meeting with Alaric, trying to reach a compromise. His demand for "a little money and some food" had been replaced with a "request" for five thousand pounds of gold, thirty thousand of silver, four thousand silk robes, three thousand scarlet fleeces, and three thousand pounds of pepper. The senators claimed they could not meet such a request, but in the early days of spring, they did provide a substantial portion of it. Alaric unlocked the warehouses as a show of good faith, and the senators, expressing sympathy for the plight of Alaric's Goths, agreed to petition the Emperor on Alaric's behalf.

In April, a courier came to Alaric's encampment with a message for Constantius. Like everyone else, he and I were living in a tent, so it took some time for the courier to find us. "Well?" I asked.

"We are summoned to court," Constantius said.

"Summoned?"

"Politely but formally requested. The phrasing is not Olympius's. It says we're to make our arrangements through Jovius. I remember him. He was *praefectus praetorio Illyrici*, that is, Praetorian Prefect of Illyricum, and appointed by Stilicho. It would seem like Honorius welcomes Stilicho's people again." Constantius grinned with satisfaction.

I was impressed. There were four praetorian prefects, one for each of the empire's four prefects. This Jovius had held one of the most important administrative positions in the empire, and now he was requesting that Constantius appear before him. Just Constantius?

"Did you say Jovius is summoning both of us?"

"Yes, the parchment mentions you by name."

We left the following day accompanied by Constantius's loyal companions and arrived in Ravenna three days later. Jovius's order authorized us to stay in the finest *mansiones* en route. I confessed to Constantius that I preferred sleeping in a quiet room on a feather mattress to sleeping in a tent on a canvas cot.

"I can see you aging day by day," he teased. "Crow's feet eyes, and wrinkled skin. Not the young beauty I married years ago." I laughed. None of that was true. We'd been married for only a year and were almost exactly the same age.

In Ravenna, we entered the palace's reception hall from the bright outdoors and waited while our eyes adjusted to the dim light. Olympius was nowhere in sight, but a man sat in a simple chair where Olympius's throne-like chair had sat. Constantius recognized him.

"Jovius?"

"Yes, it is good to see you again, Constantius. This must be your bride, Matilde."

We briefly exchanged pleasantries until Constantius asked, "Where is Olympius?"

"He has fled. To where? I'm unsure, but my sources tell me he has property on the lake at *Novum Comum*. A beautiful spot, I believe. I expect you'll want to know why he's gone." We both nodded. "The Emperor became distressed last year when our society became uncivil, with neighbors killing neighbors and slaves fleeing their masters. He hoped the people would see the vulgarity of their ways and revert to a state of decorousness, but the violence has continued. First, his nephew Eucharius was murdered, and then a gang of criminals killed his Aunt Serena. My lord asked me to investigate this chaos, and after much probing, I discovered that the instigator was none other than the Emperor's own chief minister, Olympius. Of course, it is hard to keep a secret in the palace. Olympius must have felt a noose tightening around his neck. So he disappeared, and the Emperor has asked me to take his place."

Constantius and I glanced at each other and exchanged identical thoughts. Who had set neighbor against neighbor? Who had ordered Eucharius murdered? It wasn't Olympius. It was Honorius, but when the violence finally consumed Serena, the time had come for the Emperor to find a scapegoat.

"I have summoned you here to tell you the Emperor's wish. For you, Matilde, his lordship knows that you have been seeing his half-sister Placidia. It is an open secret that he does not love his half-sister, and the same is true in return."

Does not love was an understatement. *Loathes intensely* would be more accurate.

"But," Jovius continued, "she *is* the late Emperor's daughter. Family, as it were. He is concerned for her health and safety. So you, Matilde, will lead a squad of *protectores* to Rome. There, you will extract her from whatever tenement she inhabits, install her in a suite in the imperial palace, and wait for further instructions. Do you understand?"

I was dumbfounded and could only nod.

"Constantius, the Emperor has a crucial mission for you. Tomorrow, you will leave by ship from the city harbor and go to Constantinople. There, you will arrange with Honorius's fellow Emperor, Theodosius, Second of that name, to provide ten legions or as many as he can spare. Return here with them as soon as you can. Do you understand?"

"I do," Constantius said.

"I have clerks preparing the necessary documents for your respective missions. They will be ready tomorrow. Both of you should be ready to depart by the fourth hour after dawn. This servant," he indicated a young woman who had come in after us and was standing by the room's entrance, "will escort you to your suite and bring your meals there."

Chapter 18.   410 CE. The Sacking

Matilde

It was all so unfair. I had not asked for this mission. I could understand that Placidia was in danger and that I was uniquely positioned to help her. My husband had not asked to be sent to the East for who knew how many months. We had only been married briefly, just one year, which only seemed like one week. I said as much to Constantius.

"Too short, too short," he agreed. "I had thought I would have a son by now."

"I don't want us to be separated," I said. "My life has been plagued by separations from those I love." I began to review them in my mind: Gisalric, my parents, Gainas, the list was too long.

"Nor I from you," he said. "How can I negotiate with the Easterners without you by my side? You are the clever one."

"I have grown used to having you near me. I do not think I can sleep without you," I said. My voice began to quaver. I stopped talking and leaned my head against his chest, waiting to regain my calm. "I need you by me when I awake. And in the evening, when we talk and sing." Then I *did* cry.

"And when we try to make a baby, my son and heir," he added. "Which I think we should do immediately." I laughed through my tears, and in one minute, we were out of our clothes and making love, a feverish love that would have to suffice for the months we would be apart.

In the morning, I walked down to the docks and onto his ship to give my husband a final sendoff. I cried hot tears during our last kiss. He did not. Constantius explained that he had a thousand tasks to do before his ship could sail and, while holding me close in a loving embrace, explained how very busy he was. I countered that my morning would be equally demanding. He held my hand, lifted it for a kiss, and said farewell.

As I descended the gangplank to the pier, he called out, "Grow that baby! After last night, you should be able to grow two babies." I laughed obligingly and went to the stables where my *protectores* were waiting.

I remembered that conversation in the years to come. Constantius, unlike Gainas, appreciated my cleverness. He valued me as the potential mother of his son and heir. But if he also valued my companionship, he never said so. Unlike me, he never claimed our separations made him lonely.

As my squad and I rode south, we encountered Alaric and his captains at the village of Tadinae coming the other way. We stopped just long enough for a noon meal and for me to hug my son. I described my meeting with Jovius, the downfall of Olympius, and my mission.

"Oh, so you've met this new fellow, Jovius!" Alaric said. "He has asked me to come to Ravenna and claims he wants to bargain."

"Do you think you can reach a settlement?" I asked.

"With Honorius on the throne? I am not optimistic."

Soon, we were back in our saddles and on our way.

Placidia saw my *protectores* before she saw me. We'd arrived in the Suburra, made our way to Placidia's tenement, and banged up the stairs to her apartment. No one was foolish enough to interfere with our progress. Everyone recognized the Emperor's personal bodyguards, with their black tunics trimmed in silver, cloaks, and kilts. Furthermore, the lead *protector* marched with sword drawn. When Placidia saw him, she assumed a death squad had finally come for her, and she collapsed on the floor.

"Come, sister, we're here to save you, not hurt you," I said and took her by the hand to raise her. By morning's end, we were installed in a magnificent suite in the imperial palace on Palatine Hill. Placidia was perfectly comfortable in that setting, having spent much of her life there, but I was not. Too much gold, too many sculptures, fountains beyond number, frescoes, and mosaics. Household slaves always lurked nearby to respond to any request. When I said as much to Placidia, she laughed.

"Would you trade this for my place in the Suburra? No, I thought not," she said. We quickly found activities to occupy ourselves. Placidia loved to paint and play the lyre. She had a fine singing voice, unlike me. She adopted a puppy. In the evenings, we would tell stories, sometimes true, often embellished. When I told her of my affair with Gainas, she sighed, "So romantic!" and demanded I tell the whole story again.

Several weeks later, Alaric returned. I could see his anger and disappointment even before he opened his mouth. "How was Honorius?" I asked.

"I never saw the Emperor, not face-to-face. He refused to meet me, so Jovius acted as the go-between."

"Did Jovius let you down?" I asked.

"No, no. Jovius is a fine man. His proposal was ideal. He suggested our tribe be allowed to settle in Noricum, Dalmatia, and Venetia and receive a yearly stipend of corn and gold. Perhaps Honorius would have accepted that, but then Jovius went too far. He reminded the Emperor of my good job as *magister militum per Illyricum* and recommended I be appointed *magister militum*. That made Honorius explode. He swore he would never again appoint a Goth *magister militum*."

"And then what happened?"

"Nothing. There was no point in talking anymore. We turned our horses around and came back."

W inter was coming, and with it, fierce storms on the Adriatic Sea. I resigned myself to not seeing Constantius until spring. He'd hoped to return home to see me cradling our son, but despite the passion and frequency of our love-making, my womb remained empty.

Alaric and Ataulf often met with the Roman senators, trying to reach a proposal acceptable to everyone. Their interests aligned: the Gothic leadership wanted to find a permanent home far from Rome, and the senators wanted to see the Goths as far away as possible. It was Ataulf who suggested appointing someone else to be Emperor. He visited Placidia and me in our palatial suite and explained his proposal. There was a well-known senator named Priscus Attalus, who, as *praefectus urbis Romae,* was in charge of running the city. Alaric selected him to be crowned Emperor, and Honorius would be deposed. If Honorius didn't abdicate voluntarily, Alaric would remove him by force.

As Ataulf spoke, I watched Placidia. Her attention was focused on Ataulf, nodding as he made sound arguments, leaning toward him, with her cheeks slightly flushed. Then I watched Ataulf. His speech was animated, both hands gesticulating, listening intently when she asked a question, the tip of his tongue poking out between pursed lips. She slid forward on her chair, moving a little towards him, and he did the same. They were wrapped entirely in their conversation. If I suddenly disappeared, they would not notice.

I could understand what Ataulf saw in Placidia. She was sixteen years old and in her prime. A beautiful face, thick black eyebrows, long eyelashes, cheek dimples. Her figure had filled out, recovering from her months of deprivation in Suburra. Her height was average, and her hips were broad, suggesting the potential for safely bearing many children.

But what could she see in Ataulf, a barbarian? Then, I noticed that he had changed. His golden hair was neatly cut to shoulder length and tied back with a silver band. Once long and ragged, his beard was trimmed to an inch, and his mustache reached from cheek to cheek, twisted to a point, and held with wax. When she spoke, he smiled widely at her with his almost perfect teeth.

At one point, I interjected that if Honorius resisted being forcibly deposed, my husband would be fighting Ataulf and Alaric, my stepbrother. I may as well have said nothing for all the attention I received.

When the conversation petered out, Ataulf claimed he had other pressing business, but he wished he could stay. I was sure he and Placidia would have been delighted to spend the entire day in each other's company. When he said farewell, he held her hand, kissed it, and continued holding it until I offered my hand for a kiss.

People talk about love at first sight. I had just seen it.

Ancient Source: Zosimus, in which legions arrive from the East, providing Honorius with enough courage that he felt he could ignore Alaric's threat:

[6.8.1] Upon hearing of [Priscus Attalus being crowned Augustus], the Emperor was so terrified and perplexed that he sent out ambassadors to propose that the empire should be divided between them. ...

[6.8.2] ... [Six] regiments of auxiliary soldiers arrived [in Ravenna] ...

[6.8.3] At their arrival, Honorius, as if awaked from a deep sleep, confided the defense of the walls to those who were come from the east ...

Matilde

Alaric led his fighters north from the outskirts of Rome to Ariminum, just a few miles south of Ravenna. That city had never been taken by siege, but Alaric thought having such a force on Honorius's doorstep would pressure the Emperor into a compromise. Perhaps it might have, but at this point, my husband returned, leading a fleet into Ravenna's harbor. Though it had taken a year, Constantius finally returned with four thousand legionaries. It was just one legion, not the ten

Honorius had requested, but it gave the Emperor enough courage to break off the talks. In frustration, Alaric moved his men to the Ravenna road and was preparing to advance on the city when he was attacked from the rear. It was Sarus, Alaric's long-time enemy. The engagement was short and sharp, with few casualties on either side. However, among the dead was Palvric, Wallia's lover, a loss that Wallia would never forget or forgive.

Was Sarus continuing their blood feud, or was he acting on Honorius's orders?

I never found out, but Alaric assumed the latter and, in a fury, marched his men back to Rome.

During this episode, Placidia and I had remained in the Emperor's palace in Rome. Ataulf came to see us—well, to see Placidia, actually—and explained what had happened. From my point of view, it was all for the good because my husband's legion and my stepbrother's warriors did not come to blows. Ataulf also explained that Alaric had dethroned Priscus Attalus because the entire ploy of offering an alternative Emperor to Honorius had failed utterly. Though I said nothing, I felt this was more good news. Constantius, like Stilicho before him, was loyal to a fault. He would never renounce his commitment to Honorius, though we both knew the man was a fool.

What would Alaric do next? Placidia quizzed Ataulf, but he had no answer. Perhaps Alaric himself didn't know. Meanwhile, the months rolled on, the cool Roman spring turned into a broiling summer heat, and the Gothic army remained encamped just north of the city. Alaric did not lock up the food warehouses as he did two years earlier. The city gates remained open during the day, and Goths came and went, peacefully purchasing food and other necessities.

I missed Constantius greatly. We exchanged messages periodically. In his first note, he expressed regret that our last night of passion before he left for Constantinople had not resulted in a child. I asked how long must I remain in Rome with Placidia? Or could Honorius release Constantius so he could come and live with me? In June, he did slip into the city without any fanfare, and we spent one night together, a night that tested the endurance of his love-making, before returning to Ravenna. A month later, my next message to him simply read, "No child."

I consulted two doctors in the city. The first prescribed eating rotten meat periodically. He clarified, saying, "But only meat where you can see many maggots thriving. Such meat, meat demonstrating procreative fecundity, will impart that virtue to your body." The second doctor questioned my history and Constantius's and concluded, "Your body has twice demonstrated reproductive competence, whereas Constantius has never had a child. The problem, Matilde, is with him, not you." I accepted the second diagnosis and avoided rotten meat.

Ancient Source: Sozomen (400–450 CE), a Roman lawyer, church historian, and author of "Ecclesiastical History," in which Alaric, being attacked by Sarus and blaming it on Emperor Honorius, sacks Rome:

> *Soon after, Alaric stationed himself among the Alps, at a distance of about sixty stadia from Ravenna, and held a conference with the Emperor concerning the conclusion of a peace. Saros, a barbarian by birth and highly practiced in the art of war, had only about three hundred men with him, but all well disposed and most*

efficient. *He was suspicious of Alaric on account of their former enmity and reasoned that a treaty between the Romans and Goths would be of no advantage to him.*

Suddenly advancing with his own troops, he slew some of [Alaric's Goths]. Impelled by rage and terror at this incident, Alaric retraced his steps, and returned to Rome, and took it by treachery.

He permitted each of his followers to seize as much of the wealth of the Romans as he was able, and to plunder all the houses; but from respect towards the Apostle Peter, he commanded that the large and very spacious church erected around his tomb should be an asylum. This was the only cause which prevented the entire demolition of Rome …

And Ancient Source: Orosius, describing the sacking of Rome:

Book 7.39: Alaric appeared before trembling Rome, laid siege, spread confusion, and broke into the City. He first, however, gave orders that all those who had taken refuge in sacred places, especially in the basilicas of the holy Apostles Peter and Paul, should be permitted to remain inviolate and unmolested; he allowed his men to devote themselves to plunder as much as they wished, but he gave orders that they should refrain from bloodshed.

Book 7.40: When the City was stormed, Placidia, the daughter of the princely Theodosius and sister of the Emperors Arcadius and Honorius, was captured and taken to wife by Athaulf, a kinsman of Alaric.

Matilde

I was awake even before the *protector* came into my bedroom. There was a trumpet blast, a war trumpet, a Gothic war trumpet. I'd grown up hearing them and could distinguish them from the higher-pitched Roman trumpets. The blast was followed by another and then a whole chorus of trumpet blasts. The Goths were here, inside the walls, in the dead of night. How could this happen? *How* must wait until later. My top priority was to save Placidia. I threw on yesterday's clothes and, as I opened the bedroom door, a *protector* rushed in. We darted into the hall and, a few steps later, into Placidia's room.

"Barbarians are flooding the streets," he said, "but my commander is assembling a squad to take you out of the city." The sound of screaming penetrated the palace walls, and a flickering yellow light illuminated the room. The city was burning.

"A squad? How big a squad?" I asked. "A dozen men, maybe two?"

"We have six *protectores*," he said, "but they are all expert swordsmen. We will cut a path to the city gate if necessary."

"You think those Goths don't know how to use a sword? If we resist, well, there is nothing that they would like more. We will all be killed in minutes."

"No," Placidia said, "*I* will decide what we will do. We will move to the palace chapel and stay there until Ataulf arrives."

"Why do you think he'll come?" the *protector* asked.

"He told me so. I didn't understand it at the time, but he said, 'If you fear for your life, go to the chapel, pray, and wait.'"

"He *knew* this was coming?!" the *protector* asked.

"Of course he did," I said.

We made our way out of the building and across the courtyard to the chapel. The air stank of smoke and light from burning buildings turned night into day. Once in the chapel, the *protectores* piled boxes and furniture before the door. We sat, waited, and prayed.

"Why would Alaric do this?" I asked.

"For the money," Placidia said. "By tomorrow, every jewel, every scrap of gold and silver in the city will be in some warrior's oxcart."

"I understand that," I said, "but it violates Alaric's every ambition. He has never wanted to conquer Rome or usurp the throne. His goal has always been to find a safe home for my people within the empire, as good Roman citizens."

"He has not succeeded," Placidia said. "This sacking is his admission of failure. Sacking Rome is an unforgivable sin. Do you know what this city means to the empire? Or how old this city is?"

"Yes, I know it's very old."

"It has been eleven hundred and sixty-three years since Romulus founded Rome and eight hundred years since it was last sacked. Rome was not the richest city in the empire, even before tonight. It hasn't even been the capital for more than a hundred years. But this is the *Roman* empire, and all our citizens are Romans, even if they've never set foot here." I could see that Placidia was weeping.

We sat quietly for an hour and then heard a great rapping at the chapel door. "It's me, Ataulf!" someone called. Two *protectores* cleared the door while the other four stood around Placidia and me with swords drawn.

When Ataulf entered, the *protectores* sheathed their weapons. "We thought it might be a ruse," their commander told me.

"We will wait here until dawn," Ataulf said. "It is chaos out there. Buildings are burning out of control. I've seen people robbed at knifepoint. Women raped. Anyone who resists is immediately slain, and the roads are full of corpses. I saw a patrician woman stripped bare in the middle of the street because some barbarian liked the fabric of her gown."

At dawn, things were no better. Alaric allowed the sacking to continue for an entire day. The homes of the wealthy on the Palatine and Esquiline hills were looted and burned. Only the presence of Ataulf's men kept the looters out of the palace. When his men grumbled that everyone else was getting rich, Ataulf allowed them to sack the palace, "but no fires!" he ordered.

After two days, we were allowed to leave, but with armed escorts. Placidia was shocked at the destruction, but I said it could have been worse. Alaric had ordered his men to honor the sanctity of churches. Men, women, and children had crowded into the chapels of St. Paul and St. Peter. They were safe there from physical abuse; however, the Goths confiscated their jewelry. The gold and silver plates were seized in every church and melted down. Corpses filled the Tiber River, thrown there by slaves clearing the streets.

Four days after the sack began, Alaric said *enough*. He announced that our nation would trek down to the toe of Italia, embark on ships, and make a new home in Libya. I was heartbroken and got into a heated argument with him. "The idea of sacking Rome was stupid. Stupid and counter-productive," I said. "You have always wanted a home within the empire, working with the hierarchy, to be considered a Roman, not a barbarian. Sacking Rome was brilliant if you wanted to work against those goals."

"But Honorius made me *so* angry!" It was a poor excuse, and he knew it.

"A skillful leader does not act out of anger," I retorted. "Think, Alaric! Please think of the actions that have advanced our goals and those that did not. When you were *magister militum per Illyricum*, the court respected you. When you scoured Greece and Macedonia, the court hated you. Your invasion of Italia was a disaster. I was captured and taken away from you and my family for years. Why did you not..."

Alaric interrupted me. "Please, Matilde. You might be correct. At this point, I don't know. I am sad and feel poorly. Can we talk about this when I'm feeling better?"

Such a time never came. We moved south with Alaric riding his stallion. When he tumbled from the saddle, Ataulf ordered a sedan chair for him. He was carried semiconsciously to the port at Rhegion and woke from time to time to ask about the ships he'd summoned, the ships that were to take us to Africa. A few came, but a storm destroyed the rest. It was the last straw, and he collapsed.

We lay him on a cot under a spacious tent, which protected him from the hot August sun. A cool sea breeze wafted through its open ends. The splashing and burbling sound of the nearby Busentus River soothed him. Theodoric and I sat by his bedside and wiped his feverish brow with a cold cloth. At first, we talked about our life in Moesia, growing up with Elodia and Caius, but a day came when he couldn't remember our names, and he began to call me Pentadia. He told me how he loved me, only me, and "I would never have married Matilde except you insisted." In moments of relative clarity, he summoned Ataulf and said, "My brother, I am dying. I entrust my wives and sons to your care. Be good to Pentadia. She is foolish, but she loves hard. And protect Amalric and my other son," he paused here until I could prompt him with, "Theodoric." "Yes, Theodoric. They are both good boys and will make fine kings in due time." He'd forgotten that the same fever that killed Pentadia also took Amalric.

Finally, as the first cold nights of winter approached, my dear stepbrother Alaric fell into a deep sleep and never awoke. Ataulf, Alaric's brother-in-law (by virtue of his marriage to Pentadia), took charge of the body and organized the mourning and burial rites. The mourning began immediately, with men of every rank and from every clan weeping openly, rending their garments, and tearing their hair. Ataulf and Theodoric worked together and alone to secretly bury his body in an unmarked grave by the river and then, to prevent grave robbers and Alaric's enemies from excavating and desecrating his remains, Ataulf put about a fantastic story: that he'd had the river dammed, and buried Alaric in the now-dry river bed along with a vast amount of treasure and tools, and that all the slaves involved in the burial had been put to death. Those who knew Alaric scoffed at the tale. He had been a devout Christian and had looked forward to the day of resurrection. When that great day happened, he would have no use for tools and treasure.

Like Moses, Alaric had started my tribe on the path to the promised land, but he never lived to see it.

Chapter 19. 411 CE. Dismissed

Matilde

Ataulf summoned the clan leaders to meet and choose a new king. My Theodoric, at age eleven years, was acknowledged as Alaric's son but was far too young to lead the tribe. No one was comparable to Ataulf in importance or stature, so he was duly elected.

He attempted to continue Alaric's plan of migrating the tribe to Africa, but no ships were available. Emperor Honorius had made transporting Goths a capital crime, and no ship owners were willing to take the risk despite the great sums we were willing to pay. We did, after all, have the entirety of Rome's gold in our oxcarts.

In the spring, my husband arrived leading his legionaries, a group that had grown from four thousand men to many times that number. The thought of war erupting between him and my people terrified me, but Constantius restrained the belligerent impulse of his captains. He was here to talk, not fight.

I was overjoyed to see him, but the bliss of our reunion was postponed until the leaders could converse. We met around a bonfire, which kept everyone warm during the damp spring day.

"Welcome, Constantius," Ataulf said. "We can only hope that your master's obstinacy has moderated since we last talked."

"I would never characterize my Emperor that way," my husband said. At least, he would not say so publicly. That might cost him his life, but in the privacy of our chamber, he had accused Honorius of much worse than obstinacy. "However, my master has arrived at two resolutions. The first is that there is no place in the heart of his empire, by which he means Italia, for your tribe." I could feel Ataulf and his captains bristle. "Your desolation of our capital city is an unforgivable crime. Or it would be for anyone other than our Emperor. But Emperor Honorius is a magnanimous and merciful master. He has issued an edict and requires that I read it to you. I will omit the introduction, in which he sets out his role as lawgiver, and begin at the meat of the decree. 'To ameliorate the suffering of my loyal Goths, I have instructed my marshals to allow them safe passage from Italia to Gaul, where they may settle on any open and available land.'"

Constantius's audience gasped in amazement while he paused to take a sip of wine. This is what Alaric had sought ten years earlier when I was first captured. Finally, after so much time had passed and so many lives lost, Honorius saw the light. "He instructs that your migration to Gaul should finish this year. Do you see any objection or difficulty with this, King Ataulf?"

Ataulf may have been irritated by Constantius's lofty tone, but my husband's use of the King's title softened it.

"It is a distance we can easily cover this year," Ataulf said, "but we do not have sufficient food for the journey. Can the Emperor provide us with grain and oil as we proceed?"

"I shall see that it is done. We would hate to see you mark your passage with a trail of despoiled villages, as is your wont."

"It is done from necessity, not inclination," Ataulf replied.

"The second purpose for my visit is to relieve you of the burden of caring for Lady Galla Placidia. You, Lady Matilde, daughter of Caius, have faithfully fulfilled your mission." It seemed peculiar for my husband to refer to me so formally. "You have loyally guarded the Emperor's half-sister for the better part of two years, protecting a young woman renowned for her nobility, beauty, and chaste purity. The Emperor relieves you of this burden and duty and offers you his thanks. If you will go to that lady now and aid her in gathering her belongings, I will escort her to Ravenna when we leave at dawn tomorrow."

I turned to do as he requested when Ataulf spoke, "With regard to preserving her moral virtue, no one could have done more than Lady Matilde. As for her physical safety, I assumed *that* responsibility at the time of the sacking and have continued to protect her ever since. This has been no burden. She has now reached the age of eighteen winters, well into womanhood, and is more than capable of protecting her innocence herself." I'd wondered if Ataulf would speak up.

He continued, "As a woman, she does, of course, require a man's protection, and on the day she is married, her husband will be that man. Until then, as she is an adult, I shall leave it in her hands whether she rides with you tomorrow or remains with my people—people, I should add, who have welcomed her presence. In summary, General Constantius, you may certainly take Lady Placidia with you if that is her wish."

I expected Constantius to be vexed, but he calmly said, "Can I ask that Lady Placidia be brought before me and answer the question herself? If she wishes to remain with your tribe, my master will require that she has spoken without let or hindrance."

Ataulf agreed, and I fetched Placidia to the fireside. Constantius asked her the question, and she asserted her desire to remain with my tribe. My husband then required that she sign a sworn statement to that effect. A priest fetched a scrap of parchment and wrote her avowal on it. She signed her name, and two clan chieftains witnessed with their marks.

"That is done," Constantius said, in a tone suggesting it was of no matter to him whether she stayed or went.

"Wife," he said, "can I assume you will ride with me tomorrow morning?"

"With eagerness," I said with less enthusiasm than my words suggested. "I shall gather my things—it won't take long—and have Theodoric escort me to your encampment."

He nodded, smiled stiffly, and left with his captains, walking toward the field where his men were constructing a camp.

Placidia walked with me to the tent that had been my home for over a half year. When we were alone, she asked, "Did you notice Ataulf's comment, how nobody could have done more than you to preserve my chastity?" She wore a broad smile.

I laughed. "Yes, it was a hopeless task for me or anyone else."

"Indeed, there was no stopping Ataulf. Not that I wanted him to stop."

"Please avoid getting with child until you're married." She knew what I meant. A child could be Honorius's successor, but only if he were legitimate.

"Don't worry. I have a quantity of *silphium*, enough to prevent motherhood for another year at least."

I collected all my clothes, jewels, and the pair of sandals I wore while bathing and tossed them into my trunk. I was about to call for a slave to carry it when Placidia put her hand on my arm. "Just wait," she said. "You don't have to rush. I don't know when we will meet again."

I sat on my trunk, Placidia perched on the edge of my cot, and we rested holding hands. Tears ran down her face. "Do you remember the first time you visited Serena and me in Suburra?"

"That horrid little apartment? Don't remind me of it," I said.

We sat quietly for a minute. I watched, knowing she had more to say. Finally, "You could stay too, you know. You don't have to go with *that man*."

I was not surprised. She had never liked Constantius.

"But, my dear, I want to go. I love him. I want to have his children, and we will raise them together."

She shook her head. "Words coming from a woman who spent precious little time raising her son."

I was stricken, and she saw it. "Oh, I'm sorry. I didn't mean it. I understand it was Alaric's fault."

"More like Alaric's *wish*," I said. "He was my king, and he wanted his heir near him. Especially after Amalric died."

"I know, I know. I have strayed from what I was trying to say." She got up, walked to the tent's door, peered outside for a minute, and then returned to her seat. "You say you love Constantius, and I believe you. But he is one of those men who loves only himself. You amuse him, you stir his loins, and he wants to have children with you, but Matilde, he does not love you. He does not love you like Alaric loved Pentadia or Ataulf loves me."

"Constantius loved Stilicho," I countered.

"Not romantic love, as a man loves a woman. Constantius was loyal to Stilicho. His loyalty to Stilicho was boundless. Now that he is dead, Constantius has become loyal to Honorius. Unlike Stilicho, my half-brother is a man undeserving of loyalty."

Placidia paused and then went on. "You find joy with him now, but someday he will disappoint you."

"You are wrong," I said, though I could not prove it.

She stopped arguing, squeezed my hand in hers, and said, "Here, kiss me goodbye, and promise me neither Constantius nor anything else will come between us."

I did, and so we parted. Theodoric had been waiting patiently outside my tent. I don't know how much of our conversation my son overheard. He and I held hands as we walked to the Roman camp, where he received directions to Constantius's headquarters. When we reached Constantius's tent, we kissed goodbye.

"Will you come tomorrow before we set off?" I asked.

"You will be busy. The whole camp will be busy. It would be better if we said our farewells now," he said. Theodoric was correct and very grown-up for a boy of eleven years. I could not have been more proud.

My argument with Placidia was erased from my mind when I stepped into Constantius's tent. Our lovemaking filled the afternoon and long into the night. In the pre-dawn hours, I asked my husband, "Whatever became of that horrid turd Olympius?"

I knew Constantius's deep hatred for Olympius, who had stabbed his revered Stilicho in the back.

"He met his just end," he said.

"Which was?"

"His life was already forfeit after the Emperor blamed him for the murder of Serena, which, of course, was Honorius's own fault. However, I was the only one sufficiently motivated to track him down, and I was away seeking troops from Constantinople."

"But then?"

"Then Alaric sacked Rome. Again, Honorius was at fault, but since an emperor can do no wrong, Olympius—long gone Olympius—got the blame. In his anger, the Emperor said to me, 'That Olympius! Why is he not dead yet?' and told me to 'See to it.' So I did."

"And he met his proper fate?"

In the dim morning light, I could see Constantius nod. "Informants had placed Olympius in Verona. I sent a squad of men there to find him. I ordered that they arm themselves with nothing more lethal than cudgels. When they finally cornered him, they took turns beating him to death."

I tried to picture it, thinking it should disturb me, but it did not.

Chapter 20.   411 CE. Magister Militum

Matilde

As a reward for dealing with "the Goth problem," Honorius appointed my husband *magister militum*. I was now the proud wife of the most powerful general in the empire. I mentioned this to Gaba after we moved back to Ticinum. She still lived there with her husband Nevitta and their two little girls. Gaba's response was to lecture me on hubris. "Do not tempt the gods," she said. "Serena once held your position, and remember her fate." As if that weren't sobering enough, she said, "Anyway, it's not the *whole* empire. Theodosius rules the Eastern half, and Constantine the West. Honorius rules only the middle."

But then messages arrived from Gaul, suggesting Constantine's hold on the West was shaky. His top general, Gerontius, the man responsible for seizing Hispania for his master, had betrayed him and now pledged his allegiance to *another* usurper named Maximus. With Maximus ruling Hispania, Gerontius decided to overthrow his old lord, Constantine. He harnessed the barbarians who had roamed Gaul ever since crossing the Rhine four years earlier and encouraged them to ravage Constantine's territory. When they had done their worst, he welcomed them to Hispania, where he awarded each tribe with a vast tract of land in the south and west of the peninsula.

As if depriving Constantine of Hispania were not enough, Gerontius marched his army into Gaul and besieged Constantine in his capital of Arelate.

M y husband and I led his army of ten legions over the Mont Cenis pass from Italia to Gaul. We aimed to crush the so-called Emperor Constantine and restore Gaul to the empire. It was a sunny mid-summer day, and as we wended our way through the Alpine valleys, cool breezes lifted my spirits. Until then, I'd not realized how much I hated the baking heat of southern Italia.

"I believe," Constantius said, "I can turn Constantine's men in my favor."

"Don't you think," I said in a light-hearted tone, "they will be confused by your names? Constantius, Constantine, and you tell me he has a son named Constans. The choice you Romans make in naming your sons certainly seems *constant*."

This did not amuse him. "I am Constantius because my father named me for the Emperor of that name, but the usurper wasn't born with the name Constantine. He adopted that name so people would associate him with Constantine the Great, the man who turned the empire toward Christianity."

"Still," I said, feeling slightly belittled, "it's confusing."

"It will be less confusing after I execute the usurper." His mood was grim.

"You look worried."

"Let this be our secret: I *am* worried. I believe I have sufficient strength if I must contend with only the usurper, but I have no idea of Gerontius's strength. My friend Tricostus claims that Edobichus, the usurper's *magister militum*, is recruiting men along the lower Rhine. How many men and when they might come to Constantine's aid, I do not know. I am attacking blind."

"Have I met this Tricostus?" I asked.

"I doubt it. He is an old friend, a retired legionary. We served together under Stilicho. He has a villa north of Arelate. You and I will stop there before we head south."

The legions set up an encampment near Arelate while Constantius and I were escorted by a small contingent of bodyguards to his friend's plantation. Tricostus came to the door of his villa, opened it wide, and welcomed us warmly. He showed us where we would be sleeping and provided nearby sleeping cubicles for our bodyguards. He was an old man of over fifty years, a childless widower, but he still looked healthy and energetic. When he offered to show us his orchards and fields, my husband readily accepted, but I declined. I was so very tired. Our host saw my eyes would not stay open, so he showed me to our room. I lay down and immediately fell asleep.

It was dark by the time I awoke. I heard distant voices and made my way towards them. The two men were sitting around a table, eating bread, fruit, and a pungent gravy-covered pork dish. As I entered, I overheard them talking.

"And your slaves?" Constantius asked. "Where are they?"

"They fled into the hills a month ago, afraid of being conscripted into Gerontius's army. There's not much to eat up there, so I expect they'll be back before autumn when this war is settled," Tricostus said.

"So you have no servants?"

"Just a couple of women, house slaves," Tricostus said and then looked up and noticed me.

"Wife, are you feeling rested now?" Constantius asked.

Then, the smell of the food assaulted my nose, and I could scarcely exit the room before I vomited. Fortunately, my stomach was empty, so the mess was minimal. Tricostus summoned a house slave to help me back to the bedroom and clean me up. The young woman took my hand to guide me. As we retreated from the dining room, I heard my host ask Constantius, "A baby?"

"It's about time," Constantius said.

But I knew what it felt like to have a baby. This did not feel like that. It felt more like *influentia*, a common sickness caused by the influence of the stars. As wretched as I felt, I knew it would pass in just a few days if it didn't kill me first.

The young woman helped me back into bed. "You are so kind," I said, "as is your master."

"One could not ask for a kinder master than Dominus Tricostus," she said just as I fell asleep.

In the morning, I awoke feeling much better. Not entirely whole, but not inclined to vomit again. And hungry. I found my way back to the dining room. The table was still covered with the remnants of breakfast, and I picked through the leftovers for a slice of bread and a hard-boiled egg. The villa was quiet. I finished my food and then checked the table jugs for watered wine. They were empty. My clanking around must have alerted the slave woman.

"Are you feeling better, Domina?" she asked.

"Much better. Where are the men?"

"They left at dawn. Dominus Tricostus escorted your husband back to the legion camp. My master should be back before noon. He told me to make you comfortable and said you should treat his home as if it were your own."

"Did my husband say when he would return to collect me?"

"He said you will stay here for the duration of the campaign. I am to fetch you anything you or your baby needs. He said he thought he would defeat the usurper by autumn, so you should not expect to spend the winter here, and he said, 'Tell her I'll be back long before the baby is due.'"

I felt like pulling my hair out and shouting, "I am not with child!" It would not have been helpful. Instead, I finished my breakfast and called for a bath. Noon came and went without Tricostus returning. I felt weak and tired but not otherwise ill. I napped throughout the afternoon. Night fell, and dawn arrived with no sign of my host. I ate by myself since there seemed to be no one else but the servants. I explored the villa and found Tricostus's small library. He had only three books: The Gospel of Mark from the Christian Bible, a copy of Virgil's Aeneid, and Ovid's Metamorphoses. I opened Mark but was too angry to read. Why didn't he wait? If he had to leave, he knew I could catch up! If only he'd left a bodyguard, someone to accompany me. I can ride quickly! There was nothing to do except take another bath.

At dusk, Tricostus returned. He was a kind man and pleased to see me up and about. He took my hands in his, looked solemnly into my eyes, and asked, "How are you? How is the baby? You had us quite worried."

I explained that there was no baby, to which he said disbelievingly, "Yes, of course, yes!"

"There *is no baby!* I was just sick for one day. Now, I am feeling well."

Perhaps he believed me then, but it made no difference. I was a reluctant guest and would remain so until my husband returned.

Two weeks later, one of the slave women ran into the villa and breathlessly announced, "The Romans are coming!" It took some quizzing before we learned that "the Romans" comprised General Edobichus—the usurper's *magister militum*—a small number of British legionaries, and a very large number of barbarians. The General's effort to recruit northern barbarians had been a success.

"Do you know this general?" my host asked.

"We managed to avoid him when we besieged Valentia three years ago," I said.

"He is a nasty piece of work. Two months ago, when he went north, he came onto my property and demanded hospitality. My foreman asked for his name—politely as far as all the witnesses could say—and Edobichus drew his sword and slew my man."

I was horrified and worried. "Do you think he'll return here again tonight?"

"I expect he will. He enjoyed my food, my bed, and my slave girl. She told me later that he was a beast. Though she was used to rough treatment, he was the worst."

"Then we have a problem," I said.

"Yes, if he learns who you are, you will be as good as dead."

"Better than being raped by Edobichus!"

Together, we quickly settled on a plan. My host hid all my possessions in a hayloft. The slave girl helped with my disguise, giving me some of her rag-like clothes, cutting my hair close, and smearing dirt on my face and hands. I would pose as a stable hand.

When Edobichus appeared at the villa at dusk, he barged in before the porter could open the door. A half dozen bodyguards followed him in. I tried to stay out of sight.

To no avail. After the intruder and his men had feasted and drunk their fill, one of his warriors spotted me. "I've seen that trick before, dearie," he said gleefully. "Hoping a little dirt would hide your beauty? I can see you! You're a lusty girl who would delight in warming my bed tonight!" When I protested, another warrior seized me from the first and proclaimed the pleasure would be his. They bickered good-naturedly but loudly until Edobichus and my host emerged from the villa into the stable yard to investigate the ruckus. The two warriors who had claimed me asked Edobichus to settle their argument. Then, four other bystanders declared that they, too, should have me.

My host said, "My Lord Edobichus, this girl is accustomed to keeping me warm at night. I have found I only sleep well when she is by my side."

"Of course," Edobichus said, "I would not deprive my good friend of a night's sleep. Tricostus, you *are* my good friend, are you not?"

"Of course, my lord, the best of friends."

"Then no more saying 'my lord.' I am now Friend Edobichus." My host nodded. "And I would not deprive you of a good night's sleep," he said. "Have you any other slave women on your estate?"

"Only the slave girl who enjoyed your company a few weeks ago."

"None other?"

"There were three other slave women, but when Constantius came through, they befriended his men and attached themselves to his column. With the legionaries providing protection, the women taunted me, saying, 'Better to be a camp follower than a plantation slave.' There was no stopping them, but Friend Edobichus, when you defeat Constantius, perhaps you could return them to me?"

Edobichus humphed noncommittally. He told his men to leave me alone, and I resumed currying the horses. After my host and I were alone, I asked him about the three slave women. "That was all true," he said. "One of the few true things I've told him!"

He and I discussed the peril Edobichus's force posed to Constantius and what opportunities it might provide. By my reckoning, the enemy had twelve thousand soldiers. If Constantius were fully invested in besieging Arelate, he might not be guarding his rear, which would provide Edobichus with the perfect opportunity to attack him from behind. Constantius would be crushed. But if we could get word to my husband, he would have time to lay a trap. Who should go? It had to be me because our enemy would notice my host's absence. Yet, my host was reluctant. "It is a long way to travel for a woman by herself and one who is having a baby."

I did not bother to argue but insisted I would go. He helped me make a bed in the hayloft, and I lay down for a few hours. Late that night, after Edobichus and his men were drunk and asleep, my host awoke me and helped me saddle my horse. Making as little noise as possible, I led my mount on a deer trail that ran parallel to the road. When I was well away from the plantation, I cut over to the road and headed south at a trot, one that my animal could maintain for hours.

After a day of long, hard riding, I overtook Constantius's rear guard. They had reached Arelate but had not yet surrounded the city. The outpost guard took me to my husband's tent, where I received a frosty reception. There was no look of pleasure, no hug, just a rough, "You rode down here by yourself, endangering my son?"

Not even *our* son, the son who didn't exist.

"I rode down here to save your life! Edobichus is one day north of here with thousands of men."

It took Constantius a few minutes to grasp my information.

"I could ambush him, take him from both front and rear when he arrives."

That was precisely what I was going to suggest, but ideas had more weight when Constantius thought they were his own.

"Anicius," he called. His faithful aide came to the tent. "Call my captains. We are going into battle against Edobichus, probably tomorrow morning. Find some secure place to keep my wife until the fighting is over."

Anicius located an unused tent and *asked* me to go inside. A legionary was posted at the door "to ensure no one bothers you," making it clear I would not be permitted to leave. Another soldier brought me food and water, and when I asked, a piss pot and sleeping cot. Despite my anger and the noise of a camp arming for battle, I slept. The afternoon passed, and so did the evening. My hopes that Constantius would come and release me, or at least visit me, were dashed. In the early hours, I awoke to the sound of fighting. It went on and on: trumpets sounding, clashing of arms, wounded men screaming. My husband had brought me on this campaign with the idea that I could help the medici with the sick and wounded, but here I sat, useless, sweltering under canvas in the early summer heat.

The sound died at some point, and I heard cheering and singing. I peeked out of the tent entrance. My guard was gone. I came out and walked north a half mile into the battle carnage. It was a familiar and appalling scene. The dead and wounded littered the ground, and it was impossible to distinguish friend from foe since both sides employed legionaries and *foederates*.

A medicus was examining the fallen, calling for soldiers to carry the hurt, at least those that might survive, to a medical tent where surgeons would bind their open wounds or amputate shattered limbs. He recognized me and was thankful when I stopped to help him. In the distance, I saw Constantius walking through the bodies, crying, "Where is Edobichus? Where is he?"

The men around Constantius were turning over bodies, looking for the vanquished leader. When I saw them examining barbarian's corpses, I called out, "He was dressed like a Roman *comes* with a leopard cloak."

My husband noticed me for the first time. "Why are you here?" He walked through the bloody wreckage to where I was standing.

"He has probably fled north with the other survivors," I said.

"I don't suppose there's any chance of catching him now," he said.

"He will seek shelter with a friend."

"What friend can he possibly have?"

"He seems to believe Tricostus is his friend," I said.

Constantius and I, along with a hundred other men, rode north through that day and the following night, encouraged by local farmers who confirmed that a small party of soldiers had fled that way earlier. Twice, we came across bodies, men injured in the battle who had taken flight and, with wounds untreated, died en route.

We found three pikes at the gates of Tricostus's estate, each crowned with a severed head. I pointed to the head in the middle. "That's Edobichus," I said.

Tricostus welcomed, fed, and helped us take care of our mounts. Then he explained. "Edobichus arrived at dusk. Not a happy man. He didn't talk about his lost battle, but he did go on at length about the men who had abandoned him on the road. He cursed them. All his entourage deserted him except for the other two men you met on the way in."

"How did you catch him unawares?" Constantius asked.

"He thought we were great friends. When the three men were seated at my dining table, my servers—acting on my signal—slit their throats."

Shocked, I said, "You killed your guests?"

"The law of hospitality did not protect them. I did not invite them into my home. They were ignorant British men. It is a cold, rainy land ungoverned by the laws of civilized people."

There was no point in arguing, but it still seemed wrong.

Events moved quickly after that. Gerontius's siege of Arelate had reduced the usurper to the point of collapse. Now, Gerontius himself was at risk of being surrounded by our victorious army. He fled with his army back to Hispania.

However, that did not relieve the usurper's plight because Constantius resumed the siege.

The usurper, seeing all was lost, negotiated with Constantius. He proposed to abdicate as Emperor, take holy orders, and go into exile. Constantius agreed.

But my husband lied. As soon as the usurper surrendered, Constantius had him decapitated and sent his head on a pike back to Italia, a gift to Honorius.

My husband's next target was Gerontius. To crush him, Constantius began to plan an invasion of Hispania. That became unnecessary when Gerontius's troops, unhappy at their exhausting and pointless siege of Arelate, mutinied and killed him. Now, all of the Western empire was controlled by a single Emperor, Honorius, with one exception: Britannia.

When the usurper left Britannia, he took the last Roman troops with him. When he was defeated, no forces ever returned. After barbarians began to invade that island, the British begged the Emperor for aid. He rejected their plea. For all practical purposes, Britannia was no longer a Roman province.

Chapter 21.   411 CE.   Retaking Gaul

Matilde

In the next month, when my regular blood appeared, Constantius had to admit that his longed-for son did not exist. He clung to the belief that I had been with child and that my midnight ride had caused the death of *his* son. While together at Tricostus's villa, he insisted on sleeping in separate rooms. That was a relief. The passion he once aroused in me was dead. Sadness filled me, sadness and anger that I never received any thanks or even acknowledgment for my role in vanquishing Edobichus and the usurper.

When Placidia warned me about Constantius a year ago, I had not believed her, but she was partially correct; he had disappointed me, but I had also disappointed him. To him, I was no more than a womb, sometimes a clever and amusing companion and an eager fuck, but basically just a womb. Whereas I was looking for someone to share my life with, he was looking for the mother of his heir. Neither of us had found what we were looking for.

I did not doubt that when he found his woman, he would divorce me. I understood I would never find my man. Twice, I'd been blessed with passionate relationships, but I was old now, almost twenty-eight years of age, well past my prime. It was fine if no man turned his head when I walked by. I was done with men and all the heartbreak that attended them.

After weeks of avoiding each other, the time came when he and I had to talk.

"The army has largely recovered from the fight. The men long to go home," Constantius said at breakfast one day.

I nodded. He looked at me, waiting for me to say more. Finally, "What will you do?"

I hadn't expected to have a choice, but since he offered one, I said, "I will stay here with Tricostus if he will allow me. Perhaps all summer. After that, I don't know."

He shrugged as if it didn't matter. The following week, Constantius led his tired army back to Italia. To avoid an awkward farewell, I arranged to be absent when he left, riding my mare in the western hills. I did not care if I ever saw him again.

I lived with Tricostus as his guest and watched as life on his plantation slowly returned to normal. His workforce was back up to strength. His male slaves had watched the armies leave, and with them, the risk of conscription, and once it was safe, they returned. The women, who had run off with Constantius's legionaries, had returned after deciding that life under a kind master like Tricostus was preferable to subsisting as camp followers.

Before Constantius left, he talked to Tricostus about the defense of his estate. "Lawless barbarians are still rife in the country. It will be some time before the legions can restore order." They agreed that Tricostus would hire a dozen of Constantius's veterans to stay behind as a security force.

My host made no demands on me except to provide conversation at the dinner table. I was lonely.

From time to time, travelers—mostly merchants—would stop by and, in return for a small fee, spend a night within Tricostus's compound, enjoying the safety it provided. Those coming from the north brought unsettling news. The *limitanei* along the Rhine River had mutinied again and proclaimed a man named Jovinus to be Emperor. Jovinus was, like Tricostus, a Gallo-Roman senator who owned a vast tract of land with hundreds of slaves.

"Has Jovinus restored order? Is it safe to travel there?" I asked a merchant.

"I'm not going back," he answered. "Does that answer your question? When the usurper Constantine first came, things got better for a while. He drove all the barbarians back across the Rhine or south into Hispania, and he paid the *limitanei*. But since Constantius killed him, things have worsened. The *limitanei* aren't being paid, and the Burgundians are crossing the river in droves. Anyone who travels without an armed escort is likely to get robbed or worse."

A month later, a visitor arrived from Italia, someone I was more than happy to see: my little boy, Theodoric, who was now twelve. Of course, he did not come alone; the land was far too lawless for that, but he led a small group of followers like a natural captain. Among them was Wallia, who guarded my boy as if he were his own.

I wept with joy to see these friendly faces and begged to learn their news.

"Your husband ordered us ..." Theodoric began until I interrupted him with, "Don't call him that!"

Theodoric started at my outburst. "Has he divorced you?"

"No, not yet. I'm sorry I interrupted. What has Constantius ordered?"

Theodoric picked up where I'd cut him off. "Constantius ordered Ataulf to lead our tribe out of Italia before winter, so here we are. We crossed the Alpine pass and just arrived at Vienna. Mother, you have traveled through the mountains, have you not?" I nodded yes. "Could you imagine mountains of such size? Such majesty? I kept wanting to stop and stare, but it was cold, and Wallia stood behind me repeating, 'Keep moving, keep moving.'"

I agreed that the mountains were very tall, but I did not find them majestic or noble. I said they scared me and questioned their purpose since no one could live there.

"Perhaps they scare you because you are a woman?"

I almost cuffed him before I saw the teasing glint in his eye.

"Great stones and icefalls blocked the road in several places. However, we crossed the pass and came to Vienna without losing anyone. Now, we have camped outside the town for a few weeks. My uncle—I now call Ataulf 'uncle'—has asked me to find you and invite you to join us. Would that suit you?"

"Nothing would suit me more," I said.

My son and his companions stayed as Tricostus's guests for a week. He welcomed them warmly, especially after I promised to answer for their conduct. The reputation of barbarian Goths was well known.

Theodoric, Wallia, and I gathered with our host around his dining table for a lavish repast. Wallia discussed Ataulf's plans. "He hopes to act as a mediator, a peacemaker between Honorius and Jovinus, the new usurper."

"Is that likely to succeed?" I asked. "Constantius has attacked every usurper like a dog on a snake. He is ferocious. Never gives up."

"No, it doesn't seem likely," Wallia said. "However, Ataulf is still looking for the homeland Alaric promised us, here in Gaul or perhaps Hispania. Hopefully, it will not be in Britannia, where the sun never shines. If Jovinus can promise us a land of our own, then Ataulf will forswear Honorius."

"Ataulf would turn against my hus ... Constantius?" I asked.

"Yes," Wallia said. "He would support anyone who can provide us with a home."

That was the story Ataulf told everyone, but I later learned the truth.

Ataulf led our tribe to a large, level area, clear of trees, high above the Rhine River, some ten miles southwest of Borbetomagus.

During that bitterly cold New Year's Eve five years earlier, the barbarians had crossed the river at Borbetomagus but could not take the city. They bypassed it and proceeded to destroy dozens of other towns. Their rampage ended when Constantine the Usurper crossed from Britannia with his legions and subjugated them.

Rome had not paid the Rhine *limitanei* for over a year, so the remnant that survived the barbarian onslaught gave their support to the usurper, and when Constantius killed him, they pledged their allegiance to Jovinus.

Northern Gaul was a chaos of contending barbarian tribes, mutinying legionaries, and plantation owners with private armies.

Ataulf's campsite had been a large plantation, but when barbarians came across the Rhine, they destroyed almost everything: huts, barns, fences, everything except the owner's large villa. The ground had gone untilled since then, and the forest was retaking the land.

Theodoric, Wallia, and I caught up with Ataulf there. Not just him, but with my friend for life, Placidia. Though it had been less than a year since we'd last seen each other, it seemed like decades. We threw our arms around, smothered each other with kisses, and then found a quiet place well away from all the men to catch up.

I confessed how my marriage was a ruin. My fury and grief had lost their sharp edge so I could discuss my situation calmly. She was supportive and never mentioned her earlier prediction.

I asked about her relationship with Ataulf. "We are as good as married," she said, "and Ataulf has a plan for us to actually wed."

"What kind of plan? Doesn't Honorius still oppose it?"

"It's a secret plan," she said.

"So secret that you can't even tell me?"

"Not even you," she said and kissed my cheek.

We were relaxing on couches in the great room of the abandoned villa. The room was not a complete shamble; the barbarians had not ransacked it, and its Roman aristocratic owner had deserted it only last year.

"Wallia tells me," I said, "that we have turned our back on Honorius and pledged our support to so-called Emperor Jovinus. What will you do, Ataulf, when my estranged husband leads his legions here to destroy the usurper?" I felt I could speak openly since only five of us were in the room: Ataulf, Placidia, Wallia, Theodoric, and myself.

"Wallia said that, did he?" Ataulf said. "Yes, that is what we want the world to believe. Especially Jovinus. But the man is a nothing, and I would never support him.

"Jovinus is a puppet, only kept on his throne by Gundahar, the Burgundian king. He hopes to balance the barbarian's power with the arms of the remaining *limitanei*. The border legions are no better than mercenaries, supporting whoever will pay their salary. Jovinus knows that, so he thinks to bolster his power with Sarus's clan and my warriors. It is all crumbling down. He has no money to pay the *limitanei*, no leverage over the Burgundians, and I will never ally with Sarus."

"Sarus is here?" I asked.

"Yes, somewhere north of the city, I believe. My actual goal is to destroy Jovinus and to intimidate Gundahar. What I lack is information. How secure is Jovinus's position in the city? How many *limitanei* does he have at his command? Where is Sarus? We really cannot move until we know the lay of the land."

"Perhaps I can help," I said.

It was midafternoon on a late autumn day when I entered Borbetomagus dressed as a tradesman's wife with only Theodoric for company. Initially, Ataulf wanted to send along a dozen men to provide protection, but as far as we knew, the city was at peace with Jovinus's *limitanei* in control. I planned to talk to merchants and common people, which would be impossible if I had a small mob of Gothic warriors at my back.

Theodoric, a bodyguard, and I rode to an abandoned farm just outside the town, left our horses with the bodyguard, and walked to the town gate. Our story was that my husband was a merchant, and we'd fled from Colonia Agrippa after barbarians seized our home.

I expected the gate guard to ignore us or question my story. Instead, he took one look at us and said, "Oh, you're Goths. Most of your kind have already come and gone for the day," and to my surprise, waved us through. Were there other Goths in the area?

Theodoric and I wandered around the town, observing and memorizing. The housing quarter was quiet. Most of the dwellings were empty, and a few had collapsed. Only one person on the street was willing to speak with us, and he just wanted money for a drink. The marketplace had few stalls and fewer customers. We found an inn and purchased two mugs of ale from a talkative innkeeper. "You're my only customers in the last hour," he said. "If Jovinus weren't here to keep order, the whole town would be abandoned. I know I'd shut up shop and move somewhere safer, somewhere further from the river."

"Even so," he said, "no one has confidence that the *limitanei* will protect the town whenever the next gang of

Vandals appears. The smart people have already fled. Only the legionaries and their families remain, and they are just waiting for their pay. Then they'll take off if they're smart." He wiped our table with a dirty cloth. "And who do they take orders from? Not from Jovinus and certainly not from some Emperor in Rome. It's Gundahar, king of the Burgundians, who's in command now." Shaking his head, he went on, "The Burgundians are crossing the river and settling around the town, but they are not city folk. They live out in the countryside while the city shrivels and dies."

We finished our drinks, and when the innkeeper paused his endless stream of complaints, we bid farewell and left. Across the road from the inn, I spotted someone I hadn't seen in years: Sautus. We noticed each other at the same time. He called and came over to speak. His manner was cautious, not friendly.

"Matilde, I would never have thought to see you here! Who is this boy?"

"Nor would I expect to see you! What a surprise after all these years!"

Here was the son of Sarus, Alaric's greatest enemy. Should I assume that the blood feud had died with Alaric? That Sarus would spare my life or my son's if the opportunity arose to kill us? That would be foolish. We were in danger, yet here was a chance to learn something useful.

"Do you live near here? Are you married?" I asked.

"Yes, yes, of course," he said. "I have a wife of seven years. She has borne me two daughters, and I am expecting a third one by New Year's, hopefully, a boy this time. And you? I heard you married again."

"I have, but my home is far away. It must be comforting for you to live with your whole clan near here."

"Truly. We have a settlement just five miles northwest of the town. I have a good home, which my wife and mother have made quite comfortable, although she died last year. My mother, not my wife," he babbled on.

"And has your father remarried?"

"No, though he is quite energetic for such an old man. I'm sure he would like to meet you again and see what a handsome woman you've become. But you say you are married? Is this your son?"

I'd heard everything I needed to know.

"I am married to a Roman general and have come to arrange a meeting with Emperor Jovinus." A lie.

"No doubt you learned that the Emperor is in the north until the Sabbath."

"My husband will be disappointed, but I will come back then and try again. Perhaps you will be here? We must be leaving now, though I look forward to seeing you on the Sabbath." Was that too rushed? Did he think me flustered?

My son understood my urgency and said, "Mama, Dada is waiting," then, as little boys do, he took me by the elbow and pulled me toward the town gate. Over my shoulder, I could hear Sautus saying, "Farewell!" and "Your boy is handsome. What is his name?" We just kept walking.

Sarus's settlement, northwest of Borbetomagus, was poorly defended. The wooden palisade had fallen in places. Our incursion awoke the single gate guard. We entered the settlement in the dead of night without warning and with overwhelming numbers.

For Wallia, this attack was personal. He still grieved for his dead lover. Our tactic had not been his preference. He had pressed for a general massacre. "Surround the walls, burn the place to the ground, and kill everyone as they come out the gate." But he hadn't met Sautus and learned of his young wife and two little children, with another baby on the way. I had never liked Sautus, but my distaste did not extend to a death sentence. Fortunately, Ataulf was the chieftain. He decided that only Sarus must die.

The gate guard was quickly persuaded to point out the chieftain's hut. A large group of our warriors gathered around it. Theodoric, who'd insisted on coming, stood between Wallia and me, watching attentively.

"Sarus, this is Ataulf!" Ataulf shouted. "Your doom is now. It is time to pay for your crimes. Come out! Come out by yourself. Anyone who resists will be killed!"

A few warriors emerged from nearby huts, but when confronted by dozens of Ataulf's men, they lay down their arms. I heard yelling and crying from Sarus's hut, where his women begged him to stay. He ordered them to be quiet. Soon, there was silence, except for the sound of weeping and wailing. Then the door opened, and Sarus emerged.

"What business have you with me?" Sarus bellowed into the night air.

"Justice," Ataulf said. "You are guilty of murder, of blocking a peaceful settlement between the Goths and Rome, of…"

"Oh, be silent!" Sarus shouted. "If you mean to kill me, as I'm sure you do, then do it. But don't weary my ears with tales of crimes and justice."

"So be it," Ataulf said. "Kneel, and I will end this."

"Am I some criminal, some slave that I should accept death without a struggle? Give me a sword. Let me die like a warrior."

"This is not some feud to be settled with single combat," Ataulf said. He paused as if unsure what to do next. Then he turned toward where Theodoric, Wallia, and I stood and quietly said, "Wallia." Wallia stepped forward, drew his sword, uttered, "This is for Palvric," and plunged his blade into the pit of Sarus's stomach, who gasped and collapsed. With another stroke, Wallia beheaded him. He cleaned his weapon on the dead man's tunic.

Ataulf signaled, and we all withdrew from Sarus's settlement. Would this end the blood feud? I did not believe it.

Jovinus was beside himself with anger at Sarus's death. Between his *limitanei*, Ataulf's men, and Sarus's, he thought he commanded a significant military power. Now, one-third of his force was leaderless.

He demanded that Ataulf come before him and answer for Sarus's death.

"Are you worried?" I asked Ataulf. It was the first cold day of winter, but we were comfortable in the villa's great room, where the large fireplace kept us warm. Theodoric was feeding the roaring blaze with pieces of broken chairs. The chairs were hand-carved oak, probably imported from Italia at a significant cost. I suggested it seemed shameful to waste such artwork, but Theodoric disagreed. "These chairs were never comfortable."

"No, Jovinus should be worried," Ataulf said. "He still hasn't paid his *limitanei*, the Burgundians do not respect him, and I have cowed Sarus's clan. I have an army, and he does not. He should be afraid."

"What will you say when you meet him?" I asked.

Ataulf just laughed.

A taulf invited usurper Jovinus and his brother (and co-Emperor) Sebastian to come to our encampment to parley. They did not arrive. In a narrow ravine, Ataulf's men ambushed them, slaying the two would-be Emperors with arrows and putting everyone else who resisted to the sword. Once the two brothers were dead, there was no more resistance. As had become customary, Ataulf sent the heads of the two usurpers to Ravenna. I wondered what Honorius did with this ever-increasing collection of usurper heads.

Wallia explained that Ataulf had never planned to pledge fealty to Jovinus. He had made a secret pact with Constantius that if he could terminate these last imperial pretenders, Constantius would find us a permanent home. "And," Wallia added, "finding and killing Sarus was just a bonus."

Chapter 22.   414 CE. Narbo Martius

Ancient Source: Orosius, in which he discusses the rule of King Ataulf and his marriage to Galla Placidia:

Book 7.43: The Gothic peoples at that time were under the rule of King Athaulf, who, after the capture of Rome and the death of Alaric, had succeeded him on the throne and had taken to wife, as I said, Placidia, the captive sister of the Emperor. ... [Athaulf] strove to refrain from war and to promote peace. He was helped especially by his wife, Placidia, who was a woman of the keenest intelligence and of exceptional piety; by her persuasion and advice, he was guided in all measures leading to good government.

Matilde

The next few years were quiet, happy years. Our tribe had moved south through Gaul to the vital city of Narbo Martius on the Mediterranean coast. If there was a more beautiful and gentle place to live, I'd never been there. I appreciated the warm sun, sea breezes, and the clement winter weather.

I relished the time I could spend with Theodoric. I helped him with his reading and writing when he was nearby, and our local Arian priest instructed him in our Christian faith. Theodoric and a dozen other young men of similar age learned the art of war from his uncles. Wallia would take them on week-

4

long treks into the northern mountains to build their endurance, to "make men of them," as he would say.

I was getting old, over thirty now, and the occasional cold weather penetrated my bones. I sometimes missed Gaba, who remained in Ticinum with her husband and children, though I usually found I did not need a handmaiden. But when Wallia offered me his niece, Liuva, I was happy to accept. She was a lovely young woman, well built, with long blond hair and the face of an angel. She bubbled with joy at every new experience, reminding me of Pentadia in her vitality, without Pentadia's endearing silliness. I noticed that when Liuva was by my side, Theodric would visit more often. I'd always greeted him with a kiss on each cheek. When Liuva adopted that practice, Theodoric did not object.

Our Arian priest grew up north of the Danube, not far from where our tribe had originated. He claimed many Goths were still there, people who had made peace with the Huns, paying a yearly tribute to mitigate their harsh rule. In exchange for gold, the Huns allowed them to live as they pleased. The Romans in Constantinople now referred to them as eastern Goths or Ostrogoths and us as western Goths or Visigoths. Soon, everyone used those names.

Placidia and Ataulf were finally planning their marriage. They had lived together as man and wife for over two years and addressed each other as *aba* (husband) and *uens* (wife). My particular friend spoke those Gothic words with a marked Latin accent. Ataulf was delighted when Placidia attempted to speak his language, and anything that delighted him made her deliriously happy.

Their formal union had been postponed because Emperor Honorius adamantly opposed it. He did not want his half-sister to marry a barbarian, especially a hated Goth. But it seemed that Ataulf's destruction of the usurpers changed his mind. Word finally came that the Emperor had reluctantly approved, and the wedding planning commenced.

We all lived in a stunning seaside villa outside Narbo Martius's city walls. The estate stood high on a cliff overlooking the sea. Ataulf had acquired it from its previous owner, a Gallo-Roman senator. When I asked Ataulf how much it cost, he said it was a gift. Was the senator coerced into giving it to Ataulf? Probably.

I enjoyed many tranquil days there. I strolled on the villa's long winding clifftop walkway, peering over the edge to where the surf crashed two dozen feet below. The walkway was covered with black and pink granite tiles and shaded by a wide tile roof supported by marble Corinthian columns.

Eberwulf, one of Ataulf's bodyguards, brought a couch from the villa and placed it near the edge of the walkway. I would lie for hours, listening to the waves and watching the fishing boats and the occasional dolphin. I could see the busy bustle of the town and port along the bay shore to my left. On my right, the bay ended some miles away, where mountains plunged down to the sea. At my back, I heard children splashing about in the villa's large pool, and beyond the pool, the children's nurses sat and gossiped while keeping half an eye on their charges. Seagulls practiced swooping in and boldly stealing bread from people's hands. When the day grew old and the sun dropped behind the western hills, Liuva brought me bedding and food so I could remain and watch the color drain from the sea, leaving only flashes of light where whitecaps broke far off the shore.

Theodoric came by to kiss me goodnight, and I slept under the stars.

Waking one morning, I spied five ships—Roman war galleys—entering the port. I called out in alarm, and soon Ataulf, Placidia, and Theodoric stood by my side, watching as the ships tied up at the Narbo Martius pier. Far in the distance, we could see legionaries disembarking and lining up on shore in parade order.

"What can it mean?" I asked. "Have we angered the Emperor? Is this force meant to arrest us?"

"I can guess," Placidia said. "My half-brother has changed his mind again. He now opposes my marriage and has sent a force to seize me. I *will* not return to him, to Ravenna. We must make haste, pack some food, and flee into the hills."

"Let's keep calm," I suggested. "Theodoric and I will ride to the harbor and greet this Roman commander."

"I am King of the Visigoths, so I should go," Ataulf said.

"No, Ataulf, their presence here may mean nothing. Let us presume they have stopped in Narbo Martius to ... I don't know ... reprovision their ships, perhaps, and welcome them."

Ataulf grumbled but finally agreed.

A few minutes later, my son and I passed through the town gate and trotted down the hill to the port where the last Roman soldiers had just disembarked. They were arrayed in parade formation, and at their head was a commander I recognized.

"Constantius!" I called out. Theodoric and I dismounted and walked to where my husband and his captains were standing.

"Wife," he replied. "And Theodoric! You've turned into a man. How many years have you seen?"

"Fifteen, my lord," Theodoric spoke. His voice had recently deepened, and he sounded like a man.

"Excellent! You are growing tall and stout like your father."

"What brings you to Narbo Martius, Constantius, you and this great force?" I asked. He might call me wife, but I refused to call him husband.

"It is not such a great force. Slightly less than the one cohort I'd hoped to bring, but I only had five galleys. The other one was not seaworthy. But my force is, I hope, great enough to honor the lady Placidia and her groom in their marriage. My lord Honorius, her brother, insisted we pay fitting tribute to a princess of Rome."

"Then your timing is good, my lord," Theodoric said. "The wedding is planned for three days hence."

Theodoric rode back to the villa to announce Constantius and his troops while Constantius and I walked after, with me leading my horse. Ataulf met us at the villa gate and warmly greeted him. He looked relieved that Constantius had come in friendship.

Ataulf ordered that the legionary camp be erected in a field near the villa, and he said, "We have a fine room in the villa available for you, my lord."

Constantius said, "Thank you, but I will share my wife's chamber."

I shook my head slightly, a gesture I'm sure both Ataulf and Constantius noticed, but when I said nothing, neither did they.

As we talked, Placidia arrived at the gate and exchanged chaste kisses with Constantius. She was no more than twenty-two years old, a decade younger than me, and in the prime of her life. Her cheeks were pink with happiness, her skin clear, her smile radiant. A sea breeze blew back her silk cloak, revealing a plump figure that filled out her purple tunic. Its neckline was cut low, revealing the top of her generous breasts. A gold cross on a delicate necklace lay between them, drawing one's eyes to her beautiful form. In all the years of our friendship, I had never seen her looking more attractive or joyful.

Constantius stepped back from her to get a better look. "You have changed greatly," he said.

"As have you," she said. "I think the last time we met was before the sacking." She meant the sacking of Rome, an event of momentous importance, with people giving such dates as "so many years" preceding or following "the sacking." She addressed Constantius coolly, knowing every detail of our failed marriage and having taken my side in any dispute, as a best friend should.

We spent the day talking and eating in the villa, with Ataulf explaining the wedding plans to Constantius, and he offering a parade of his forces. The musicians among them had brought their instruments so that the parade would be similar to a triumph, he said, although nobody had been conquered. Ataulf joked that he was a victor, having persuaded Placidia to marry him. She countered, saying that was not much of a victory since she'd lain down her arms (and in his arms!) when they first met.

At dusk, I went to my room, where Liuva was waiting to help me undress for the night. Without an invitation, Constantius followed along, and when we entered the room, he ordered Liuva to leave. She looked to me for confirmation. I nodded. She shut the door as she went, and I waited for him to speak.

"Wife," he said. A poor start, in my opinion. Why hadn't he started with "Matilde"? Was I still not a person, worthy of a name? Instead, I was "wife," a role, a role with responsibilities, notably to provide him with a son.

"It is true I have come to honor Placidia's marriage, but I also hoped to repair ours. After we last parted, I consulted doctors to learn whether your barrenness could be my fault. I know it is unlikely, and yet there *are* men who are incapable of fathering a child. The doctor recommended I contact other women and try to get a child on them. But I did not. If I am to father a child, I want it to be with my wife. I have been faithful to you."

I understood where this conversation was leading. I moved toward the cupboard where Liuva stored the bedding I used when sleeping out of doors on the cliffside colonnade.

"I have seized this occasion, this wedding, as an opportunity, perhaps our last opportunity, to live together as man and wife. We are, you must admit, aging, but for men a few more years will not affect my ability to get children. But you must be nearing the age where further motherhood is impossible. For your sake, for both of our sakes, is this something you would consider? I will not force you, but I beg that you give it honest consideration."

I knew my answer. It hadn't changed in the last few years. But I had questions.

"If you want a son by a lawful wife, why not divorce me and find another woman? It only takes a simple declaration on your part."

"This wedding between Lady Placidia and Ataulf demonstrates something I've known for years: that the future of Rome depends on our embracing the barbarian races. You come from royal Gothic lineage, which I honor. Our child would demonstrate that honor."

"I wondered if that was your motive," I said. "There was a time when the sight of me stirred your loins—when you couldn't wait to bed me and, having done it, bed me again."

"Alas," he said, "the bloom is off that flower. Flowers of thirty years of age have wilted blossoms, and their perfume becomes rank."

"I suspected as much," I said as I gathered up my bedding.

"If I wanted a young flower, I would choose Lady Placidia. She exudes such a beauty as you never had. If Ataulf were elsewhere, I do not doubt she would be attracted to me."

I laughed. "Oh, how little you know my friend Placidia." With that, I left the room, went to the colonnaded walkway, and settled onto my couch for a sound night's sleep, serenaded by the swell of the surf.

The wedding ceremony passed without incident. The Roman soldiers paraded from their camp, down through the city, and back to the villa, marching in time to the music of their trumpets, flutes, and kettle drums and accompanied by an army of delighted children who beat sticks in time. The couple's vows were officiated twice by separate priests, one Catholic and one Arian, in recognition of Placidia's and Ataulf's respective faiths.

At the wedding banquet, Ataulf rose to salute Constantius, emphasizing the importance of this marriage and how the merging of Goths and Romans would strengthen the empire.

"At first, I wanted to erase the Roman name and absorb all Roman territory into a Gothic empire," he said. "I longed for Romania to become Gothia and for myself to be what Caesar Augustus had been.

"But long experience has taught me that the ungoverned wildness of the Goths will never submit to laws and that without law, a state is not a state. Therefore, I have more prudently chosen a different glory, that of reviving the Roman name with Gothic vigor." He went on to say that he hoped that future generations would view him as the creator of a new, restored Rome. The audience cheered, and even Constantius clapped politely. I shook my head, marveling at Ataulf's hubris. The gods punish men who rise above their station. Would this be the zenith of Ataulf's fortune?

Chapter 23. 415 CE. Barcino

Ancient Source: Orosius, in which Constantius embargoes the Visigoths:

> *Book 7.43: Count Constantius, who was occupying the city of Arelate in Gaul, drove the Goths from Narbo, and by his vigorous actions forced them into Spain, especially by forbidding and completely cutting off the passage of ships and the importation of foreign merchandise.*

Matilde

W as I responsible for what followed? When King Ataulf had finished defeating the usurpers, the barbarians had devasted much of Gaul, and we Visigoths faced starvation. As a reward for Ataulf's good service, Honorius agreed to send grain shipments to the Mediterranean ports in Gaul. These shipments suddenly ended after Ataulf and Placidia's wedding. Now, in a complete reversal, the Emperor demanded that Ataulf return his bride to Ravenna.

"I won't go; I would rather die," Placidia told me. It was never an issue because Ataulf would never release her. Besides, the bulge in her belly showed that a Romano-Visigothic child was in the offing. "Why would he change his mind?" she moaned. "I thought the matter was settled, especially after he sent Constantius here to represent him at the wedding!" When Placidia talked to me, she never referred to Constantius as *your husband*.

I thought I knew the answer: Constantius wanted Placidia for himself. He'd seen her at the wedding and liked what he saw, and as a member of the royal family, she offered a route to power. It was a small matter for him to persuade stupid, weak Honorius that the marriage was invalid or should be annulled and Placidia must be returned home to Ravenna. If that succeeded, Constantius would divorce me and arrange for Honorius to offer him Placidia.

I could have changed all that at the wedding. If I had slept with Constantius as he requested, if I had borne him the son he demanded, then none of this would have happened. This was all my fault.

But it was just a theory, and I saw no merit in discussing it with my friend.

Ataulf refused to surrender his wife, and Constantius increased the pressure. His war fleet returned, and his soldiers occupied Narbo Martius and closed the city gates. All trade was blocked. Constantius's war fleet destroyed any boats caught trading along the coast. He reinforced the garrisons in the other Mediterranean coastal cities. We Visigoths were isolated.

In desperation, Ataulf moved his court to Burdigala in Aquitania, beyond Constantius's reach. Access to the Atlantic coast helped alleviate the food shortage. Even there, with fifty people in the King's entourage, the city could not host us for long. After a few months, we moved to Tolosa, in Gaul. From there, we planned to move to Carcasso until Wallia learned that the Vandals had killed our garrison and occupied that city.

Constantine the Usurper had done a good job of flushing all the barbarians out of Gaul. These were the barbarians—Vandals, Alans, and Suebi—who crossed the upper Rhine river seven years before. After roaming at will around the province for several years, Constantine the Usurper drove them south into Hispania, where they took vast tracts of land for their own, killing or displacing the Hispano-Romans who lived there. However, a few barbarians remained behind in Gaul, and some now claimed ownership of the critical fortress at Carcasso.

Ataulf was eager to move his court to Hispania, along the Mediterranean coast, where provisions were abundant, and the coming winter would be less onerous on his quite pregnant wife. Most of us proceeded east along the *Via Aquitania* to Narbona Martius, where Constantius's garrison still denied us entrance. Then we turned south on the *Via Domitia*, which ran along the coast into Hispania. But Ataulf left many troops behind to retake Carcasso from the Vandals. Wallia led that army with my son Theodoric as an advisor. I knew there would be fighting, so I prayed to Jesus to look after my boy. He was as tall as my father and strong as an ox, but he was only fifteen. Just a boy.

With winter on the way, we were eager to reach Barcino, where Ataulf was having a palace built. But one cold night, dusk found us at Baetulo, not far from Barcino. I was reluctant to stop there and even suggested we carry on through the dark to Barcino. "It's only another dozen miles," I said.

After we'd killed Sarus, an uneasy peace reigned between his clan and Ataulf's. Ataulf let it be known that the blood feud ended with Sarus's death, and there was no need for further killings. I waited in vain for Sigeric, Sarus's successor, to make a similar proclamation from Sarus's kin. Chieftain Sigeric said nothing, but there were no reprisals. In the following years, Sarus's people paid a token tribute to King Ataulf, and when they moved south, they took possession of the city of Baetulo.

Ataulf understood my worries and tried to assuage them. "They have been loyal subjects for years," he said.

The city gates were already closed, but Eberwulf hammered endlessly until someone came to the postern door and opened a peephole. "The gates are closed," came a voice. "Come back in the morning." The speaker spoke Latin with a strong Gothic accent. I said as much to Eberwulf, who said, "One of Sigeric's men."

"Tell Sigeric that King Ataulf is here and wishes accommodations for the night," Eberwulf said.

"Tell your master that we are closed. This gate does not open until dawn, not for kings and not for Emperors." The peephole slammed closed.

Eberwulf hammered again on the door and shouted, "This is Eberwulf, here with King Ataulf and his party, and I demand you admit us immediately."

I did not understand why the name of Eberwulf might have more authority than Ataulf, but a few minutes later, the main gate slowly swung open. A man stood in the gateway waving us in and said, "Welcome, welcome, I am Chieftain Sigeric. Please excuse my porter's rude speech. He is drunk and will be beaten in the morning."

When I tried again to raise my concerns, Ataulf said, "They have done nothing to raise my suspicions. Accepting their hospitality for one night will demonstrate that the past is past, and we are all one tribe."

Placidia heard the anxiety in my voice. "Can we, at the least, have some bodyguards in our sleeping chamber?" Ataulf agreed.

Now, here was Chieftain Sigeric welcoming us into his city with open arms. Roused from their sleep, his servants lit torches, woke the cooks, and prepared lodging for our party.

We did not keep our hosts up for very long. They provided us with a hearty last-minute meal and showed us to our rooms. Sigeric and his wife gave their chamber to Ataulf and Placidia, and I was shown to a small room just down the hall.

The night passed without incident. At breakfast—a healthy repast of fish, bread, cheese, and eggs—Ataulf leaned over to me and whispered, "Do you see? There was nothing to worry about."

Placidia mouthed, "Perhaps because we *did* post two warriors in our chamber?"

"Or," I added, "because we came unannounced, and they had no time to plan some treachery."

We left Baetulo at the third hour after dawn. It was cold, with a frigid breeze blowing off the sea into our faces. I kept looking over my shoulder at Sigeric's men on the ramparts, always expecting to see an arrow winging my way. I did not feel safe until we reached Barcino.

Placidia was thrilled with the new palace her husband had built for her. She was too gracious to mention that the palaces she'd grown up in dwarfed it, but despite its size, it was an actual stone and wood palace with marble floors and gilded sculptures. She would be sleeping under a proper structure, not a length of canvas. Living in camps had sufficed when she first traveled with Ataulf, but she had a baby due soon and wanted it to come in a proper home.

The chamber she shared with Ataulf had a sunken bath, and somewhere in the palace was a furnace that piped hot air under the tub to keep it warm. "Better than Ravenna!" she exclaimed. Their room had an antechamber assigned to me, a sleeping room as big as the one I'd had in Narbo Martius. There was a passage doorway between the two rooms, so she and I could visit without stepping into the public hallway.

I kept myself busy, ensuring my friend remained comfortable during the last month of her pregnancy. We were rewarded when she delivered a beautiful little boy toward the end of the year. She named him Theodosius in honor of her father.

There have been times in my life when I prayed to Jesus and the other gods, begging them to stop time. I would thank the gods for bringing me to this happy place and suggest that if they let my life continue precisely as it was now, I would never ask for anything else, ever again. The day I helped deliver baby Theodosius, I made such a prayer.

But the gods don't listen.

Three months into the New Year, little Theodosius died. His tummy bloated, he wouldn't suck on Placidia's swollen breast, and he cried and cried until he died. Placidia was devastated, and Ataulf failed to hide his tears. They placed the tiny body in a silver-lined coffin and buried him under the cathedral floor. For months, Placidia attended Mass daily, kneeling on the floor above her boy and praying for his soul.

Just the thought of losing my own child reduced me to tears. I prayed to Jesus to keep Theodoric safe, and if my boy couldn't be with me now, let the siege of Carcasso end soon so we could be reunited.

A month later, Placidia began to sleep with me in my antechamber. "I want to sleep with Ataulf," she explained, "to start a new child. But the midwife has warned me to wait. 'Wait until your womb is ready," she advised. Matilde, is she right? Must I wait?"

The midwife recommended waiting six months. That seemed too long to me, but I was no midwife and had no answer. Placidia was really asking how long I'd slept apart from Alaric after giving birth, but it was so long ago I couldn't remember.

"I miss being with Ataulf so much," she sobbed. "I need his arms around me at night."

She had to make do with my arms around her. It wasn't the same.

One month later, Placidia confided in me that she could wait no longer. She and I were undressing for bed when she said, "Do you hear that? My love is lounging in his bath. Listen as he splashes about!"

I listened, and he seemed to be enjoying the deep, hot water. We'd often heard him bathing, but never this loudly. "I have waited long enough!" Placidia said. "I will join with him." She grinned at the double meaning of her remark. She dropped her silk nightgown to the floor and, in her beautiful nakedness, opened the passage door.

And screamed.

I pushed past her and witnessed an appalling sight. Eberwulf stood knee-deep above Ataulf in the tub, using one hand to keep the King's head underwater and the other to stab him repeatedly. Already, the bath water was opaque with blood.

Placidia collapsed in the doorway, softly mouthing "treason!" I took up the cry but at the top of my voice, screaming, "Treason! Murder! Treason!" Water thrown up by the struggle had flooded the floor around the tub and flowed toward my door. I heard bodyguards pounding up the outside hall, but the door was locked. The assailant had barred it. The bodyguards hammered on it to no effect.

I stepped over Placidia's prone form back into my room and reached under my bed, fumbling for the *gladius* I always kept there. I drew it from its scabbard and returned to the larger chamber. A glance at Ataulf told me he was dead. I took one step forward to confront Eberwulf as he tried to step out of the bath. He waved his bloody dagger at me, forcing me to keep my distance.

I was armed with a sword, and he had only a dagger. I should have the advantage, but he was a man, a trained warrior, and I was only a woman. I was cautious.

"I mean no harm to you," Eberwulf said, "but do not stand between me and the Roman girl," meaning Placidia. "The end has come when Goths sell their lives and souls to the Romans. We are not Romans, and no marriage or little dead babies can turn us into Romans."

I watched with alarm as he hefted himself out of the tub, leaving Ataulf's body to float lifelessly in a red sea. He was vulnerable as he got his feet under him and stood to his full height. He was two hands taller than me and a hundredweight heavier. I watched and despaired, trying to imagine how I might defend Placidia and myself. I glanced toward the hall door. Perhaps I could unbar it and let the bodyguards enter.

He saw my glance. He shook his head at me, grimaced, and moved to block my path. Then he slipped on the wet floor, fell with a clatter while still holding his dagger, but struck his head on the floor. The blow did not knock him out. He looked up at me with an embarrassed grin. "Clumsy," he said.

I did not wait for him to say more. I stepped forward and plunged my sword into his stomach. He screamed with pain and dropped his dagger. Then, I proceeded to chop off his head. It took many blows, so many blows that I lost count. I screamed at his body and, in my fury, hacked it and kept hacking and would have continued if Placidia hadn't come up behind me and said, "Stop. He's dead. Very dead."

She moved over to the tub and stepped in, taking her husband's gory body in her arms and pressing it to her own. She rocked back and forth, clutching him and moaning softly. I unbarred the door, and men swarmed into the room.

I did not recognize the men, but I did know their leader. It was Sigeric. He entered, looked around, and said, "Is he dead?"

Was he stupid? I pointed at Eberwulf and spewed, "Are you jesting? I chopped his head off!" One of Sigeric's men had tripped over the head, and it was now at some distance from his body.

"Not him. Ataulf." He took a moment to look at Eberwulf's remains. "Though I regret *his* loss. He was not good for much, but in the end, he provided a good service."

I was completely confused. One of Sigeric's men struggled with Placidia to haul her away from her husband's body, but she clung tightly to it. "No, no, no!" she screamed and would have continued, except Sigeric called out, "Gag her and bind her. And throw a blanket around her." I'd forgotten that she was still naked. Another man struck my sword from my grip and picked it up where it fell.

Then, I began to understand. "You traitor!" I shouted at him.

"Gag and bind her too," he said, meaning me. One large warrior seized me by my shoulders as another wrapped a rough cord around my head and into my jaw, and more of the cord to tie my hands behind my back. I struggled, but it was pointless.

I watched as two men dragged Ataulf out of the bath by his heels. They grappled him out the door and down the hall. When Placidia and I were bound, men roughly walked us to the palace courtyard, forced us to sit on the ground, and left. I watched as my good friend sat quietly, head on her bent knees. I expected her to moan, or writhe, or shake, but she sat still, eyes closed, not even crying. We heard shouting and the clashing of weapons from inside the place. From time to time, men would emerge from the building, dragging bodies into the courtyard and out the gate into the dark. Sigeric was murdering all of Ataulf's men. Finally, the commotion ended, the torches died, and Placidia and I were left alone and shivering in the dark. I looked eastward into the night sky, but it was still many hours before dawn. Finally, to my surprise, I fell asleep.

A kick in my ribs awoke me. The blackness was not total, so I could tell it was still an hour before dawn. Someone untied my gag. Sigeric was standing over me, hands on his hips. "The Roman bitch is only alive," he said to me, indicating Placidia, "because I can use her to bargain with the Emperor. But *Lady Matilde*," he hissed my name, "give me one reason why I shouldn't kill Alaric's wife."

I had trouble speaking. I spat bits of cording from my dry mouth. When I finally worked up some spit, I said, "I am not—and you know it—Alaric's wife. He divorced me years ago. I am married to *Magister Militum* Constantius."

"Not a real marriage, by all accounts."

"Real enough, as you'll learn if you murder the spouse of Rome's most powerful general."

"When was the last time you slept with him?"

"That is of no matter. Even if Constantius despised me—which he does not—I am still his wife. If you mean to send him a deadly insult, then harm me. He would not forgive such an affront."

Sigeric studied me and tapped his foot. Placidia had not moved. "Get them on their feet," he said to his men. "We leave now!"

"Leave?" I asked. "Where are you taking us? At least first give us water."

"Give them water," he ordered. "We're not *taking* you anywhere. You are taking yourselves on your own feet." Our feet were bare. They unbound our hands so we could drink and prodded us into moving across the courtyard and out the palace gate.

Ancient Source: Orosius, in which Visigothic Kings Athaulf and Sigeric are killed:

Book 7.43: While [Ataulf] was thus eagerly occupied in seeking and offering peace, he was slain at the city of Barcinona in Spain by the treachery, it is said, of his own men [i.e., Sigeric's Visigoths].

After him, Segeric was proclaimed king by the Goths, and, although he likewise was inclined towards peace by the will of God, he too was nevertheless killed by his own men [i.e., Wallia's Visigoths].

Matilde

Dawn finally broke as we left the city and walked north. Three dozen of Sigeric's warriors walked alongside our column, generally bored, occasionally open to brief conversations.

"Is Sigeric taking us back to Baetulo?" I asked one.

"He is now King Sigeric. You must be respectful."

"By what right is he named king?"

"By right of conquest. He killed the old king. A good thing, too. That man would have treated with the Romans, making us subject to all their customs and laws."

A voice came from in front. "No talking with the prisoners."

The warrior whispered, "Yes, we are heading for Baetulo, Sigeric's stronghold. That will be the new capital of Visigothia."

It was only a dozen miles to Baetulo, but we had made no more than half the distance when Placidia stumbled.

I called, "Stop! We must stop. Lady Placidia's feet are raw and bleeding. At least let me bind them with bandages. And more water."

Sigeric provided me with bandages but no water, and soon, we were marching again. I could see she was struggling. Up all night, thirsty, grieving, and bleeding. If she could convert her grief into anger, as I had, she could cope better. Instead, she began to fall regularly. Once, Sigeric rode back to where she lay on the ground and struck her with a whip. How I longed to have my hands free and my *gladius* in my grip.

In another mile, it became clear that Placidia could walk no further. Sigeric ordered her to be thrown over a horse's back like a sack of flour. I looked up the road, hoping to see signs that we were nearing Baetulo. The bright dawn sun made seeing difficult, but I thought I saw something ahead. It was not a town, but some men coming toward us. We continued forward, with me leading Placidia's horse.

Sigeric ordered, "Warriors, line in front!" and a dozen warriors moved to the front. They screened my view of the approaching men and their view of me. But the oncoming men could see Placidia lying semiconscious on a horse when they were a hundred steps away.

"Halt, who are you?" a voice called from across that distance. I recognized it as Wallia's. *He* was here and perhaps with my son. And a small army that would put things right.

"King Sigeric orders you to stand aside, clear the road, out of his way," a warrior returned.

"We are twenty to your one. *You* stand out of the road," shouted a young voice. It was Theodoric. I did not hesitate. In one explosive motion, I jumped, hurled a leg over Placidia's horse, and landed right behind her prone body. I pulled myself on top of her and gave her mount a mighty kick. It leaped through the warriors clustered ahead of us onto the clear road separating Sigeric and Wallia's forces. Before Sigeric could act, I was among friends.

"Sigeric is a traitor," I gasped. "He has murdered Ataulf, killed all his men, and declared himself king." If Wallia needed proof, he had only to look at Placidia's ruined state. But nothing more was required. He turned to face his troops and shouted, "Kill them! Kill the traitors! Kill them all!"

The chronicles claim that Sigeric was King of the Goths, having succeeded Ataulf, whom he murdered. If that was true, his reign lasted for less than a day. Wallia's men quickly surrounded Sigeric's and set to work with ruthless energy, butchering every traitor and accepting no calls for quarter. My son did not hold back but emerged with a sword every bit as bloody as mine, for I found a weapon and attacked, shouting "Ataulf!", furious and weeping and laughing at the joy of our revenge.

Chapter 24.   418 CE. Queen Mother

Matilde

After that brief battle, we stood on the road just a few miles south of Baetulo, looking at the carnage we had dealt. The bodies of Sigeric's force covered the ground. I helped Placidia down from the horse and found her some decent garments. After fetching her water to drink, I helped bandage our few casualties' wounds, then sat beside my friend, exhausted. My son and other fighters came and sat by us and watched as Wallia stood to address the troops.

"Our revenge for the murder of Ataulf does not end with the death of Sigeric," he began.

"Ataulf was a fool, thinking he could end a blood feud by killing one man. He knew that Sarus had family, people who were honor-bound to avenge his death. Now Sigeric has family, and the feud will continue until they are destroyed."

With that declaration, he turned the army around, and we took Baetulo by surprise. We killed all the men and boys over twelve years old and sold all the women and children into slavery. I don't know what happened to Sautus. I never saw his body.

This brutal and decisive nature would be Wallia's hallmark. Theodoric explained that their appearance on the road was just a matter of luck. The siege of Carcasso had succeeded when the trapped and desperate Vandals, facing starvation, had opened the city gate and charged out. They met the same fate as Sigeric's people: death and slavery. Wallia's force was leisurely making its way to Barcino after that victory when they encountered Sigeric. They had no notice of the previous night's drama.

As was their custom, the Visigothic chieftains gathered for a summit to pick their next king, and Wallia was duly elected. We moved back into Ataulf's palace but into different quarters. Placidia refused to live in the same rooms as before. She and I shared a large chamber, and I held her at night when nightmares ruined her sleep. Theodoric told me that Ataulf's bath had been filled with concrete. No one would ever be murdered there again. I refused to enter that room.

My friend surprised me with her resilience. She continued to grieve for her lost husband and baby, but her grief did not rule her life. She filled her days with activity and study. When Theodoric arranged hunting parties, she would join. She and I would study the Bible and other literature on hot summer afternoons. Only at night would her sorrow bubble to the surface, and I would find her face washed with tears. "I keep looking around expecting to see him," she said one day. "A tunic, a goblet, a saddle, almost anything might recall some memory, and I would glance about, thinking he must be nearby. But he never is." She was terribly lonely.

Ancient Source: Orosius, in which Wallia makes peace with Emperor Honorius:

Book 7.43: Thereupon Vallia succeeded to the kingdom. ... [Wallia] concluded a very favorable peace with the Emperor Honorius giving hostages of the highest rank; he restored Placidia, whom he had treated with decency and respect, to her imperial brother.

To ensure the security of Rome, he risked his own life by taking over the warfare against the other tribes that had settled in Spain and subduing them for the Romans.

Matilde

Three months after Wallia became king, Constantius's war fleet sailed into Barcino's harbor. Our relationship with the Romans was cool and not openly hostile. The trade ban continued, and food was in short supply, but there were no armed clashes. From the palace walls, I watched the ships maneuvering, wondering whether the Roman commander intended to land troops and seize the city, as they'd done with Narbo Martius. Wallia vowed there would be bloodshed if that was their plan.

A white flag of peace went up on the lead galley as it reached a harbor pier. Dockworkers rushed out to help secure the ship's mooring lines. A wooden gangway appeared, and the Roman commander came ashore. Even from afar, I recognized Constantius. Theodoric went down to the pier to welcome him. They embraced warmly, which did not surprise me. Their bond had formed when my son was very little and Constantius played the role of father.

With Theodoric leading, Constantius and a small party of his captains and bodyguards made their way to the palace. Wallia was just out of the city, visiting a large estate he'd acquired. Theodoric sent a message asking him to return. Until then, Theodoric hosted Constantius in the palace's great room, with Placidia and me in attendance. Slaves brought food and drink, and we made small talk. There was little of our news with which Constantius was unfamiliar. He knew of Ataulf's murder, and he offered Placidia sincere condolence for her dual losses.

I was cool toward him, but he addressed me warmly, calling me his dear wife and asking after my health. We talked but exchanged little of substance; Constantius was waiting for Wallia. When the King finally arrived, the two men retired to the palace roof, where they could speak privately while enjoying the cool sea breeze. We waited in the great room until a servant appeared after a few hours.

"Lady Placidia, their lordships request that you join them. May I lead you?"

She disappeared, and my son and I waited impatiently for two hours. We had chores we wished to do but dared not leave for fear of missing something important. Then the servant reappeared, returning with a sober-looking Placidia and requesting that Theodoric follow him. Constantius was involving everyone but me in these important discussions. Why should he include me? I was just a wife. I fumed.

Placidia took my hand and led me to the palace courtyard. I could hardly wait to hear her news. "Well? Well?"

She waved to a servant to bring us wine. "Wait, just another minute. Give me a chance to drink. I am parched from all the talking." She carefully sipped her wine while I swallowed mine in a gulp and sat impatiently, bouncing a knee up and down. Finally, she began.

"There is to be a permanent peace between Romans and Visigoths. Wallia and Constantius will sign a *foedus*. That will end the trade ban, and Wallia will commit his warriors to act on Rome's behalf."

I gasped. "What does 'on Rome's behalf' mean?" I protested. "I've seen this all before! This is the kind of agreement that cost us ten thousand dead at Frigidus River."

"That was a civil war. Wallia will only attack the enemies of the empire."

"Such as?"

"The Vandals, Alans, and other barbarians who have turned Gaul and Hispania into a wasteland."

"And what do we get in return? Besides plunder, slaves, and the usual?"

"Honorius will give you the Garumna River valley in Aquitania, from Tolosa to Burdigala, and the Atlantic coast from the Pyrenees mountains to the Loire River."

I considered this. The Garumna was a fertile and beautiful valley. If only Honorius had agreed to this decades ago, so much suffering could have been avoided. Then, something struck me.

"You said, 'Honorius will give *you*.' Not give *us*?" My voice quavered as I spoke. "You won't be here, will you? You're leaving with Constantius." It was a statement, not a question.

"Yes. That was his price. A *foedus* and a homeland in exchange for me."

I could feel my face turn red. "And Wallia agreed to this? How could he?" I groaned. I was so angry. I stood and stamped my feet in frustration.

"Wallia only agreed when I said yes. Initially, he said 'no,' and the talks almost ended there. Then Constantius said, 'Let me ask Placidia.' So they summoned me. Wallia left us alone, and we talked."

"And he browbeat you, didn't he? Threatened you?"

"Of course not. Matilde, did he ever browbeat you? Threaten you? You've never said so. He spoke gently, kindly. Matilde, why do you hate him so much? Just because he disrespected you?"

I had no ready answer. I sat back down beside her and wrung my hands. She was my dearest friend in the world, and she was going to leave me.

"I don't hate him," I said. "Or just a little bit. He blamed me for not bearing him a son. He blamed me for killing a baby in my womb when there was none. Whatever about me he first found attractive vanished with those charges. I was nothing but a failed mother. It was so unfair, and he has never acknowledged it. If he had, things could have been different."

"Matilde, you expect too much from a man, especially a great soldier like Constantius. His world is black and white, and he's a Roman. A wife either produces sons or she is not a good wife. Your brilliance and other qualities were interesting but not essential. They attracted him at first and that you'd already borne a son. But then, for him, you failed. He does not hate you or blame you, but he wants to go on with his life."

"He said that?" I asked.

"In so many words."

"You understand," I said, "that 'going on with his life' means marrying you? You are his route to power. To the throne. Are you willing to be that—and only that—to him? Is that what you want?"

"Matilde, unlike you, I am still young." That jarred me. I was only thirty-four and still turned men's heads. "I miss my lost baby. I weep daily for little Theodosius. But I long to have more babies. There is no man here for me, certainly not Wallia!" We laughed. Our king had once fathered a daughter, but rumor said it was not a pleasant act for either him or the woman. Wallia much preferred men. "And if I should join with some beautiful Visigothic warrior, Honorius would certainly go to war. No, I need to go with Constantius. He will treat me kindly and, if Jesus wills, give me many children. That's what I wish for."

I began to cry. "I will miss you," I said.

"Do not miss me. Not yet. Come with me to Ravenna, and bring your new handmaiden, Liuva, and stay while I settle in. For a year, maybe two. Then return to your son and your people."

I agreed, and when asked, young Liuva said she would be happy to come. Her eagerness to see the world refreshed Placidia's spirit and mine. She was like a young puppy, where everything was new and fascinating.

Wallia signed the *foedus*, which Constantius must have anticipated because two grain ships arrived even before we sailed for Ravenna. Our farewell was largely tearless. Everyone accepted that it was time for Placidia to go. The only tears I witnessed were shed by Liuva as she clung to Theodoric before they separated. He kissed her chastely on both cheeks, making me wonder if theirs was a chaste relationship. He was only seventeen years of age, and she about the same, so I was inclined to dismiss this as a spring flower of love, quick to bloom and soon to fade. But then I remembered Gisalric. That flower still blossomed in my mind and smelled heavenly decades later.

Everything in Ravenna had changed since my last visit, except for the beaches. There were parks and sculptures everywhere. The palace was vastly enlarged, with the new buildings constructed of marble rather than wood. I saw where colorful mosaics had replaced simple tile floors. Almost every palace room had a fresco depicting some tale of the ancient Greek gods and heroes. My room's fresco showed Penelope's joy when she first realized her strange guest was her long-lost husband, Odysseus, finally returning from the Trojan War. Had Constantius purposely chosen this room for me? Penelope had remained faithful to her husband, as had I, but she was elated to see him, and I was not.

The beaches were unchanged. They remained sunny and sandy and inviting to anyone who loved sea bathing. Liuva loved the bright smell of salt air and demanded that *we* spend every spare hour splashing in the surf. By *we*, she meant Placidia, herself, and me. Still, of course, it also involved several dozen legionaries to ensure our privacy and safety. Placidia insisted the men stand a hundred steps away from where we frolicked. No men were permitted to see us as we swam nude. Liuva said she wouldn't mind if *some particular* man were present. She didn't mention Theodoric by name, but their connection was an open secret between the three of us and the subject of much gossip and teasing.

Placidia also wished to conceal the growing bulge in her belly. Constantius had not waited long before making his case to Honorius. As the most successful general in recent history, the man who (Constantius claimed) had driven the Goths from Italia, crushed three (perhaps four) usurpers in Gaul, and whose *foedus* with the King of the Goths had finally brought them under imperial control, Constantius claimed he was entitled to the ultimate reward, Placidia. He had returned her from Gothic captivity and restored her to her loving half-brother.

Constantius's arguments were sound if one ignored certain facts. She had not been a captive but Ataulf's contented wife. But because he was dead and there was no surviving offspring—a good thing in Honorius's opinion—that whole episode, the happiest in Placidia's life, could conveniently be forgotten. Also, Honorius did not love his half-sister, and she could hardly bear to be in his presence. They were estranged due to something that had happened years earlier, something that no one would mention aloud but which Constantius had divulged to me long ago. Placidia was the only woman ever to arouse Honorius. She knew it and found him disgusting.

Honorius duly awarded his *magister militum* with Placidia. Constantius immediately divorced me, an act I'd long anticipated and one that required only a public declaration, and they were married on New Year's Day. Six months later, as we women bathed in the warm Adriatic sea, it was evident that the marriage's consummation had been swift.

Their baby, Justa Grata Honoria, was born in the autumn. Placidia was thrilled. Constantius was not present. He'd taken an army into Gaul to crush the *bacaudae* criminals, including the small group that had befriended us during our retreat from Valentia. Notwithstanding their kind treatment, they were lawless men who robbed or demanded bribes and illegal tolls from merchants. In Constantius's empire, such illicit liberties were punished by death.

He was pleased that his wife had demonstrated her ability to bear his children, but he was quick to say that he needed and expected their next child to be a boy and that that should happen soon. Placidia tolerated him, and she could afford to. *She*, not he, was a member of the imperial family. I avoided him. He was such a prick.

Little Honoria was healthy and ate well. Placidia waited fearfully, worrying the new baby would die at the same age that little Theodosius had. A needless concern.

When spring arrived and the winter storms had passed, it was time to go home. I might have remained longer, but Liuva was anxious. "Do you think he might have married already?" she asked.

Constantius and Placidia accompanied us as we rode to Pisae, where a galley ship awaited us. Placidia and I shed fountains of tears as we parted, knowing that this farewell would be forever.

Constantius sailed with us. "I have business with Wallia" was the only explanation he deigned to give me. When we arrived in Barcino, Theodoric was waiting on the pier. Liuva was so eager to disembark that she almost pushed ahead of Constantius.

"Patience, girl," I counseled. "Let him see joy in your eyes, not your action."

Theodoric was equally joyful, and he did not hesitate to act on it. Only when he'd kissed both Liuva's cheeks, forehead, and mouth (at length) did he turn to greet his smiling mother. Young people in love, I sighed.

My story is now coming to a close. Events continue, but they are part of other people's stories. Theodoric and Liuva were married within weeks of our return, and little Thorismund arrived the following year. My grandson might have arrived earlier, but his father spent too much time away from home at war. *That* was Constantius's business with Wallia. The Roman *magister militum* called on Wallia to eradicate the barbarians in Hispania, a project which Wallia gladly and successfully prosecuted. Within two years, he restored Hispania to Roman rule, leaving the barbarians only a shadow of their former power.

The Visigothic army was so powerful and effective that it alarmed Rome. Constantius feared Wallia's force might pose a threat to the empire, so he ordered the Visigoths to leave Hispania and settle in the land that Honorius had given us, in the Garumna valley. Wallia reluctantly agreed. He'd killed many barbarian kings and wanted to finish the job. Perhaps the gods found him greedy for glory because an old war wound re-opened, and King Wallia died without ever returning to Aquitania.

Theodoric moved his family and followers to Tolosa and summoned the clan chieftains, who duly elected him king. My son, the son of Alaric and grandson of Fritigern, both Kings of the Goths, was now himself King of the Goths. I felt I might burst with pride.

Word came from Ravenna periodically. We learned when Placidia gave birth to a second child, a boy they named Valentinian. Next came word that Constantius had finally achieved his ultimate goal when Honorius appointed him co-Emperor of the Western Empire. He was now Augustus Constantius, Third of that name.

Placidia was honored with the position of *Augusta*. My best friend was now Empress of Rome.

But the gods take as well as give. Within nine months, Constantius, my third husband, lay dead from a fever. I did not weep.

I had no job, no responsibility except to be a grandmother, to sit with my growing flock of grandchildren, sing them songs, and tell them stories. I told them of my father, Caius, a Roman legionary and a giant of a man who my mother, Elodia, almost slew. She was an archer who never missed her target except once when the target was a giant Roman legionary, the one time when it truly mattered. I told them of her ruse that saved the lives of all the Gothic chieftains.

I told my grandsons of King Alaric, who started my tribe on its long journey from the frigid land of Moesia to our current home, Aquitania, where the soil is fertile and rain and sunshine are plentiful. I sang the memory of Brutus, a strong, silent man who gave his life to save mine.

For my granddaughters, I told them the sad story of Gainas, my first lover, one who tried to grasp beyond his reach.

Perhaps a granddaughter will tell her children my story. For now, it is finished. My tale is told.

Chapter 25. 422 CE. And Yet …

Matilde

A message has come from Placidia. "He insisted on touching me," she writes, speaking of Honorius, "and when I called my soldiers to protect me, his soldiers fought, and blood was shed. I can write no more. I must flee. Please, my dearest friend, come to my aid. If I am gone from Ravenna, look for me in Constantinople."

Of course, I will go. My next adventure is just beginning.

~ FINI ~

260 ROBERT S. PHILLIPS

Glossary

(Fictional persons or relationships indicated by '†')

Alamanni — Germanic barbarian tribe
aba — Gothic for "husband"
Ad Pirum — Pass in the Julian Alps
Adrianople — Ancient city in Thracia, modern Edirne, Bulgaria
Aetius—Became *magister per Illyricum* after Honorius's death.
     Assembled a force of Romans and Visigoths who, in 451 CE at
     the Battle of Catalaunian Plains, finally broke the back of Hun
     power
Alans — Iranic barbarian tribe
Alaric — Gothic Chieftain of Balti clan, later King (Reiks) of Visigoths
Alfsthan — † Gothic Chieftain
Amalric — † Son of Alaric & Pentadia
amicus publicus — Friend of the people
amphora quadrantal — Volume measurement, ~26 litres
Anatolia — Large peninsula in western Türkiye
Anicius — † One of Constantius's officers
Apennines — Mountain chain, Italy's backbone
Apollo — Greek god of music, prophecy, and healing
Aquileia — Ancient city in Venetia province, near Venice, Italy
Aquincum — Ancient city in Pannonia, modern Budapest, Hungary
Aquitania — Roman province in eastern Gaul, modern Aquitaine,
     France
Arcadius — Emperor of Eastern Empire, reigned 383-408 CE
Arelate — City in southern Gaul, modern Arles, France
Argentarius — Silversmith Pass in the French Alps
Arianism — Christian heresy that held Jesus distinct and inferior to
     God the Father
Ariminum — Ancient city in Italia, modern city of Rimini
as — Very small Roman coin

Asia — Roman province on the east bank of the Bosporus
Ataulf — King (Reiks) of Visigoths, Alaric's successor
Athens — City in Greece
Augusta Taurinorum — Ancient city in Italia, modern Turin, Italy
Augustum — Ancient city in Gaul, modern Aoste, France
augustus, plural *augusti,* feminine *augusta* — Emperor(s), Empress
Aurelianus — Eastern Roman Politician, Chief Minister, anti-Gothic
aureus, plural *aurei* — Gold coin

bacaudae — Groups of peasant insurgents in the Western Roman
   Empire
Baetulo — Ancient city in Hispania, modern Badalona, Spain
Barcino — Ancient city in Hispania, modern Barcelona, Spain
Bononia — Ancient city in Gaul, modern Boulogne, France
Bononia — Ancient city in Italia, modern Bologna, Italy
Borbetomagus — Ancient city in Gaul, modern Worms, Germany
Bosporus — Waterway connecting the Black Sea and the Aegean
   Sea
Brundisium — Ancient city in Italia, modern Brundisi, Italy
Brutus — † Gothic warrior, Matilde's bodyguard
Burdigala — Ancient city in Gaul, modern Bordeaux, France
Burgundians — Germanic barbarian tribe
Busentus — River in southern Italy

Caius — † Ex-Roman legionary, Elodia's husband, Matilde's father,
   Alaric's adoptive father
Colonia Agrippa — Ancient city in Gaul, modern Cologne, Germany
Carcasso — Ancient city in Gaul, modern Carcassonne, France
Carthage — Ancient city in Libya
Castra Regina — Ancient city in Gaul, modern Regensburg,
   Germany
Catholicism — Branch of Christianity believing Jesus and God the
   Father are of the same substance and co-equal

cenatio — Dining room

Chariobaudes — Roman general

comes — Count

comes rei militaris — Count of the Military

constant — The Latin word for "constant," which conveniently makes all the puns on "Constantius", "Constantine", etc. work

Constantine III — Usurper Western Roman Emperor, 407-411 CE, not to be confused with Constantius III

Constantinople — Capital city of the Eastern Roman Empire, on the Bosporus, modern Istanbul, Türkiye

Constantius III — General and Western Roman Emperor, reigned 411 CE, not to be confused with Constantine III

Corinth — City in northern Peloponnese, Greece

Cotian — Pass in the French Alps

Crotona — Ancient city in Italia, modern Crotone, Italy

Danube — Major European river that runs from Southern Germany to the Black Sea, the Northern border of the Eastern Roman Empire

Daphne — Nymph in Greek mythology

Dumnorix — † *Bacaudae* town leader

duumvir, plural *duumviri* — Mayor(s), cities usually had two

dux Pannonia Secunda — Leader of Lower Pannonia

Dyrrhachium — Ancient city on Adriatic coast, modern Durrës, Albania

Eberwulf — Gothic warrior

Edobichus — General under usurper Constantine III

Eleuthō — Greek goddess of childbirth

Elodia — † Gothic woman, Caius's wife, Matilde's mother, Alaric's adoptive mother

Emona — Ancient city in Pannonia, modern Ljubljana, Slovenia

Epirus — Historic region in western Balkans, in Greece and Albania

Eucharius — Son of Stilicho

Eudoxia — Augusta Aelia Eudoxia, Eastern Roman Empress, 394-404 CE

Eugenius — Usurper Roman Emperor 392-394 CE

Eutropius — Eastern Roman Politician, Chief Minister

fabricatus, plural *fabricati* — arms factory

Florentia — Ancient city in Italia, modern Florence, Italy

foederate allies, foederates — Allied troops, per terms of a *foedus*

foedus — Military alliance

Franks — Germanic barbarian tribe

Fravitta — Roman general, ethnic Goth

Frigg — German goddess of marriage

Frigidus — River in the Julian Alps, possibly modern Vipava River, Site of civil war battle in 394 CE

Fritigern — King of Visigoths, † father of Alaric

Gaba — † Slave companion to Matilde

Gainas — Roman general, ethnic Goth

Galla Placidia — See entry for Placidia

Garumna — Garonne River in Aquitaine, France

general — High-level Roman commander. The Romans had no rank equivalent to 'General.'

Gerontius — General under usurper Constantine III

Gildo — General in Western Roman Empire, rebel

Gisalric — † Young Gothic warrior, Matilde's youthful crush

gladius — Short sword. Origin of the word 'gladiator'

Godigisel — King of the Hasdingi Vandals

Goths — Germanic barbarian tribe, western branch known as Visigoths, eastern branch as Ostrogoths

Gratian — Western Roman Emperor, reigned 367-383 CE

Greutungi — Gothic tribe, horse warriors

Guitabert — † Gothic warrior

Gundahar — King of Burgundians
Gunderic — King of the Hasdingi Vandals, Son of Godgisel

Hasta — Ancient city in Liguria, modern Asti, Italy
Hatria — Ancient city in Veneto, modern Adria, Italy
Honorius — Western Roman Emperor, reigned 393-423
Horreum Margi — Ancient city in Illyricum, near modern Ćuprija, Serbia
hostis publicus — Enemy of the people
Huns — War-like tribe, horse warriors from Central Asia

Illyricum — Roman province in northwest Balkans
Indos — Modern India
influentia — influenza, "the flu"
Italia — the Roman province of Italy

John — Officer in Eudoxia's court and possibly the natural father of Emperor Theodosius II
Jovinus — Usurper Western Roman Emperor, 411-413 CE
Jovius — Western Roman official, *praefectus praetorio Illyrici*, 410 CE
Julian — Mountain range that stretches from Italian Alps to Slovenia
Justa Grata Honoria — Daughter of Placidia and Constantius III, 418 -~455 CE
Justinianus — General under usurper Constantine III

Larissa — City in Thessalia (Thessaly), Greece
Lauriacum — Ancient city in Noricum, modern Enns, Austria
Libya — Roman Province in North Africa
Limenius — Western Roman official
limitanei — Roman frontier border legions
Liuva — † Young Gothic woman, Matilde's handmaiden
Lugdunum — Ancient city in Gaul, modern Lyon, France

Macedonia — Roman Province in the Balkans
magister equitum — Master of cavalry
magister militum per gallias — Master of the military for Gaul
magister militum per illyricum — Master of the military for Illyricum
magister militum, plural *magistri militum* — Master(s) of the military
magister officiorum — Master of Offices
magister scrinii — Master of the Imperial Secretaries
magister utriusque militiae in praesentalis — Master of the army and
     cavalry in the Emperor's presence, Commander-in-chief
mansio, plural *mansiones* — Inn(s), official stopping place(s)
Maria — Older daughter of Stilicho, married to Roman Emperor
     Honorius from 398-407 CE
Maritsa — River that drains Thracia (Bulgaria) into the Aegean Sea
Mascezel — Gildo's brother and enemy
Matilde — † Young Gothic woman, daughter of Elodia and Caius
Maximus — Usurper Western Roman Emperor, 409–411 CE
medicus, plural *medici* — Doctor(s)
Mediolanum — Ancient city in Italia, one-time capital of Western
     Roman Empire, modern Milan, Italy
militiae praesentalis — Emperor's own legions
Moesia — Roman province, north of Haemus Mountains, south of
     Danube River
Moguntiacum — Ancient city in Gaul, modern Mainz, Germany
Mons Silicis — Ancient city in Italia, modern Monselice, Italy
Mont Cenis — Alpine mountain in France

Narbo Martius — Ancient city in Gaul, modern Narbonne, France
Nebiogast — General under usurper Constantine III
Neoterius — † Shipowner
Nevitta — † Roman husband of Gaba
Noricum — Roman province in Austria

Noviodunum — Roman fortress on the lower Danube, modern Isaccea, Romania

Novum Comum — Ancient city in Italia, modern Como, Italy

Odysseus — Mythical Greek hero, the protagonist of Homer's "The Odyssey"

Olympius — Western Roman Politician

optio, plural *optiones* — Roman military rank, just subordinate to a *centurion*

Ossa — Mountain in Thessalia, Greece

Ostia — Port for the city of Rome on the Tiber River

Ostrogoths — Eastern Goths who did not enter the empire in 376 CE, remaining north of the Danube River

Palvric — † Wallia's lover

Pannonia — Roman province bounded on the north and east by the Danube River

Patavium — Ancient city in Italia, modern Padua, Italy

Pella — Ancient capital of Macedonia, Greece

Peloponnese — Large peninsula in southern Greece

Penelope — Wife of Odysseus, known for her fidelity

Pentadia — † Sister of Ataulf, wife of Alaric, mother of Amalric

Philippi — Ancient city in Greece, modern Filippoi, Greece

Pisae — Ancient city in Italia, modern Pisa, Italy

Placentia — Ancient city in Italia, modern Piacenza, Italy

Placidia — Half-sister of Emperor Honorius, later Empress in 421 CE, aka Galla Placidia

Po — Major river that drains much of northern Italy

Pollentia — Ancient city in Italia, modern Pollenzo, Italy

praefectus praetorio Illyrici — Praetorian Prefect of Illyricum, a chief aide to the Emperor

praefectus urbis Romae — chief civil officer of Rome

Proculus Tatianus — † Commander of Western outpost at Ad Pirum *protector,* plural *protectores* — Personal bodyguard(s) of the Roman Emperor

Radagaisus — Ostrogoth chieftain

Raetia — Roman province in Switzerland

Ralamunda — † Young Ostrogoth woman, wife of Guitabert, daughter-in-law of Radagaisus

Ravenna — City on the Adriatic Sea, one-time capital of the Western Roman Empire

reiks — Gothic king, elected, not inherited

rhabarbarum — Rhubarb

Rhegion — Ancient port city on the "toe" of Italy, modern Reggio Calabria

Rhine — Major European river that runs from Switzerland to the North Sea, Eastern border of the Western Roman Empire

Rhône — River that drains from the Swiss Alps, through France to the Mediterranean Sea

Roman — Citizen of the Roman Empire (East or West)

Rufinus — Eastern Roman Politician, Chief Minister, Goth-friendly

Sarus — Visigoth chieftain, enemy of Alaric

Sautus — † Son of Sarus

Serena — Wife of Stilicho, Niece of Emperor Theodosius I

Serica — Modern China

Servilia — † Wife of Gainas

Sigeric — Gothic clan chieftain

siliqua, plural *siliquae* — Roman coin, 1/24th of a solidus

silphium — a herbal contraceptive, worth its weight in silver, derived from some unidentified and possibly extinct plant

Sirmium — Ancient city in Pannonia, just west of modern Belgrade, Serbia

Sparta — Ancient city in southern Peloponnese, Greece

spatha — Roman long sword

Stilicho — Western Empire command-in-chief
Suburra — Ancient neighborhood in Rome, Italy
Sueves — Germanic barbarian tribe
Synesius — Greek bishop, who opposed recruiting barbarians into
    the Roman army

Tadinae — Ancient town in Italia, near modern Gualdo Tadino, Italy
Tanaro — River in northwest Italy
Tarsatica — Ancient city in Illyricum, modern Trsat, Croatia
Theodoric — King of the Visigoths, reigned 418-451 CE, † son of
    Matilde
Theodosius I ("the Great") — Roman Emperor, reigned 379-395 CE
Theodosius II — Eastern Roman Emperor, reigned 402-450 CE
Thermantia — Younger daughter of Stilicho, married to Roman
    Emperor Honorius, tenure 408 CE
Thessalia — Modern Thessaly, Greece
Thessalonica — Modern Thessaloniki, Greece
Thorismund — King of the Visigoths, reigned 451-453 CE, son of
    Theodoric and † Liuva
Thracia — Roman province of Thrace, southern Bulgaria, also
    Türkiye, Greece
Ticinum — Ancient city in Italia, modern Pavia, Italy
Tolosa — Ancient city in Gaul, modern Toulouse, France
Tricostus — † Retired legionary, a friend of Constantius

uens — Gothic for "wife"
Uldin — Hun chieftain
Ulpiana — Ancient city in Illyricum, modern Graçanicë, Kosovo

Valentia — Ancient city in Gaul, modern Valence, France
Valentinian — Son of Placidia and Constantius III
Vandals — Germanic barbarian tribe
Venetia — Roman province in northeast Italy

Verona — City in northern Italy

Via Aemilia — Road from Placentia (Piacenza) to Arminium (Rimini)

Via Annia — Road from Venetia along the northern shores of the
   Adriatic Sea

Via Aquitania — Road from Burdigala (Bordeaux) to Narbo Martius
   (Narbonne)

Via Domitia — Road from Italia to Hispania

Via Egnatia — Road from Dyrrhachium (Durrës) to Constantinople

Via Militaris — Road from Singidunum (Belgrade) to Constantinople

Via Popilia — Road from Ariminum (Rimini) to Atria (Adria)

Victorianus — Roman general, *magister equitum*

Vienna — Ancient city in Gaul, modern Vienne, France, not to be
   confused with Vienna, Austria

Vincentia — Ancient city in Italia, modern Vicenza, Italy

Vincentius — Western Roman General, *magister equitum*

Visigoths — Western Goths, Goths who entered the empire in 376
   CE, also Radagaisus's people, and others who joined with Alaric

wagon train — Group of ox, mule, or horse-drawn wagons traveling
   together, usually single file

wagon-fort — Wagons arranged in a circle, a defensive configuration

Wallia — King (Reiks) of Visigoths, Ataulf's successor

Sources

Gibbon, Edward, "The History of the Decline and Fall of the Roman Empire," London, 1776-1788

Hughes, Ian, "Stilicho, The Vandal Who Saved Rome," (Pen & Sword Military, 2010, ISBN 978-1-84415-969-7) http://www.ianhughesma.com/

Socrates of Constantinople, "Historia Ecclesiastica," (written ~439 CE, translated by Socrates Scholasticus and Philip Schaff, 1819-1893) http://www.ccel.org/ccel/schaff/npnf202.html

Sozomen, "Ecclestical History," (written ~518 CE, translated Hartranft, 1890) https://www.newadvent.org/fathers/2602.htm

Zosimus, "New History," (written ~500 CE, translated R.T. Ridley, 1982) https://www.livius.org/sources/content/zosimus/

Bonus Content: The Great River

In the following short story, a family of Goths flee for their lives from the invading Huns, seeking refuge in the Roman Empire by crossing the Danube River. The story won First Prize in the 2023 Chanticleer International Book Awards for Short Stories.

"Old mother, can you walk?" my daughter-in-law asked with a sneer that suggested she hoped I could not.

"Of course." And I proceed to demonstrate it. Not fast, perhaps, but adequate for the journey ahead. Odd that Gerta should ask. She herself could no longer keep up with her grandchildren as she chased them around the campfire. So many great-grandchildren, too many names. Now just *boy* or *girl*.

I remember the names of the eight children I bore and the secret names for the four little ones who died in the year before their naming day, names I have never divulged. Of my three daughters, only Sinda remains to care for me. I lost one to the agony of childbirth and another to the coughing sickness. I still have two sons, brave Gothic warriors both. Of the others, one died years ago on the tusks of a boar; the other two fell only ten days ago to the swords and arrows of the merciless horsemen from the east, the Huns.

My husband of countless years, Hathus, led my boys and the other men of our village to its defense. Sinda says many were killed including Hathus, but I know this cannot be true. Since the battle—just a skirmish, really—he comes most evenings to my bedside, and we talk. My eyes are cloudy now, but when he sits and puts his cold hand in mine, he looks no older than when we first met by the fishing stream.

I'd had my first blood just a few months earlier, and my breasts were small and high. Hathus, the son of a nearby village headman, was lean, strong, and already as tall as my father. He showed me a quiet pool where tall trees hid the trout from the afternoon sun. We lay together there, and afterward, we talked. We conspired about how he would come to my hut in the dead of night and steal me for his bride. I told my father, who approved and arranged for Hathus to be welcomed with a feast, not weapons. We lived through many years, endless days of plenty or hardship, joy or grief—and countless nights of comfort and pleasure. And so it went until the Huns arrived.

Sinda says we must move. The horsemen are gone for now, but they will return. Our wooden palisade is damaged, and even were it whole, we no longer have enough warriors to man the walls. When they attack again, they will breach our defenses and slaughter us all. That is their way.

Hathus told me last night that we must move south to the Great River, which the Romans call *Danubius*. Once we cross it into Roman territory, the Huns will not follow, being as fearful of the Romans as we are of them. This morning Sinda told me the exact same plan. When I asked if she'd learned of it from Hathus, she said, "Don't be ridiculous."

I find walking more and more difficult. We have been on the road for a week, and my hips hurt. I am slow, and the others see it. Yesterday, I overheard Gerta saying I should be left behind. "She has had a good life. Her years have exceeded the number Jesus allots to each human. She is using years that should have gone to Atto." Atto was her husband, my son. His body lies in a grave back in our village, mutilated by a horseman's sword. I do not resent Gerta's words. I understand grief. I will struggle harder to keep up.

Hathus tells me that we are making good progress. The Danubius River is only another week or two away, and the Huns are not pursuing us closely.

Every day the road becomes more crowded. People join the throng walking to the river. Some come as individuals, others as entire villages, all fleeing the horsemen. There are more women than men and grievous wounds often afflict the men. I help rebind wounds, one of the few things I can still manage.

We meet a young man who, Sinda says, comes from a village near our own. I do not recognize him. But his sword hand is badly wounded and smells of rot. I tell him the limb must come off, or he will die. He says he'd rather die.

The land here along the road is no different from our home. It is flat and featureless, though in the far distance we can see the foothills of the Carpathian Mountains. Spring is arriving quickly. The snow has melted, but the runoff has nowhere to go because the ground is still frozen. It covers the road deeply in mud. Because we knew it would be so, we did not bring any wagons or carts. Other folk were less wise. We find their carts abandoned, mired up to the hubs in gray, sticky clay.

Though it still freezes every night, the early flowers have bloomed. First, the crocuses appeared almost overnight, their purple blossoms providing a splash of color in a bleak landscape. Within a few days, they were followed by wild daffodils and tulips. While colorful, they don't compare with the ones I grew by my hut, flowers I will never see again. Bushes line the road. The tips of their branches show a splinter of green. I expect to see new growth and leaves within the next few days.

We were fortunate enough to bring provisions for several weeks. Other families were less lucky. I see little children crying for food. I feel very sad, but have lived through hard times and watched youngsters starve to death. Once you witness it, you grow a callus on your heart. Sinda has no callus. She insists we must share the food we have with the small ones. Gerta has not witnessed what I've seen, but she was born with a callus on her heart and says we have little enough remaining for ourselves and nothing to share with others. She watches me as I eat. I do not eat very much, but I can tell she begrudges me my small portion.

Some people are dying. The very old and young are most affected. The ground is still too frozen to bury them. Regardless, people reserve their energy for walking, not digging. The dead are gently, reverently laid beside the road. Reverence is no protection against the scavenging of foxes and birds. We see them feed and avert our eyes.

Finally, after weeks of walking, we arrive at the Great River. It is wide and flows swiftly. There is no boat traffic across it. We had expected to see ferries moving our people to the far bank. And there are so many, many people wishing to cross. My family cannot get closer to the river than a hundred paces, a distance filled with the people of our tribe who have preceded us here. As I look up and down the river, I see the same disorder everywhere: Thousands of people milling about, a makeshift tent city, the endless buzz of people talking, weeping, shouting, and the unimaginable smell of crowded unwashed humanity. The ground is a churned mixture of soil and human feces. There are no animals; they have all been eaten.

Where are the Romans? I look across the river to a great fortress, which I'm told is called Durostorum. There are red and green pennants flying from the battlements. A neighbor, who is camped near us, says the Romans are still negotiating with our leaders to allow us to cross. The negotiations have been going on for a month, waiting for them to grant us asylum.

As I look at this squalid mass of humanity, I wonder how anyone could survive here for a month. If the emperor waits longer, we will all starve. Or perhaps the Huns will catch up to us. At some point, that might be a preferable death.

Last night as I lay down to sleep, Hathus came to me. He said he has crossed the river, and it is good. The land is green and fertile. Summer is further advanced there than here. New leaves of bright green adorn the maple and walnut trees. The forsythia bushes are blossoming a brilliant yellow.

I asked about the plum trees and whether any of my favorite fruit is ripe yet. Hathus laughed, saying it is far too early. There are many plum trees, but they are still adorned with their early dark red leaves, leaves that are only beginning to unfurl and turn green.

He is building me a hut like the one we made together when we were young. Next to it is a field of winter wheat, ready to be harvested. He does not say who planted the crop, but it is there for the taking. He has found a stream where we can fish together. He says I should hurry. There is so much he wants to show me.

My neighbor has returned, saying the emperor has finally given us leave to cross, and the Roman rivercraft will begin ferrying people tomorrow. Some men, while waiting for permission, have built rafts. They are not waiting for tomorrow. They load their rafts and push off. The rafts are crudely constructed, and the men overload them with their families and possessions. I watch many cross halfway to where the current is strongest before they capsize. There is no way to help the passengers as they are swept away.

Sinda says we will find room on a safe Roman boat and cross tomorrow at dawn. I lie down to sleep, feeling very happy. This journey has been far too long and hard on an old woman like me.

But I don't have to wait for dawn. Hathus comes to me. He takes my hand and helps me to my feet. Together we walk past all the sleeping people to the water's edge, where he has arranged a private boat for us. The crew of two, a beautiful man and woman dressed in white robes, lift their paddles, and we push off from shore. As we reach the river's center, the water becomes calm, and we finish our passage easily.

Hathus helps me from the rivercraft, and we walk hand-in-hand to the hut he has prepared for me. It is all as he promised.

Acknowledgments

I would like to thank the many people who helped and supported me while I wrote both *Matilde's General* and *Matilde's Empress*: my editor Joseph Donley; the Village Books Fiction Writers group (Lee Brown, Sandy Lawrence, Patti Thomas, Kim Owen, Delaney Peterson, Christy Rommel, Nathan Dodge, Jared Mattox, Kathy Smith, George Murray), and my Beta readers (Alice Campbell, Jamie Good, Kari Lisa Johnson, Kristina Smith, Jana Dunn, Graham Phillips, Ian Phillips, and Frances Pickett).

Also my daughter Martha, who gracefully surrendered half of the kitchen table to my manuscript drafts, history books, and miscellaneous scribblings.

And to Bob Paltrow for the cover design and Audra Mercille for the author photo.

Author's Biography

Robert S. Phillips was an avid reader and history buff. Born in Vancouver, BC, Robert lived in many places in Canada and the United States, only returning to the Pacific Northwest in the last decade. Home was Bellingham, WA. He has three grown children of whom he was very proud. Robert passed away shortly after finishing *Matilde's General* and *Matilde's Empress*, which are sequels to his debut novel, *Elodia's Knife*. That story won first prize in the 2023 Chanticleer Book Awards for Historical Fiction.

Made in the USA
Columbia, SC
25 September 2024

43018619R00159